LETHAL
TRACKS

ALSO BY MERISSA RACINE

The Crawford Mystery Series
Silent Gavel
Shadows of Doubt

A CRAWFORD MYSTERY

LETHAL TRACKS

MERISSA RACINE

WIND DRIVEN PRESS

ISBN (Print) 978-0-9993033-4-4
e-ISBN 978-0-9993033-5-1

Cover Design: Nick Castle
Book Design: Maureen Cutajar

This book is funded in part by the Wyoming Arts Council.

This book is dedicated to Chris Gordon
A wonderful brother
You are missed every day

Chapter One

"I am *so* over this, Maverik. I want sunshine. I *need* sunshine. And ... I need dry roads for the drive to Cheyenne for work tomorrow."

Lauren's large mixed-breed dog's response to anything she said was a quick swish of his tail. If a dog could trot happily, Maverik did just that on his way to the back door, where he nudged the knob with his black nose. He glanced back at her.

"Yes, yes, I know." Lauren pushed off the kitchen counter and had barely gotten the door open when Maverik squeezed his large frame through and dove off the back deck into the whiteness. She watched him momentarily disappear. "At least he's enjoying this."

Lauren flipped the cream-colored switch on her arthritic coffeepot. While it sputtered and hissed, she went to the kitchen window and peered out. New, higher drifts from Thursday's powerful storm added to the mounting piles of snow already there. Since mid-January, one winter storm after another had pummeled Crawford, Wyoming, creating a bleak month of gray. The snow easily reached three feet in spots in her backyard. The weatherman on the radio sounded almost gleeful that more snow was on the horizon.

Maverik's distressed barks caused Lauren to stick her head out the door and glance around. He stood at the side fence, the one separating her yard from her neighbor's, Twila Nash. Ms. Nash's granddaughter, wearing a thin white hoodie, plaid pajama pants, and a pink knit cap, closed the side gate that led to her grandmother's backyard. She made her way toward the deck and Twila's back door.

"Quiet, Maverik. It's just Ruby."

The teen reached the deck, turned in Lauren's direction. She lifted her shoulders in an "I've been caught" gesture, offered a shy smile, then raised her hand and wriggled her slender fingers in a small wave before disappearing inside her grandmother's house.

Lauren and Maverik retreated into the warmth of the kitchen. Lauren poured herself a cup of coffee and Maverik ran into the living room. Before she could take her first sip, Maverik's deep bark interrupted her. It was too early on a Sunday for Maverik to chase shadows.

"Hey, you, what are you barking at now?" Lauren called out as she went to investigate. Maverik stood by the window that faced the front yard, hackles raised. His low and repetitive growls were aimed at the rumble of a diesel engine coming to life. Lauren tried to get a glimpse of the vehicle, but couldn't with the cloud of thick, charcoal exhaust billowing in the still air.

"It has to be a pickup with that much exhaust, right?" She spoke to Maverik but he was already trotting into the kitchen. Lauren followed. She caught the time on the microwave. Seven ten. Maverik sniffed his empty dog dish. Lauren scooped out two cups of dry food from the large bag and filled his bowl with the kibble. While she closed the bag, she asked, "Why was Ruby going in through the back like that? Like she didn't want Old Lady Nash to know she was just coming in?"

I did that once or twice in high school. She lifted her chin at Maverik. "Must be a boy."

Maverik crunched his breakfast, oblivious to her comments. Lauren had stumbled upon a good four-legged companion. Any would-be intruder would think twice before breaking into her house after hearing his deep bark. Plus, he listened to her endless ramblings, thankfully never disagreeing with what she said.

She popped open kitchen cupboards and typed a grocery list into her phone. She wanted to stock up on essentials in case Crawford ended up with the forecasted ten inches of new snow. She typed in Double Stuf Oreos, an essential to get through the never-ending cold days of winter.

After a breakfast of toast topped with chunky peanut butter and a sliced banana, Lauren poured herself a second cup of coffee, taking it upstairs to her home office. She'd been working on an expedited transcript from the remote deposition she had taken Friday afternoon. *A court reporter's job is certainly not Monday through Friday, eight to five.* She had only a few more pages to edit, then she would proofread the transcript before emailing it to the attorneys. Charging extra for the fast turnaround made up for a weekend married to her computer.

* * *

Maverik, who had been sprawled on the carpet next to her desk, jumped up and barked before disappearing downstairs. Lauren's hand went to her throat. "Geez, Maverik." She checked the time on her computer screen. Eight forty. Lauren went downstairs, cell phone in one hand, empty coffee cup in the other. Maverik pawed the back door.

"Just a minute. Just a minute." She opened the door. Piercing winter air rushed in as Maverik rushed out. He ran to the same side of the yard as earlier, his bark anxious and nonstop. Lauren listened for any sounds coming from Twila's yard that would explain Maverik's behavior, but heard nothing. She didn't see anything unusual.

"Maverik, come here."

He didn't.

"Come here. *Now.*"

He ignored her commands. Any moment Lauren expected her phone to ring, or worse, Twila Nash to appear on her back deck, yelling for that "damn dog to shut the hell up." For an old woman, she had a bark as loud as Maverik's. Lauren shoved her feet into her unfashionable yet warm snow boots. She snatched her black parka off a hook by the back door and, not bothering to snap it up, dashed outside, pulling the door shut behind her.

Maverik continued his chorus. Lauren shivered and pulled her coat tightly around her.

"*Quiet,*" Lauren hissed as she trudged through the snow until she got closer to her dog, now on his hind legs lunging at the fence. Lauren's gaze turned in the direction of her neighbor Twila's place. She saw nothing other than bare branches and pyramid-shaped snowdrifts piled behind the apple trees growing in Twila's backyard.

Lauren reached and swiped at Maverik's collar, ready to physically drag him into the house. Instead, she grabbed air and fell to her knees. The cold immediately seeped through her sweats. She cussed as she stood. Maverik turned his head to look at her, as if saying, "Keep up." The slight hesitation on his part gave her enough time to grab his collar.

"There's nothing over there. Let's go." Before turning to go back inside, Lauren glanced one more time into Twila's yard. Something pink caught her eye. It hung from a low branch of her neighbor's bare crab apple tree.

Chapter Two

"Is that what you were making all the noise about?" Lauren pointed. "Whatever's hanging from that tree?"

In response, Maverik wrenched free of her grip and did something she had never seen him do before. He scaled the chain-link fence between her and Twila Nash's backyards and ran toward whatever hung in the tree.

"Son of — damn it." Lauren couldn't tell if the goosebumps on her arms were from the cold seeping into her coat or the anxious whines of Maverik. She ran inside, grabbed a leash off a hook by the door, and hurried to her neighbor's yard. The side gate Ruby had entered through earlier stood wide open. *Maybe Ruby didn't shut it hard enough?*

Lauren trudged through the deep blanket of white, tall enough that it got inside her boots. She ignored the cold, wet feeling. As she got closer to the tree she saw a pink knit hat, the one Ruby wore earlier. It must have caught on a branch when she went inside and she didn't bother to retrieve it.

Maverik had stopped barking. His muzzle twitched over the snow, sniffing the ground beyond the trunk of the tree near the bottom step of Twila's back deck. Lauren stepped toward him. That was when she saw what had caused Maverik's frenzy. Ruby lay on her back, her head tilted to the right, her short violet-tipped blonde hair contrasted against the snow. She still wore the same plaid pajama bottoms, but instead of the white hoodie, she had on a thin T-shirt.

"Ruby?" Lauren knelt and leaned toward the girl, checking for signs of breathing. It was only then that she saw Ruby's soft blue eyes were open, unblinking with a faded glimmer of surprise in them.

I think I'm going to be sick.

Lauren swallowed hard. "Ruby? Ruby?" She forced herself to press her fingertips to the teen's neck, not surprised when she didn't feel a pulse.

Ruby, what the hell happened?

Lauren straightened, pulled her cell from her coat pocket, and with shaky fingers, tapped out 911.

In a rush of words, Lauren told the dispatcher the address and what she'd discovered. No, the girl wasn't breathing. The voice on the other end told her not to hang up, and while Lauren didn't, she had forgotten to wear her gloves and her fingers were numb. She shoved her hands into her coat pockets along with the phone. She stomped her feet to keep warm. Tears pricked her eyes.

7

Maverik's nose sniffed Ruby. For some reason she didn't understand, the sight of him doing that made Lauren queasy.

"I need to get you away from here." The snow around the teen's body had been completely trampled and covered in Maverik's pawprints. And now her own boot prints.

Does it matter? Lauren glanced around where she stood. *Were there other boot prints? Or are all of these mine?* Lauren couldn't tell, she only knew she should get her dog home before the EMTs and police arrived.

"Let's go." This time Maverik didn't struggle or try to pull free. She led him the way she came, out the side gate to her own deck, and opened the back door for Maverik. He went into the living room, sat by the couch as if expecting her to stay with him. She ruffled his cold ears.

"It's okay. I'll be right back." Before leaving, Lauren zipped her coat, shoved her hands into a pair of gloves and started toward her neighbor's house. It looked easier to simply retrace Ruby's steps to the back deck, so that's what Lauren did. No one had taken a shovel to Twila's deck. Her dog's tiny paw prints dotted the snow, along with boot prints from someone walking in and out of the house, and up and down the few steps leading to the backyard.

Lauren rapped on the kitchen door. Percy's sharp, high-pitched barks answered from the other side. While she waited for Ms. Nash to answer, she glanced around. A small round metal table stood on the deck, covered in snow. In the middle of it sat a round terra-cotta saucer filled with cigarette butts.

The kitchen door swung open. Before the Papillon could race past her, Lauren bent and scooped him up and held him in her arms.

8

"Ruby, what's going on? Why are you knocking? Did you lock yourself out again?" Twila squinted through thick glasses. "Oh. Lauren." She clutched her robe. "What are you doing here?" She stuck her head out and called for her granddaughter. "Ruby?"

"Twila, I — I came over to tell you your granddaughter's hurt. Badly." *It's so much more than that.* "I've already called 911. They should be here any minute."

"What do you mean hurt? Did she slip and fall? I thought she finally went out to shovel a path for Percy. She'd been promising to do that for days. Percy's been having a heck of a time going out and doing his business."

Twila tried to move past Lauren. "Ruby, are you okay?"

"I'm not sure what happened, but she's laying in the yard." Lauren used her body to shield Twila's view of Ruby. "You should go inside and wait for the EMTs. It's really cold."

"Don't tell me what I should do. You sound just like my granddaughter, thinking you know what's good for me." Twila stepped onto her back porch, craning her neck to locate Ruby. The elderly woman, dressed in a thin pink robe, began to shiver.

Lauren handed Percy to Twila.

Maybe now she'll go inside.

Papillons were not a breed for Wyoming winters, neither was the elderly woman, but Twila stood there rooted in place. Lauren gently put her hand on her neighbor's elbow, ready to guide her inside, when the faint sound of sirens broke through the quiet.

Chapter Three

Detective Sam Overstreet stood in the break room pouring a cup of coffee when Nancy, the receptionist on day shift, came up behind him. "Sam, there's a report of an unresponsive female found outside a residence. Officer Peterson is requesting a detective."

The Crawford Police Department had one detective per shift. That meant Sam this morning. He poured his coffee down the drain. "Tell dispatch I'm on my way."

"Will do." She gave him a thumbs-up and returned to her desk. Sam resigned himself to the fact that his morning wouldn't include sitting in his warm office, drinking coffee and catching up on writing reports on the latest rash of break-ins at the retirement center.

He stopped at Officer Fuentes's cubicle. "Let's go."

She pointed at herself with a questioning look.

Sam nodded.

Lola Fuentes grabbed her coat and followed. "What have we got?"

"Unresponsive female. Ben's on scene. He just called it in." As he passed Nancy's desk, she handed Sam the address. He read the location and his heart beat faster.

That's gotta be Lauren's neighbor, Twila Nash.

He quickened his pace. Officer Fuentes jogged to keep up.

The snowplows wouldn't be clearing secondary roads for at least another day, maybe two, if at all. He tried going the speed limit, but every time he did, the vehicle fishtailed and threatened to send him into a parked car. Sam cussed under his breath as he maneuvered his police-issued SUV toward the 911 location.

Sam turned onto Hancock Street and followed in the tracks Officer Ben Peterson had made with his vehicle, and parked behind him.

"Coroner en route." The dispatcher's voice crackled inside the vehicle.

Shit. Sam opened the glove box, removed two pairs of latex gloves, handing one set to Officer Fuentes.

The EMTs must have called the death in, confirming that, yes, whoever lay in the yard was deceased. Most likely the old woman herself. Maybe she stepped outside and for some reason couldn't get back into her home and succumbed to hypothermia. He and Fuentes would be in the cold for a while. The only bright spot — if Sam even dared call it that — would be the experience it gave to Officer Fuentes, who rode shotgun. He saw the eagerness spark in her eyes when he had asked her to assist him.

Sam pulled his blue knit cap low on his head, his wavy brown hair disappearing underneath.

"Let's go see what we've got." Before Sam even got out, Officer Fuentes was closing the passenger door. She stood between the two parked vehicles, waiting for Sam's lead.

They trudged through the eight inches of new snow toward Ben Peterson. The tall officer stood by the four-foot chain-link gate that separated a small patch of Ms. Nash's front lawn from the back.

Sam glanced at Fuentes, her cheeks pink either from the cold or the excitement, maybe both. Sam knew that she'd been a patrol officer in Powell, Wyoming, for three years before accepting the job with the Crawford PD. She was twenty-six, the same age he'd been when he began his career in law enforcement. Hard to believe he'd been on the force twelve years now. So much life had happened since that first day. *Was I ever that young and eager?*

Sam still remembered feeling excited and nervous arriving on the scene of his first death. Cops were taught the proper protocol for investigating a death in the police academy, but no classroom lectures could prepare anyone for the reality of death. Sam knew it would be the same for Fuentes. Adrenaline pulsed through Sam, but having been to the scene of dozens of deaths over his career, he no longer described what he felt as excitement. He wouldn't describe it as dread. Or maybe it was. No, more like resignation. He shook off any more thoughts of the past.

Sam mentally noted the wobbly tracks from a gurney, and the multiple shoeprints in the packed snow as he made his way through the gate and into the backyard. He called out, "Peterson, what do we have?"

"Back here, sir. A deceased female. Young. No obvious signs of trauma."

Young? Not Lauren's neighbor, Twila Nash. Sam picked up his pace, his mind thinking the worst, that Lauren lay in the snow. She'd been a suspect, only briefly, in a previous murder case, but the thought of her now out in this cold made his chest ache. He quickened his pace.

When he reached Officer Peterson, Sam put up a hand to catch his breath, then asked, "What do we have?"

"Sir, the reporting party, a Lauren Besoner, identified the deceased as Ruby. Didn't have a last name. Said the female lives at this residence with her grandmother, a Twila Nash."

Sam closed his eyes for the briefest of moments, taking a calming breath, letting his heartbeat return to normal. *Not Lauren. Thank God.*

The gangly officer led the way, talking over his shoulder as he went. "The RP and Ms. Nash are inside. I told them they didn't need to wait in the cold, that someone would be in to talk to them shortly."

Sam rounded the corner and almost bumped into Peterson, who had stopped short, pointing to the young woman, as if anyone could miss her.

Sam bent slightly, hands on thighs, and conducted a mental inventory. Late teens, possibly early twenties. Thin T-shirt, no coat. No blood, no obvious abrasions. No signs of trauma.

Two male paramedics stood beside the gurney in heavy black coats, bright yellow reflective strips across the backs. The younger of the two confirmed he'd notified dispatch that the female was deceased.

"Coroner is on her way," said Sam.

The older EMT nodded.

Sam knelt next to the young woman with purple spiked hair. Officer Fuentes approached from the other side and leaned closer. He heard the sharp intake of her breath before she straightened and backed up. It's a shock, coming upon your first death. Even more so when they're young. Lola would be seeing this girl's face in her dreams for some time to come.

His gaze swept the yard. Paw and boot prints trampled the snow around the victim's petite frame. Sam stood and could see into Ms. Nash's window, the layout of the house identical to Lauren's, so he knew he was looking into the elderly woman's kitchen. Lauren stood there with her back to him, her silky brown hair dipping past her shoulders. She appeared to be cradling something in her arms, head bent slightly. *Probably Percy.* Lauren swayed rhythmically right, then left. She turned to look out the window. Sam's eyes widened. It wasn't a dog Lauren held. She held a baby.

Chapter Four

Lauren's jaw relaxed when she spotted Sam walk toward the house. Until that moment, she hadn't realized her teeth were clamped tight. She opened the back door with her free hand, ushering Sam into the overly warm kitchen. A female officer she didn't recognize trailed behind. The officer pushed her hood back, revealing long, sleek black hair pulled into a tight ponytail.

Sam stopped in front of Twila, who stood beyond the doorway.

"Ms. Nash, Officer Peterson said that that's your granddaughter Ruby outside?"

Ms. Nash nodded. "Yes."

"I'm very sorry to have to inform you that Ruby is dead."

Twila shook her head. Lauren had told Twila that Ruby was hurt, not dead. Lauren had lacked the courage to say those words. Sam spoke to Twila with warmth and compassion. It was a professional side of Sam Lauren hadn't witnessed before. It made her eyes prick with new tears.

Lauren's heart ached for Twila.

Twila cupped her cheek with her hand. "I don't understand. What do you mean she's dead? How could that be? Are you sure?"

"We're still assessing the situation, Ms. Nash," Sam said in a gentle voice. "We need to get some basic information from you, if you feel up to answering a few questions."

The old woman, in her tattered pink terry cloth robe, stroked her dog. She seemed both frail and stoic, simultaneously in shock and denial. Twila closed her eyes, inhaled, then let out her breath. When she opened her eyes she nodded.

Lauren went to the sink. With one arm holding the baby, she used her free hand to fill a chipped daisy-print ceramic teakettle and place it on the burner. "Let me make you some tea."

"I don't need no damn tea." Twila sank into one of the kitchen chairs, releasing Percy from her arms. She covered her face with leathery hands, fingers knotted and twisted like a bonsai tree. Barely above a whisper, Twila said, "Not again. Not Ruby."

Sam reached into the inside pocket of his parka and pulled out a notepad and pen. He tipped his head toward Officer Fuentes.

The officer opened her phone and tapped on the screen.

"Did Ruby reside here with you?" asked Sam.

Twila nodded.

"What's Ruby's full name?"

"Ruby West. That's Evie." Twila lifted her chin toward the baby. "Ruby's child."

"What about Ruby's parents? Do they live in Crawford?"

"Cynthia … her mother, my daughter … is dead. Her father lives in town. Bill West."

"What about the baby's father?"

"It's Carson … I can't think of his last name. But Evie … Evie has been here on a trial home placement with Ruby. The state has legal custody of her."

Sam turned to Officer Fuentes. "You better let DFS know what's going on."

Officer Fuentes nodded, turned, and walked a few steps away from Sam. She spoke into the mic attached to her jacket on the shoulder and notified dispatch to contact the Department of Family Services.

"Do you know what Ruby was doing outside?" Sam asked.

"I didn't realize she was out there. When Lauren knocked on the door, I thought it was Ruby, that she locked herself out. I thought maybe she was shoveling an area for Percy to do his business. That snow's getting too much for him. I'd been on her for a while now to do that. Or maybe she went out for a cigarette."

Sam gave a small nod.

Twila's explanation made sense, why Ruby might be outside. The snow was taller than the small dog. But there were no signs that any area had been shoveled, only trampled snow that led from the back door and the steps leading to the yard.

Lauren wanted to do something for Twila but didn't know what. She placed her free hand on Twila's shoulder. "I'll shovel it for you."

Twila tilted her head at Lauren. The withering look on the old woman's face made Lauren remove her hand as if she'd touched a live wire. "I'll just go put Evie in her crib."

The baby was asleep in Lauren's arms. Even though Evie was too young to understand anything going on, for reasons Lauren couldn't explain, didn't understand herself, she didn't want Evie present as they talked about her mother.

Lauren, cradling Evie, walked toward the staircase and whispered, "Where did you get such long eyelashes?"

* * *

Lauren entered Ruby's bedroom, realizing today was the first time she had gotten to see Evie up close. There had been glimpses of Evie from Lauren's living room window as Ruby went in and out of Twila's house, but Evie had always been in a carrier and covered up to keep out the cold.

She placed Evie in the bassinet, covered her with a blanket, and slowly backed out of the room and returned to the kitchen.

Sam approached Lauren. "Officer Peterson said you found Ruby?"

Lauren nodded. "Yes."

"Tell me when and how you found her."

"It was actually Maverik." Lauren thought Sam might give an eyeroll, as if to say, *Of course he did.* Maverik had come across a dead body once before. "He must have sensed something, because he started barking, so I let him out. When I did, he jumped the fence. He's *never* done that before. Never ever."

"Did you touch *anything*, Lauren?" Sam asked.

Lauren knew that look, that questioning in his eyes. Almost expecting her to say, "You know me, of course I did." But she hadn't touched anything. She shook her head. "But I did see something in the snow next to her."

Sam dipped his head, eyes focused on Lauren.

Lauren held his gaze. "It looked like a syringe. You didn't —"

Without letting her finish, Sam turned to Officer Fuentes, who had been listening and taking the occasional note. She spoke into the body mic secured on her parka at shoulder level, asking Officer Peterson if a needle had been recovered.

"No," came a distorted reply.

"Are you sure that's what you saw?" asked Sam.

"Well, I'm pretty sure that's what I saw. There was definitely something lying near her arm." Lauren tilted her head to the left, then to the right. "Left side. Left elbow area."

Sam flipped his notebook shut. "Ms. Nash, why don't you let Lauren make you that cup of tea. We'll be right back."

Lauren watched Sam rush out the back door with the very pretty officer following close behind.

Chapter Five

S am retraced his steps to where Ruby lay and surveyed the area around her.

Brianna Reese, the coroner, clad in a thick white parka, appeared at the back gate and trudged toward the small group gathered around the deceased.

Sam turned from his inspection. "Anyone come across a syringe?"

Ben Peterson and the EMTs shook their heads in unison as he continued to search the ground around Ruby.

"What are we looking for?" asked Coroner Reese as she approached.

"Found it." Officer Fuentes smiled as she pulled out latex gloves and an evidence bag from her coat pocket. With her gloved fingers she gently reached around the syringe, its needle barely visible in the snow.

"Detective, I've already made a call to the medical

examiner in Loveland, Colorado." Coroner Reese rubbed her gloved hands together. "The pathologist is expecting her. I checked with Road and Travel. The highway's closed, from here to the state line. You know what that stretch of road is like, all that damn wind causing ground blizzards, black ice. A whole smorgasbord of shitty driving weather conditions."

Sam nodded, picturing a couple of semis blown over, making the decision to close the road a no-brainer.

"We'll get her down there as soon as we can," Coroner Reese assured him.

As if on cue, they all peered up at the clouds, then toward the west, where a streak of blue sky sat just above the horizon, a sign that, at least for today, there would be no more snow. Maybe the wind would die down as well. Sam prayed it would.

Sam exhaled, his breath visible. "Let's hope they clear the roads soon." He knew the closure would cause a delay in the autopsy being performed. He hated waiting, but knew getting annoyed wouldn't change anything. Patience. One of the things he'd been working on in counseling. Some days he felt like he was making headway, understanding he could not control everything. And then something like this happened, a delay out of his control. His anger would flare, setting back any headway in controlling his emotions. *Why even bother with the damned counseling?*

"I'll make a note about the syringe so the pathologist will know to follow up, do a complete toxicology panel." Coroner Reese pointed to the bagged needle.

"Thanks," Sam replied. "And, Peterson, secure this area."

The officer nodded.

The coroner went over to the two EMTs who stood on either side of the gurney awaiting her further instruction.

Officer Fuentes stood beside Sam. "Looks like she OD'd?"

Sam heard the question in her voice, seeking confirmation of her theory. He obliged with a slow nod. "It looks that way but remember, no jumping to conclusions. Let's finish talking to Ms. Nash." He turned and walked toward the house, not looking forward to asking Twila Nash some hard questions about her granddaughter.

Chapter Six

Lauren sat across from Twila at the kitchen table, their cups of tea untouched and growing cold. Lauren wanted to reach out and squeeze Twila's hand, offer her words of comfort, but Lauren knew nothing she said would help. Not right now. They sat in silence waiting for Sam to return.

The doorbell chimed. Twila didn't get up from her chair but Percy raced toward the ancient sound, letting out a series of sharp yips.

"I'll see who it is." Lauren picked up Percy and shushed him before swinging open the door.

"Taryn?"

The woman's blue eyes widened. "Uh, hi, Lauren. What are you doing here?"

Lauren pointed in the direction of her house. "I'm Twila's neighbor. I live next door."

"Oh, I didn't realize that."

"What are you doing — wait. Is Ruby involved with the Department of Family Service?"

"Yes, she's one of my clients. I'm on call this weekend. I was getting ready to go to the gym when I got notified. Thought I was going to get lucky and make it through the whole weekend without something coming up, but ..." Taryn lifted a shoulder.

Lauren stepped back to let Taryn Biggs enter. Percy's bark became nonstop, his attempt at protecting his territory failing. He wriggled and tried to get free from Lauren's embrace.

"Percy, no."

Percy growled in response. Weighing only seven pounds, he held no menace. Nevertheless, the corner of Lauren's mouth twitched with a smile at the wannabe protector.

"You've turned into quite the guard dog for Twila, haven't you?" said Taryn.

More sounds came from deep in his throat, erupting into another round of high-pitched barks.

"You should recognize me by now," said Taryn. "Must be a little dog thing, huh, fella?" The social services worker stomped one foot, then the other against the cement step, knocking snow from her boots, then entered the house. Cold air slunk in behind her, clashing with the almost hot air of the living room. She pulled a tissue out of her coat pocket and wiped her nose.

Lauren was surprised to see her friend Taryn here even though she shouldn't have been. Social service caseworkers did attend juvenile court hearings, but that was a byproduct of their many duties. All of Lauren's professional interactions with Taryn came during Lauren's time working in the courtroom as the official court stenographer. She learned one of their jobs involved taking children out of their current living situation, when necessary, and placing them in the Department of Family Services' custody. And children needing to be removed from their homes didn't just occur Monday through Friday. It happened at all hours, and wherever the child happened to be at the time. This up-close view of Taryn in action made Lauren have new respect for her friend.

"I'm here to take Evie." Taryn pulled off her fuzzy ear warmers, the static causing loose strands of her strawberry-blonde bob to stick straight up.

"Oh, okay. I just put her down." Lauren gestured to the stairway. "She's asleep."

"You sure didn't waste no time getting here."

Lauren turned to see Twila in the open doorway leading to the kitchen, a pained expression on her face.

"Hi, Ms. Nash. I heard what happened. I'm so sorry for your loss," said Taryn.

Twila waved a dismissive hand.

"I'm sure you know why I'm here. I have to take Evie."

"I know, I know. She's in Ruby's room." Twila pushed her eyeglasses up the bridge of her nose. "She'll be fussy if she gets woke up though."

"I understand but I do need to take her." Taryn spoke softly to Twila, whose watery blue eyes held unshed tears. "She'll be well taken care of, Twila."

Twila managed to jut her chin. "You got a job to do. Go ahead and do it." She turned and shuffled toward the stairs, talking as she went. "I'll pack her things."

"Do you need some help, Twila?" Lauren asked.

"*No.*"

Taryn kept her voice low. "I've discussed this with Ruby and Twila before. They both were aware that Twila would not be a suitable placement if for some reason Ruby couldn't take care of her daughter. She's just physically incapable due to her age and health."

"I'm sure you're right but it's still sad."

Taryn nodded. "Welcome to *my* world."

Voices from behind them grew louder. Sam walked into the living room, Officer Fuentes right behind him. Sam stopped abruptly and she bumped into the back of him.

"Sorry," mumbled Fuentes.

Sam ignored the apology as he stood there, mouth open, eyes wide. "Taryn?"

"Hello, Sam," Taryn replied.

"What are you doing here?" he asked.

"My job. Just like you." Taryn's words were quick and to the point.

These two know each other. Exes? Lauren watched them, searching for a clue as to what their relationship was. Or is.

"I'm here for Evie," Taryn said.

"Can't she just stay here with Ms. Nash?" asked Officer Fuentes.

"No," said Taryn. "The department had made it clear in the past that this was a suitable home for Ms. West and Evie. But it was also made very clear to Twila and Ms. West both that Ruby had to be the one taking care of her daughter. Ms. Nash is not an appropriate placement without assistance. Ms. Nash is well aware of that."

When Lauren first met her neighbor almost a year ago, the old lady's frosty demeanor made it clear she didn't want neighborly banter between the two of them. Twila's prickly exterior and independent streak made Lauren's offers to help with grocery shopping, yard work or any assistance impossible to accept. Lauren agreed with Taryn's assessment. Caring for an infant would be too much for someone Twila's age.

The sound of Evie's crying interrupted Lauren's thoughts. "I'll go see if Twila needs some help." *Why did I just volunteer? I don't know a thing about babies.*

Chapter Seven

The muffled crying stopped before Lauren stepped into the dimly lit bedroom. Twila was bent over a bassinet, changing Evie's diaper. Next to the bassinet, against the far wall, was an unmade single bed with an old-fashioned pink chenille bedspread crumpled at the foot. A dresser stood perched beneath the only window in the room, its shades drawn. Baby wipes, bottles, and stuffed animals were piled on top of the scuffed white dresser. A hamper overflowing with dirty clothes sat at the foot of the bed. The bedside table held a hand-painted leaf-shaped ceramic dish with an assortment of earrings, bracelets and rings. An open pack of gum sat beside it.

"Well, I guess it's time to say goodbye," Twila said. She bent closer to Evie and whispered, "I'm going to miss you."

She cleared her throat, then spoke louder. "You won't be waking me up at three o'clock in the morning anymore, will you?" Twila patted the little girl's belly with her gnarled fingers. "I'm just joking. You are such a good baby, sleeping straight through the night. I never heard a peep out of you. Besides, at my age there's no such thing as a good night's sleep."

She stroked the barely there blonde hair on top of the infant's head. "You've been such a joy to have here." Twila ignored a tear as it traveled down her wrinkled face. "And I know Percy is going to miss you, too."

Twila tucked Evie's plump legs into her onesie, pressed the snaps closed, and gave Evie a forced cheery smile. "There now. All dry and clean."

Lauren stepped beside Twila. "Do you mind if I carry her out?"

Twila straightened as much as her naturally hunched back would allow and placed Evie in Lauren's arms. "Go ahead. Just be careful. Make sure you cradle her head."

"How old is she?" *I'm so clueless when it comes to babies.*

"Three months." Twila reached for a pacifier attached to a soft plush unicorn and handed it to Lauren. "This is her favorite."

"Thank you." Lauren held her close. Evie's eyes opened, her gaze settling in on Lauren's hazel eyes. She smiled at Evie, all the while thinking how tragic this little girl's life is starting out.

"Is she ready?"

The women turned to find Taryn in the doorway.

"Uh, yes," Lauren said.

"Did you want a moment to say goodbye, Ms. Nash?" Taryn asked.

"I've already said my goodbyes." Twila turned her

attention to the bassinet. "I've got cleaning to do." She tugged at one corner of the sheet.

Taryn took Evie and started for the door.

"Does Evie have a coat?" Lauren asked. *She'll be cold with just what she's got on.*

Taryn glanced around the room. "It's probably in the car seat that I saw in the living room. I'll come back for the rest of her things later, Twila."

Twila took a baby blanket and handed it to Taryn. "It's awfully cold outside."

Lauren stood in the doorway. It had felt good, felt right, to hold someone so tiny against her and breathe in her fresh baby scent. She exhaled a shuddering breath, holding back tears. Evie would never know the feeling of being held by her mother. And Ruby would never have the chance to see her daughter grow up into a young woman.

Hold it together, Lauren. Hold it together.

Chapter Eight

Officer Fuentes and Sam were huddled in the living room, talking in low voices. Sam took a step back from the officer as Taryn and Lauren emerged from the hallway.

"I'm sure you don't need anything from me, Sam." Taryn placed Evie in the car seat, tucking the blanket around her and giving her a pacifier.

"No, I don't. We're good here. But keep me posted about where she's placed."

Taryn raised a questioning eyebrow at Sam.

"This is an active investigation with moving parts, Taryn. I just want to know where she'll be living, who will be taking care of her."

"I'm sure you already know from experience that she'll be in the legal custody of the Department of Family Services. When I get back to the office I'll be making calls to my fosters. I'll let you know when and where she gets placed. For the time being, she'll be with a non-relative foster family."

"Do you have information about the father?" Sam pulled out his notebook and pen. "Or any other familial relationships, besides Ms. Nash, I mean?"

Taryn's lips pulled into a straight thin line. "I will contact you when I have more information."

"Thank you," said Sam. "I have your phone number, so maybe I'll just check with you later. Unless it's changed."

"No, still the same number." She pulled a business card out of her coat pocket. "But it would be better to call on my business line."

Lauren listened to the exchange between Sam and Taryn. They were professional but held an undercurrent of something more. Taryn's tone was as icy as the temperature outside. She knew from the way the two greeted each other and this cold interaction that they knew one another. *What past do they share?*

Taryn draped the pink elephant-print baby blanket Ms. Nash had given her over the carrier. *This scenario, having to remove a child from a home, isn't new to Taryn*, thought Lauren. She watched her friend hold the baby carrier like an oversized Gucci bag, the handle in the crook of her arm, and texting with her free hand. When Taryn finished she dropped her phone into her coat pocket and said a curt goodbye.

What a hard job she has. It was one thing to sit in a courtroom or in a deposition and listen to tragic stories being shared, something Lauren had done as a regular part of her job. But being here, in Twila's home, seeing Taryn in action, caseworkers lived the story, were a part of the story. At times a horrific story.

Lauren slowly shook her head. *I could never do what Taryn does.* When Lauren worked for Judge Brubaker and reported her first shelter care hearing, a newborn taken away from its mother after being born addicted to heroin, Lauren almost cried. Almost. Instead, she kept her head down, focused on writing every word spoken. It didn't stop her, however, from breaking down when she got home. It had taken a year before her mind had become calloused enough to where the painful stories stopped following her home, invading her thoughts daily. She didn't know if that was a good thing or not.

"Lauren?"

She turned.

Sam's dark brown eyes focused on her face. "Are you okay?"

"Uh, yeah, I'm fine. It's just so sad, you know?"

He nodded. "It always is. Listen, I'd like you to write out a statement of the events. If you have time to do it now, that would be great. But it's not urgent, I understand if you need a little time. You can drop it off at the station later today."

"I'll … I'll do it now while it's fresh in my mind." *What the hell are you saying? Fresh? You're never going to forget what you saw this morning. Ruby sprawled on the snow, face toward the sky. Her mascaraed lashes shiny with frost. And her eyes. Those cloudy blue eyes.*

Lauren sucked in a ragged breath. "I'm just going to say goodbye to Twila."

"Sure. We're going to ask Ms. Nash a few questions and then head back to the station."

Twila shuffled into the living room, her mouth in a pinched line, her eyes red rimmed behind her glasses. She clutched Percy against her chest. "I don't need anything, Lauren. You can go."

"If you change your mind, just call. I'm right next door. I can come right over."

"I know where you live." Twila made a point of turning her head and attention toward Sam. Lauren had been dismissed.

"Go ahead, Detective, ask your questions."

Sam motioned with his head, his way of saying goodbye to Lauren. She knew he was on duty, in work mode. He couldn't hug her, even though that's what she desperately needed, to feel the warmth of his body as he wrapped his arms around her. His deep baritone in her ear, telling her it will be all right.

"Please, why don't you sit down. I know this is very difficult for you, Ms. Nash."

Twila lowered herself into a well-worn recliner, the overstuffed cushions swallowing her shrunken frame.

Percy ran into the kitchen. He yipped. Lauren followed. He sat by two blue bowls. His feathery tail swished back and forth across the scuffed and faded linoleum flooring. One bowl held kibble crumbs, the other a few drops of water. A small bag of dog food sat on the counter. Lauren opened it and poured some into the empty bowl. She took the other bowl to the sink and refreshed the water. She lingered for a moment in hopes of hearing the conversation in the living room but their voices were muffled.

She placed Percy's water next to his food. As she straightened she heard Twila's voice, loud and strong. "I don't care what you found out there, my granddaughter did *not* use drugs."

Chapter Nine

Lauren trudged through the snow, head down, her thoughts on Ruby, Evie, and Twila. She let herself in through her unlocked back door, took off her coat and boots, and placed them in their designated spots by the door that led to her garage.

She made herself a cup of hot chocolate, took it into the living room and sank onto the couch. She barely had time to put the hot drink on the end table before Maverik jumped on the sofa. He pressed his bulk against her thigh before curling up next to her. She absently stroked his head.

The deposition sat on her computer upstairs needing to be finished but right now it would have to wait. Lauren knew she wouldn't be able to concentrate. Instead, she stared through the open living room curtains, thinking of Ruby and the syringe by her side. Lauren hadn't known her, but Taryn had been her caseworker and took Evie with her. It meant Ruby had a case plan. The only way that happens is if the state found her neglectful of Evie. In Lauren's world that meant most likely by using when she gave birth.

With the syringe by her side, her death could only mean one thing. Ruby accidently overdosed. But why was she even using? She must have known that there's always a chance of overdosing. And why would she risk testing positive and losing her daughter again? But maybe when you have a child and you're a teen mom, you feel overwhelmed. Or maybe it had nothing to do with her age. Whatever Ruby injected herself with was the final Satan-like grip it held on her, like a snake wrapped around Ruby's mind, squeezing out her last breath.

Lauren wiped her eyes with her shirt sleeve. "It's going to happen again, Maverik. I just know it." Her dog's ears twitched at the sound of his name and he lifted his head. "You should know what I'm talking about. You were the one who lead me to Alden Bates's body." She dug her fingers into Maverik's thick fur. He placed his head on her lap so she could continue the massage. "That was awful. I guess it's not the same for dogs. But I just know the nightmares are going to start up. Just when life was beginning to feel a little normal again." Lauren closed her eyes and breathed in on the count of four. She held the breath, then slowly let the air out of her lungs.

Calming breaths. Calming breaths. After a moment she opened her eyes.

Maverik rolled onto his back exposing his belly for a rub. "Is this your way of trying to take my mind off of what happened this morning? Or do you just not care how I feel?" She shook her head slowly, a resigned smile tugging at her mouth as she took her dog's hint and scratched his black-and-brown stomach.

Chapter Ten

Sam and Officer Fuentes returned to the station after spending the bulk of the morning at Ms. Nash's home. He woke the computer on his desk, swiveling in his chair, thinking about what the old woman said. She'd held back angry tears and insisted her granddaughter had not started using again. Twila admitted Ruby had what Twila referred to as an issue in the past, but had been clean and sober ever since she moved in.

Twila was, like most family members in a situation like this, in denial. Every parent wanted to believe their child, or grandchild, when they said they were no longer using drugs, that they kicked the habit and were clean. The syringe at Ruby's arm told a different story. It spoke of someone actively using. Though early in his investigation, he knew DFS had legal custody of Evie. It meant Ruby most likely had been a drug user, at least during the time of the baby's birth. There were other reasons children were removed from their parents, but drug use was the most common one. Teen moms were no exception.

In Crawford, there had been six accidental overdoses in the last three months, three resulting in death, two female, one male. With the town's population hovering at the thirty-thousand mark, three deaths was a significant number. The toxicology reports for the ones that died were positive for illicit substances in their system. The one nagging thought, the one variant, different drugs appeared in each tox screen. Other than an overdose resulting in death, there weren't any other connections, anything in common tying the cases together. Nothing as simple as a bad batch of meth laced with fentanyl showing up on the streets causing the uptick in OD numbers.

Sam heard the now recognizable approach of the new chief of police, Harrison Finch, heading in his direction. His boss no doubt wanted an update about this morning's death.

Four months ago, Ray Newell stepped down as the chief of police. In exchange, the county attorney didn't file criminal charges against him for aiding and abetting after the fact of a murder. Lieutenant Alan Pacheco served as the interim chief for three months. Instead of selecting him as the new chief, the mayor hired someone on the outside, citing wanting a fresh outlook on policing in Crawford. In this case, it meant not only outside of the department but searching outside of Wyoming.

Harrison Finch had been recruited from Richmond, Kentucky. They were still feeling each other out, Sam still getting used to a new boss. So far from what Sam observed,

Chief Finch had the right temperament to oversee a police department, and the smarts. Maybe it was adjusting to a new town, or adjusting to the fact that he was a minority, only one of three black men in the small police department, but the man's helicopter-mom management style had Sam grinding his molars whenever the chief talked to him about an ongoing investigation.

"What's the story with the deceased, Overstreet?"

"It's looking like a drug overdose, sir. No obvious signs of trauma. Teen mom. In the court system. The Department of Family Services had been working a case plan with her. Right now, I assume it's because she had a history of drug use. Of course, we'll know more when we get the autopsy and tox screens back."

Chief Finch nodded. "When do y'all expect that'll be?"

"Sir, I have no idea. Right now, the body is chilling at the hospital because the roads in and out of town are closed. Once she gets down to Loveland, I'll make a call and see what their estimate is."

"Loveland? Where is that exactly?"

"Colorado. It's south of here, right off the interstate, about an hour and a half drive."

"Cheyenne is, what, less than an hour east of here? Isn't there an ME or pathologist there? I mean, it's the biggest city in Wyoming. Surely the state has their own pathologist."

"No, we don't." Sam added, "And sometimes we have to use someone in Denver if Dr. Grant, the pathologist in Loveland, is too backed up."

The police chief's expression said he wanted to argue with Sam, to say that just couldn't be, but instead he replied, "Well, keep on it."

"Of course, sir."

"I understand there's been several drug overdoses in the last few months."

"Yes, sir."

"Have you been in contact with the DEA? It's important that we get a handle on this."

No shit, sir. "Officer Blain was taken off patrol and assigned to work with the Southeast Drug Enforcement Administration team. He's been reporting back to us. And I've got a call in to DCI. They should have more information about the drug situation as well. The only thing DEA knows for sure is that it isn't a single or specific batch of methamphetamine that's made its way into Crawford."

"And they know this how?"

"The path reports on some of the victims showed different drugs in their system; meth in a couple, fentanyl and meth combined in a few others. It's not looking like it's from one bad batch."

Chief Finch slowly shook his head, letting a long breath escape. Sam knew the importance for the new chief to show the mayor he had not made a mistake in his choice when he hired him. The police chief not only wanted results, he needed them.

"Keep me updated."

"Of course, sir."

"That was one hell of a snowstorm we had Thursday, Overstreet. I don't think I've ever seen that much snow come down at once. Took me a heck of a long time just to shovel my way to the car."

"Don't get snow like this in Richmond, I imagine. Too far south?"

Chief inch nodded vigorously. "We never get this much snow."

"Welcome to Wyoming, sir." Sam gave him a wry smile. "And I'm pretty certain this storm is just a teaser for what's to come."

"What do you mean? It's almost March. Spring is just around the corner."

"It is. But Mother Nature treats us special this time of year."

The chief's amber eyes locked on Sam's, as if he were waiting for Sam to laugh or say, "Just kidding." Sam did neither.

"Our snowiest months of the year are March and April, sir, so don't put that shovel away just yet."

The chief closed his eyes and shook his head. "That's just plain wrong."

He turned and walked out of the cramped space, leaving Sam to say to the man's retreating broad shoulders, "Our weather is going to be a test for you."

Sam turned toward the wide window behind him. He couldn't wait to move into the new public safety center slated to open in September.

Snow pressed against the garden-level glass panes filtering out any natural light, his claustrophobia threatening to emerge.

Chapter Eleven

Sam alternated between taking bites of his roast beef sandwich and entering the scant information he had on Ruby West into the computer. After he swallowed the last of his lunch, he crumpled the paper wrapper, tossed it in the trash can and continued typing. As he did so a shadow crossed his desk. Officer Fuentes hovered in the doorway. "Hey, Lola. What's up?"

"I came to see if there's anything you want me to do on the West case."

"Why don't you finish inputting data into her electronic file."

"Um, sure, I can do that."

He heard the disappointment in her voice. Simple data entry. Officer Fuentes had sat for her oral boards for the open detective's position on the force last month. Her responses in the interview, which Sam sat in on, showed an insight into what it takes to do the job well. She'd been selected.

Officer Fuentes needed to gain experience so she could take on her own caseload, and Sam needed to work on letting go of doing every single aspect of an investigation himself. He'd heard the whispers in the station. *Sam's a workaholic.* When he married Ashley, everyone assumed he'd loosen the reins on handling his cases and not work so hard. It hadn't happened. He'd come to realize, grudgingly, yes, he worked too much. That had been one of two reasons for the short-lived marriage. The second had been his own stupidity, remarrying so soon after his late wife's death. For not grieving properly for Abby. At least that was the consensus of the people in group therapy. *What do they know? Besides, being a workaholic in this profession isn't such a bad thing, is it?*

"I'll go get started on that," said Lola.

He blinked. "Wait a minute. We need to set up a time to talk to Ms. West's caseworker. See what they have to say about how her case plan was going, any concerns they might have had about ongoing drug use. Or if they thought things were going well." He rubbed his clean-shaven chin. "We'll go together, you taking the lead."

Lola bounced a little on her toes. "Great. What time?"

"Why don't you call DFS and find out who her caseworker is. Taryn Biggs was there this morning as the on-call person but it's probably someone else who is actually working Ruby's case. Let me know when you've set up a time."

"I'll get on it right now." The young officer did an about-face and strode out of his office, her sleek black ponytail swaying with each enthusiastic step.

*   *   *

Sam checked the time before shrugging into his parka, pulled his knit cap and gloves from his coat pocket, and walked to the lobby area, passing Nancy on his way out. "See you tomorrow."

The round-faced woman dragged her attention away from her computer screen. "Is it that time already, Sam?"

"For me it is."

"Don't you go rubbing it in that you're done for the day, young man."

Sam glanced at the clock on the wall. "You've only got another ten minutes left in paradise."

Nancy glanced around the room with exaggeration, her head moving up, down and sideways. "Paradise, huh? Is that what this place is?"

He let out a laugh. "Of course it is."

"If you say so. You drive carefully out there, Sam."

"Yes, ma'am, I will."

Nancy returned her attention to the information on her computer screen and Sam walked toward the front entrance.

"Detective, wait."

He glanced over his shoulder to see Officer Fuentes jogging toward him.

"We have an appointment at eight thirty in the morning with Ms. West's DFS worker."

"Good job, Lola." He continued toward the exit sign. "See you tomorrow morning." He knew if he turned around right this very moment he'd see a big grin on the officer's face.

Chapter Twelve

"These chicken enchiladas are amazing," Sam mumbled as he chewed.

"Thanks. They are *really* good, aren't they?" *Should I tell him the truth?* Lauren knew he assumed she had made them. Lauren took a sip of her wine. "I didn't actually make them myself." She gave him a sly smile. "But I did reheat them all by myself."

Sam arched an eyebrow at her, his fork in midair.

"Aunt Kate made these. I called her and explained what happened today. She doesn't know Twila, only what she's heard me say about her, but she made Twila some comfort food." Lauren lifted one shoulder. "At first Twila refused, but my aunt insisted ..." Lauren tipped her glass toward the empty pan on the table. "... and made an extra casserole. I did have every intention of cooking tonight. I really did."

"I get it, Lauren." Sam gave her a warm smile. "After everything that happened this morning, cooking was probably the last thing on your mind."

Lauren did a slow nod. "Yeah. And I still can't believe it. I mean, I didn't really know Twila's granddaughter or her situation. I introduced myself when I saw her out front one day but the wind was blowing, so we didn't talk long. I assumed Ruby was staying with Twila because I saw the teen driving Twila's car, coming and going with the baby for the last couple of months."

Ruby, lying in the snow, her expression of surprise flashed in Lauren's mind. Her stomach knotted at the image. She placed the hardly touched glass in the sink. *I really am not a wine drinker.*

"Aunt Kate and I went over to Twila's but we didn't stay. Twila said she was fine and didn't feel like company. I asked if I could call anyone for her. She said there was no one in town to call. We dropped off the food and left."

Lauren sucked in a long breath, fighting off the onset of tears. She'd been feeling on the verge of crying all afternoon. It didn't make sense. Lauren hardly knew Ruby. Maybe it was the sight of Twila who always came off as tough, stoic, mean even. Today she looked lost — lost, vulnerable and somehow defeated. "How sad is that?"

"We've found out some of Ruby's history as well. You were there when Ms. Nash mentioned Ruby's mother, Cynthia West. That was Ms. Nash's daughter."

That explains a lot about Twila and her permanent gruffness, thought Lauren. She suffered the loss of her daughter.

"According to Twila, Ruby's father is a real piece of work.

After going to his house to give him the death notification, I agree with Ms. Nash's assessment."

"Why? What did he say?"

"That he wasn't surprised she ended up dead. He said he knew she'd been doing drugs before he kicked her out of the house. And his final remark as I was leaving was the kicker. He said, 'And now I suppose I gotta put out money for a funeral.'" Sam raised his eyes to Lauren and slowly shook his head. "I should be used to hearing all kinds of shit, but people never cease to amaze me."

"Who's going to end up with her baby?" *Evie is so sweet, so perfect, with her fine blonde hair and those chubby little hands.*

"It's too early to know. I did find out that Ruby and a Carson Millwood were seeing each other for quite some time. That might be who the dad is but it's not a definite. I have a call in to DFS to find out where we are on that front. But as you know from your time in court, DFS has a procedure they have to go through. They have to establish paternity, of course, and see if he's a viable candidate for placing Evie with him. If he is the father, find out if he's interested in stepping up and being a dad."

"And sometimes they're not," Lauren added. "They just sign away their parental rights. If that happens with Evie, the only good thing is she's so young she'll easily get adopted."

Lauren gathered their plates and placed them in the sink. She spoke as she rinsed each one and loaded them in the dishwasher. "Thanks for coming over tonight. I know that was the original plan but that was before ... before this morning. I thought maybe you wouldn't be able to make it." She glanced over her shoulder at him. "Which would have been perfectly understandable. I mean …"

Sam came up behind her, reached for the glass in her hand and set it in the sink. He placed his sturdy hands on her shoulders and pulled her close, his breath warm on her ear. "Lauren, you've had a shock today. I didn't want you to be alone tonight."

He rested his chin on her head and wrapped his arms around her. She leaned into his chest and into his words, feeling her body and mind relax for the first time that day.

Chapter Thirteen

Officer Fuentes slid behind the wheel of her patrol car as Sam dropped into the passenger seat. She started the engine, letting it idle before turning the heat and defrost on high.

Sam peered into the back. A plastic bin rested on the seat filled with various items including Fuentes's police-issued laptop, a clipboard, and an open box of latex gloves.

"I cleared off the passenger seat for you, Detective."

"I see that. Thanks. And call me Sam."

Lola nodded. She drove out of the parking lot with warm air spewing from the vents.

"Do you know where the DFS office is?" Sam asked.

"Um-hum. I drive past it on my way to work."

It took ten minutes to arrive at the Wyoming DFS field office, and that included sitting at two red lights. Other than talking about the weather, the drive had been quiet.

Sam thought about telling Officer Fuentes what questions needed to be asked of the caseworker but decided to let her take the lead completely. He would observe her first interview and see if she asked the questions he would have.

Officer Fuentes parked in a visitor spot in the small parking lot and killed the engine. Before getting out, she said, "Thanks for letting me do this."

"No need to thank me. You need the experience. Only one way to get that." He shifted in the seat and faced her. "This should be relatively simple. You're here to gather any information that will tell us what Ruby's life was like, at least from this person's perspective. Find out the status of Ruby's case, if she was following her case plan. See if her caseworker had any concerns, and if Ruby had been testing clean."

"Does it really matter?" asked Lola. "I mean in the long run? Even if she had been clean, she certainly wasn't that morning."

"On the surface I agree, but it doesn't hurt to have a better picture of what Ruby was like."

The detective-in-training nodded, then slid her sunglasses onto her face. "That makes sense."

"Who was her assigned caseworker, by the way?" asked Sam.

"It's the same woman that was at Ms. Nash's yesterday. Taryn Biggs."

Sam nodded. "Taryn should have answers for you."

They got out of the vehicle and were greeted with the blinding brightness of sun and snow. Lola pressed her key fob and the car doors locked with a chirp. Sam pulled out his sunglasses and slipped them on. The two made their way toward the entrance of the one-story office building, the only sounds the distant hum of street traffic and the squeaking of their boots as they hit the hard-packed snow.

"You must be Officer Fuentes." Ms. Biggs stood in front of the receptionist's desk in the lobby. She walked over and reached out to shake the officer's hand.

"Yes," said Officer Fuentes, as she removed her shades and pocketed them.

"Nice to meet you," Taryn said. "I know you were at Ms. Nash's house yesterday but we weren't formally introduced. Understandable under the circumstances."

"Nice to meet you as well," Officer Fuentes said. She turned and gestured with her hand. "This, as you probably know, is Detective —"

"Overstreet." Taryn forced a tight smile on her long face. "Yes, I know. He and I go way back."

"Good to see you, Taryn." Sam dipped his head.

"I was just on my way to the break room to get some coffee. Would either of you like a cup?"

"No thanks. I think we're good." Officer Fuentes stole a glance at Sam, as if seeking confirmation.

"We're good," Sam agreed.

Taryn pointed with her mug. "My office is the second on the right. Have a seat and I'll be right in."

Ms. Taryn Biggs. It felt odd thinking of his ex-sister-in-law in such a formal way. Not too long ago she had simply been Taryn. She barely acknowledged his presence yesterday. He chalked it up to the fact that they were both at Ms. Nash's house in their professional capacities, but still...

Sam and Officer Fuentes entered a room that contained a small faux wood desk, an office chair, two visitor chairs, a child-size plastic table and chair, and not much room for anything else. Cold fluorescent lighting filled the room. A short bookcase sat in a corner, its shelves filled with children's books. There were botanical prints on the wall opposite Taryn's desk. The wall behind her desk contained children's drawings on white sheets of paper secured by clear tape. One of different-size colorful stick figures, one of a smiling sun, and one of what might have been a dog or a cat on green grass. Artwork of the children who visited while Taryn met with their parents.

The two sat in the visitor chairs. Officer Fuentes pulled her phone out of her jacket pocket, looked at Sam, a nervous excitement in her eyes.

Sam jutted his chin toward Officer Fuentes's phone. "I should start taking notes on my phone. Not sure why I haven't switched yet."

Officer Fuentes raised one shoulder. "If it ain't broke, don't fix it, maybe?"

He smiled. "Nice of you not to tell me I'm on my way to becoming a dinosaur."

Taryn walked in, set her cup down on the desk. She blew out a breath, causing her blonde curtain of bangs to rise. "It's so sad about Ruby. I had hopes that she would be one of the ones to turn her life around." She coughed and took a sip of coffee. "On the phone you said you had some questions." Taryn woke her screen up with a tap of a key. "I went ahead and pulled up the case file with all my notes. "Officer Fuentes, what would you like to know?"

"I have a few background questions. Ms. West had been a client of DFS. When did that begin?"

"I've been her caseworker ever since Evie was born. Let

me see when we opened a file for her." Taryn nodded at the screen. "Yes, November 15."

"Had there been any contact with Ruby before that time?"

"No, the department's first contact with her was at the hospital when she gave birth."

"I see. And so you've been her caseworker for approximately three months?"

Taryn enlarged the calendar function from the task bar. She appeared to be doing a mental calculation in her head. "Almost three months to the day as a matter of fact." She scrunched her brows together and sighed. "Though technically I'm now no longer her caseworker. DFS's efforts now are to place Evie with her father once he's identified, and if we don't have any luck in that department, an eventual adoption."

Sam had his notepad out but had yet to write anything in it. Instead he took in Taryn's demeanor. Her back ramrod straight, shoulders back, head tilted up. If she had worn glasses she would be looking down her nose through them. He suspected his presence had something to do with the ultra-professionalism she displayed.

"And when was your last contact with Ms. West?" Officer Fuentes asked.

Taryn checked the notations on her screen. "It looks like I paid her and Evie a visit on the Friday before her death."

Fuentes tapped on her phone and without looking up asked her next question. "And how did the visit go?"

"It went" — Taryn cocked her head — "okay is the best way to say it. It was an unannounced visit. That's where I just show up without advanced notice to see how things are going. Ruby told me Evie had just woken and been fed. The baby had on clean clothes, wasn't fussy. So that part was good. But another reason I was there was Ruby had failed to show up for a drug test the day before. And the previous week she failed to show for her random. Meaning she missed testing twice in the last two weeks." Taryn tapped on her keyboard. "Let me revise that. She did reschedule the previous week. But she also had a positive UA the first week of January." Taryn swiveled in her chair to face Officer Fuentes again.

"How often was she required to drug test?"

"She was down to once a week random. That had been going on for" — Ms. Biggs turned to the monitor again — "a month. Before that it was two times a week." Taryn took a sip of her coffee. "I asked her why she missed testing." Taryn read the notes contained in the online file. "It's just marked on here that she was a no-show. The day before I showed up, Ruby said the roads were too bad to travel." The caseworker leaned in, almost squinting at the monitor. "Let's see. She told me she rescheduled and would be testing on that coming Monday." Taryn cocked her head, waiting for Officer Fuentes's next question.

As the questions and answers flowed, Sam thought back to the last time he had seen Taryn. Ten or so months ago, right before she and his brother separated. Sam had invited them over for a family cookout, along with a few friends. Kyle and Taryn spent the whole afternoon apart, and Taryn hadn't been her usual bubbly self. She'd sat on the fringe of conversation nursing a glass of wine. She'd also put on some extra pounds, and her blue eyes lacked their spark, their usual playfulness. When he and his brother Kyle had the chance to be alone, he told Sam that he and Taryn had hit a rough patch in their marriage. He hadn't gone into detail but said it revolved around the usual topic of conversation, wanting to start a family and Taryn not being able to get pregnant.

Sam shifted in the chair, returning his attention to Fuentes's latest question.

"Were you concerned that Ms. West might be relapsing?"

Taryn scrolled through the document, her silver-ringed index finger effortlessly spinning the wheel of the mouse. "The trial home placement had been going well. But missing a UA test, even if it's made up the next day, yes, I was. It's always a concern when someone starts missing tests. I emphasized to her the need to continue testing and not miss any more if Evie was to continue in her custody."

Officer Fuentes glanced at her phone. "What do you know about Carson Millwood, the baby's father?"

"The only thing I know for certain is there is no father listed on the birth certificate."

Officer Fuentes raised one perfectly plucked eyebrow. "No one?"

Taryn nodded. "You must be new to this sort of work, Officer Fuentes. That's not uncommon, certainly not in the world we live in today." She rested her fingers on the edge of the desk. "When a woman gives birth and she's not married, she can't just put anyone's name down as the father. The man has to agree, and not only agree, he has to sign an affidavit as well. Otherwise the line for the father is left blank."

"Oh, I see," Officer Fuentes said.

A few more questions were asked before Officer Fuentes pocketed her phone. She caught Sam's slight nod, his way of telling her that, yes, she could end the questioning.

Officer Fuentes rose and reached over to shake Taryn's hand. "Thank you for your time, Ms. Biggs. This information is helpful." She rooted in her coat pocket and produced a business card. "If you think of anything else, please call me. My cell number is on the back."

"I will. And if there's anything else I can help you with, please let me know. Again, it's such a shame that Ruby started using again. I really wished things turned out differently. And especially for Evie." She gave the officer a sad smile. "Such a beautiful baby. She deserved a better start in life."

Sam rose and stuck his hand out to shake Taryn's but she had turned her attention to the computer screen in front of her, either not seeing or ignoring his outstretched hand.

Chapter Fourteen

Officer Fuentes buckled her seatbelt and started the car. "So, how did I do? Did I ask everything I should have? Or I should say, everything you would have?"

"You did great. You got some useful information."

"Like Ms. Biggs thought Ruby might have started using again?"

"Are you stating your opinion? Or are you asking me?"

Officer Fuentes didn't answer right away. When she did, she said, "From what Ms. Biggs said, it's likely she started using again. But the autopsy will give us definite answers."

Sam nodded. "I agree with your assessment of what Taryn shared. And your conclusion, to wait on the lab results."

"If Taryn is right," Officer Fuentes went on, "Ruby's grandmother may not have known her as well as she thought. Ms. Nash didn't believe she was using again."

"Yes, she was pretty adamant. But that could just mean Ruby was good at hiding it."

The two talked about the interview until they pulled into the police department parking lot. Officer Fuentes found a spot close to the entrance and parked. She got out and joined Sam on the sidewalk. "So what's the history with you and Ms. Biggs?"

Sam didn't answer, just kept walking until they reached the steps leading down to the station entrance. As he opened the door for her, he said, "You're going to make a good detective, Lola." Sam watched a small smile cross Officer Fuentes's lips. "Taryn was married to my brother."

"Oh."

"And they haven't been divorced all that long."

"That explains her dislike of you."

He let out a snort. "Dislike? Is that the vibe you got?"

Officer Fuentes nodded vigorously. "Oh, yeah."

And here I thought it was just an awkwardness of seeing her ex-brother-in-law.

They entered the department, waved to Nancy. As they made their way back to Sam's office, Officer Fuentes said, "Whenever you glanced around her office or were busy writing something down she'd sneak a sideways glance at you. And those blue eyes were prit-tee steely."

Maybe Lola is right about her disliking me.

"Very observant of you, Lola. Why don't you write up your notes, or transfer your notes, or do whatever it is you do, to get it off your phone and into the file."

"Will do," said Officer Fuentes with a quick salute.

Sam watched her retreat down the hallway, her shiny ponytail in motion.

Chapter Fifteen

Lauren towel-dried her hair, then dressed in yoga pants and a well-worn brown-and-gold hoodie with the University of Wyoming's logo, a cowboy on a bucking horse stitched across the front. She'd woken before dawn. The image of Ruby in the snow had wormed its way into her subconscious, making her jerk awake more than once throughout the night. Each time it took a while for sleep to overtake her. The last time it happened she didn't try to go back to sleep. Instead she got dressed, made some toast, and as soon as the sun broke the horizon, she went and shoveled snow from her sidewalk and then cleaned Twila's walkway as well. She'd worked up a sweat and told herself it counted as exercise so maybe she'd skip the gym today.

In the kitchen, she stirred creamer into a large mug of coffee, took the warm drink and sat at the small kitchen table. Maverik lay at her feet, his body pressing against the chair legs, a chew toy between his paws.

She cradled the mug in one hand, checking her phone with the other, hoping to see a text from Sam. He'd left her house a little after ten o'clock last night, after she asked him if he wanted to stay. She thought she covered her disappointment well when he said he shouldn't. He gave the right reason. He had to get up early to work on Ruby's case. Lauren had no confidence in her ability to read a boyfriend's feelings or emotions. Tell if a person lied on the witness stand and under oath? Sure. She could do that with her eyes closed, figuratively speaking. But relationships were a different matter. She'd been wrong too many times before and found it difficult to trust her own gut.

Before going to bed last night she had texted Sam a GIF of a sleeping dog. She had expected a meme of a cat and dog cuddled together in return, what she thought of as their semi- evening ritual. She got nothing in response. She'd told herself he was already in bed asleep. He had a busy day ahead. But then she remembered the officer that was with him yesterday. The very pretty one. The one with a shiny mane of black hair, dark brown eyes and a skin tone Lauren wished she'd been born with, not her pale complexion that burned easily in the summer sun. Maybe he texted *Lola* … that was her name, right? … after he left her house, and they went for a drink. What if Sam were attracted to her? Heck, he'd be crazy not to find her good-looking. And Lola had been literally by his side the whole time yesterday.

"Stop it."

Maverik stopped chewing on his pitted nylon bone, his ears back.

"Sorry. Not you. Me." *I'm once again filling my head with silly thoughts. But are they silly?*

Her audience went back to gnawing his toy.

Her ex-husband Tony had told her she'd had a jealous streak. He made the comment that green wasn't a good look on her. Only, in hindsight, it turned out she'd been right to be jealous of her ex. Tony cheated on her during their marriage, though she hadn't known at the time. After their divorce she moved to Denver, Colorado, in search of a new start. She thought she found that in Kevin, an attorney. Lauren had begun to feel good about her life again, until one day she didn't. She consoled herself with the fact that at least she hadn't made the mistake of marrying him. Lauren came away with a vow of never dating an attorney again.

Admit it, Lauren, you not only gravitate to Mr. Wrong but Mr. Really Wrong.

She put her cup in the sink. The clock on the microwave read eight forty-five. Not too early to drop in on her neighbor. After what happened to Ruby, and then Evie being whisked away, Lauren assumed Twila wouldn't have gotten any sleep either and would be awake.

Before leaving her neighbor's house yesterday she told Twila to call if she needed anything but knew the old lady well enough to know there would be no phone call.

Lauren grabbed her parka off the hook. She had a deposition in Cheyenne to cover but it didn't start until one thirty. As she shoved her arms inside her coat, part of her hoped the attorney taking the deposition would call and say they had to cancel. Southeastern Wyoming had been digging itself out of the snowstorm they'd recently had.

Snowplows were finally able to clear the interstate, but the road being open didn't mean it would be an easy drive. The high wind warning that showed up on the weather app on her phone added to her anxiety about driving the fifty miles to get to Cheyenne. Days like today made her long for her previous job as an official court reporter. Working in the same courtroom every day. Working for one judge. No traveling shitty roads.

Maverik trotted over. "No, *we're* not going out. I am." She put on her boots and was about to slip on her gloves when her phone pinged with an email. She read it, then let out a little whoop. "Good news, Maverik. The depo just canceled." She tilted her head back. "Thank you."

Lauren put on her gloves. "I'll be right back." She shut the door behind her and walked down the freshly shoveled sidewalk to her neighbor's house. The door opened before Lauren had a chance to knock.

"Get out of that cold," Twila snapped. She wore the same pink robe that she'd had on yesterday. Her dyed red curls hung limp around her slack face. Even the thick lenses of her glasses couldn't hide her puffy eyes.

"I hope you don't mind me stopping by."

Percy wriggled in Twila's arms until she put him down. He danced on his hind legs and Lauren picked him up. He licked her face. "Okay, okay. She pulled herself loose from his tongue. "Thank you, but no more licking, please. Oh, and Maverik says hi."

Percy stopped licking Lauren but at the sound of Maverik's name his feathery tail went into overdrive wagging. At times it surprised Lauren that a mere five months ago Percy came into her life. She more or less fostered him after her boss, Judge Murphy, had been murdered, leaving Percy with no one to care for him.

Lauren had been shocked when Twila agreed to take him in. Lauren discovered that Ms. Nash, hard and crusty as a stale baguette on the outside, had a soft spot inside for little dogs in need.

The old woman appeared to have aged five years since yesterday. Lauren instinctively reached out to hug her, but with Percy nestled in her arms Lauren settled for an awkward side pat on the woman's bony shoulder. *At least she didn't pull away.*

"Since you're here, might as well come on in." Twila led Lauren to the kitchen, where she let Lauren make them some hot tea. While the teakettle heated, Ms. Nash sank into a chair at the small Formica-topped table. In a raspy voice just above a whisper, Twila said, "I still can't believe she's gone. I just can't." She picked a loose hair of Percy's off her robe. "Evie too. It's so quiet now. At least I won't have to take my hearing aids out to get some peace and quiet around here." She gave a humorless laugh. "Either way, hearing aids in or out, all I hear is silence. I miss that little one's …" She broke off, covering her face with a wrinkled hand.

Lauren turned to the cabinets, searching for mugs and struggling to hold back her own tears. She found two mismatched cups, reached for a box of tea bags on the counter and busied herself. Lauren placed a cup of tea in front of Twila and joined her at the table. "I can't imagine how hard this is for you."

Twila absently dunked the teabag in the hot water. "This getting old stuff stinks. First I lost my daughter. Now my granddaughter."

"I'm sorry for your loss." Lauren knew the words were inadequate as soon as they were out of her mouth.

Lauren tugged at the collar of her hoodie. The temperature in the house had to be close to eighty degrees, but Twila didn't seem to mind.

Twila nodded. "It's been three years now since my Cynthia passed. Ruby was only thirteen when she died." Twila gazed out her kitchen window, her focus on the past. "Cynthia was a good daughter. Came by to check on me all the time. Picked up my groceries if I was under the weather. Had me over for dinner."

"This has to be so hard on you. I'm really sorry."

Ms. Nash stood, turned away from Lauren and reached for the sugar bowl on the counter, and placed it on the table. "I don't need nobody feeling sorry for me, including you." She added a heaping teaspoonful to her tea and pushed the bowl toward Lauren.

Lauren helped herself to a spoonful. *That's why you're so gruff all the time.* Losing another loved one might turn that hardened shell of Twila's into concrete, thought Lauren.

Twila narrowed her eyes at Lauren. "And I'll tell you, I didn't like the way that detective friend of yours ignored what I had to say about Ruby." Her voice returned to its normal deep rasp. "I don't think he believed me when I told him that she was a good girl, that she hadn't been using drugs while she lived with me."

Lauren sipped her tea and let Twila talk. They were the most words the woman had spoken to her since Lauren moved in next door two years ago. That is if you didn't count Twila's complaining to her about Maverik barking all the time, which Lauren didn't.

"I'm old. I don't know all the things young people are into, but my granddaughter" — Twila's voice cracked — "and my great granddaughter lived with me for over two months. I got to know Ruby real good. She didn't take whatever drug they say she did. She wouldn't have. In my heart, I just know." For emphasis she patted the hollow of her chest.

A knock on the door interrupted their conversation. Percy scampered out of the kitchen, his nails tap-dancing on the kitchen floor before running into the living room. He jumped onto the back of the sofa, his nose pressed against the window, and let out several high-pitched yips.

"I'll go see who it is." Lauren looked through the peephole of the door, then opened it. A short figure stood on the porch encased in a pink puffer jacket, its faux fur hood covering her head. The only things visible were the large-framed glasses and a startled look in her eyes.

"Uh, hi. Is Ruby home?"

Chapter Sixteen

Lauren gestured to the girl to come inside. Cold air whipped around and made its way in, along with the teen.

This has to be a friend of Ruby's, a friend who doesn't know what's happened to her, thought Lauren. She glanced back toward the kitchen. Lauren didn't know whether she should break the news to her or let Twila do it, it being her granddaughter, after all. At the same time she didn't want to witness Ms. Nash fall apart as she tried to explain what happened to Ruby.

"Hi, I'm Lauren. I live next door." Lauren gestured with her hand in the direction of her house.

"I'm Makayla, a friend of Ruby's. She hasn't answered any of my texts, and she wasn't in school today. I know I'm probably overreacting ... my mom says I get that way sometimes ... but I just wanted to make sure she's okay. Is she sick?"

"Come on in, Makayla," called Twila from the kitchen.

"Hi, Ms. Nash," said Makayla as she entered the kitchen. "I just came over to see Ruby. Is she here?"

"No, dear." Twila took a steadying breath and said, "She … she died yesterday, dear."

"*What?*" Makayla clamped a hand over her mouth and stared at Twila. She backed up a couple of steps, as if distancing herself from the words would somehow make them less true. "Ruby's dead? No. That can't be true."

Lauren cast her eyes down, her way of giving the girl mental space to process the horrible news. Makayla's sobs filled the small kitchen. After several moments, Makayla's crying subsided. Between gulps of air she asked, "How? How did she die?"

"I found her yesterday morning," Lauren said.

Makayla's brows shot up over her frames. "You found her? Where?"

"In the backyard," Lauren said.

"What — what happened to her? And where's — where's Evie?"

Twila cleared her throat. "The police say Ruby died of a drug overdose. The state took Evie."

"An overdose? No, that can't be right. No. Ruby was clean. I know she was."

Twila crossed her bony arms over her chest. "I told that detective the same thing, only he don't believe me."

Makayla swiped at a tear, insistence in her voice. "Ms. Nash, you have to tell the police that Ruby wasn't using drugs. She wasn't."

"I was planning on calling that detective and asking

him what's going on. I'm going to give him a piece of my mind," Twila said, her voice strong.

Lauren handed the girl a tissue. "Makayla, maybe you can speak to the police, tell them what you know about her. Tell them why you don't think Ruby was using drugs."

Makayla shook her head resolutely. "No. No, I can't do that." She backed up. "I — we — my mom wouldn't want me to get involved. She'd be super mad at me." She stared at the floor. "I'm sorry but I gotta go. I need to get back to school."

Lauren grabbed a napkin and pen from the kitchen counter, jotted down her cell number and handed it to Makayla. "If you change your mind about talking to the police, let me know. I can arrange a meeting." She held the front door open and watched the teen hurry down the sidewalk to her car.

Chapter Seventeen

"Thanks for coming over," Lauren whispered as she ushered Sam into her cozy living room. Since she and Sam started seeing each other on a regular basis three months ago, he'd been to her house many times. But today, two days since Ruby's death, when he stepped inside, his presence was different. She reminded herself, *Of course it's different, he's here as a professional. It's what he does. It is business. Sam's a detective investigating Ruby's death.*

"No, I should be thanking you," Sam said.

"I tried to get Makayla to go down to the station to talk to you. I even offered to go with her." Late yesterday afternoon Lauren received a text from Makayla. She wanted to talk to the detective. Lauren contacted Sam, and they arranged to meet at Lauren's house.

"That's okay." Sam lowered his voice. "It gives me a chance to see you. Always a good thing."

Not all business then. Lauren's cheeks grew warm.

"Makayla, this is Detective Sam Overstreet," Lauren said.

"Hi, Makayla." Sam approached the girl on the sofa. Her head was bent over Maverik, her frizzy brown curls falling on the dog's muzzle as she buried her hands in his thick coat. She continued petting him as Sam took a seat in the overstuffed chair opposite her.

"Hi." Makayla made quick eye contact with Sam, then just as quickly returned her attention to Maverik.

"Lauren said you have some information you want to share with me."

The teen nodded.

Sam reached into a pocket of his coat and produced a pen and notepad. He cocked his head at Lauren, signaling for her to leave them alone.

Lauren walked toward the staircase. "I've got transcripts to work on. I'll be in my office if you need anything."

"Do you have to go?" Makayla pushed her chunky glasses up on the bridge of her nose. "Is it okay if she stays?"

Sam nodded. "Sure. She can stay."

Lauren mouthed, "I'll be quiet," to Sam, then took a seat on the other end of the sofa. Maverik took this as a signal to make himself comfortable and jumped between her and Makayla, walking in a tight circle and finally settling his large body on the middle cushion, his head resting on Makayla's lap. Makayla pressed her fingers into his fur.

"Yeah, I do have something to tell you. Ms. Nash said Ruby died because she was doing drugs, but I know that's not true. And kids at school are already talking about what happened to her."

"I just need to get a little information from you before we discuss Ruby. What's your name and your age?"

"Makayla Dixon. I just turned eighteen last week."

Old enough not to need parental consent. "What school do you attend, Makayla?"

"Crawford High School."

Sam gave a nod. "I used to go there."

"Yeah, it's a really old school. I was hoping I could go to the new one they just built. If we lived one street over I would have been in the right boundary." She lifted a shoulder. "Doesn't matter now. I'll be graduating soon."

"I haven't been in the new one yet. I'm sure it's nice." Sam asked for her address and phone number, which he wrote down. "You were starting to tell me about what people are saying at school. Go ahead."

"I can't believe how quickly people found out. Some people were saying she was using again. But it's all rumor. She wasn't. I saw Ruby a lot, ever since she came back this semester. We were in a lot of the same classes. We've been best friends ever since seventh grade."

Sam wrote something down, then asked, "And you're a senior, you said you're graduating this year?"

Makayla nodded. "We were … we were supposed to graduate together." Her hands balled into fists on her lap. "It's not right. She shouldn't be dead."

"I know you said Ruby didn't do drugs, but the preliminary toxicology reports show illicit substances were in her system. Those reports are usually accurate."

Makayla shook her head. "I don't care what it says. She was clean ever since her baby was born. Ruby loved Evie *so* much. That's all she talked about when I saw her at school. Ruby was going to prove to everyone — including her caseworker — that she could be a good mother. She was doing *everything* DFS told her to so she could keep her baby. Did you know Ruby had Evie in a trial home placement?"

Sam nodded.

"That proves she was doing everything right."

"I'm afraid the tests don't lie." Sam softened his tone and continued. "Unless something unusual happened, I suspect the final report will confirm that methamphetamine was in her system. Maybe it was laced with something else as well." Sam shifted in the overstuffed chair.

"If she died from a drug overdose, then someone gave them to her without her knowing." Makayla's voice rose. "I wouldn't put it past Carson to do something like that. Or Carson's mother."

Chapter Eighteen

"Why do you say that?" Sam asked.

"Carson's mom hated Ruby. She even told her if Carson was the dad they were going to fight to get custody. Ruby was scared. She said she was probably in for a battle with the rich bitch." Makayla's eyes flickered with defiance at Sam. "That lady was really horrible. And how was Ruby going to fight her? She has no money. At first Carson's mother is, like, all nice. 'Oh, you'll stay with us. You're family now.' Then after Ruby had the baby, for no reason at all she turned on Ruby."

"Can you be a little more specific? And this is Stephanie Millwood you're talking about, right?" Sam asked.

Makayla nodded. "See, Ruby had got in a big fight with her dad when he found out she was pregnant. Her dad said really mean things to her, told her he didn't want no whores living in his house. Told her to get out."

He called his own daughter a whore? Lauren's eyes darted to Sam's, then back to Makayla.

"You probably already know, Ruby's mom died a couple years ago. After her dad kicked her out she came and stayed with me but my mom said she could only stay for a few days, until she found another place to live." Makayla rolled her eyes. "My mom just doesn't understand. I felt so bad for Ruby. She didn't have any place to go. She didn't even have a phone. Her dad took it away from her when he threw her out."

"She didn't have a phone?"

"Not until just recently. Her grandma got it for her. Some cheap refurbished thing." Makayla shrugged. "But it was better than nothing. I don't know how she survived all those months without one. Anyway, her brother and sister — they're a lot older than Ruby and live — I think her sister lives in Iowa or Nebraska, someplace like that, and I'm not sure where her brother lives. But then Carson's mom invited her to live with them." Makayla was nodding at the memory. "I know Ruby didn't want to move in with Carson."

"Why was that?" Sam asked.

"Because Ruby and Carson weren't getting along by then. They were always fighting. He was just a jealous, controlling jerk. Ruby was finally starting to see that. Carson accused her of sleeping around on him. She told me she never did. And I believed her." Makayla sighed. "But Ruby had nowhere to go. She had to move in with him."

Sam raised a questioning eyebrow. "Was there any truth to that at all? That Carson wasn't the dad?"

Makayla leveled her gaze on Sam. "Like I said, Carson was just super jealous."

"Do you know how far along she was by the time she moved in with him?" Sam asked.

Makayla tilted her head from side to side. "I'm not sure. Not too long before Evie was born. I think."

"Can you narrow it down? Was she six, seven, eight months pregnant, do you remember?"

Makayla's eyebrows scrunched together as she thought. "She was maybe ... maybe seven months. I know she tried to hide it as long as she could, but I'm not sure. I hardly saw her at all after she moved in with Carson. The only time I did was at school. We had one class together back then. English."

Sam flipped a page in his notepad, then locked eyes with the teenager. "Makayla, what was Ruby's drug history?"

Makayla broke eye contact. The living room filled with silence. No one spoke for a long moment.

"Did she use regularly? Do you know what her drug of choice was when she was using?" Sam asked.

Makayla tugged at the sleeves of her coat, her hands disappearing inside. "No. I mean I — I don't know."

"I'm only asking, Makayla, because it's important to get to know Ruby and what was going on in her life. You're the best person to tell me. It sounds like you two were best friends."

Makayla nodded. She used the cuff of her sleeve to wipe at her eyes, and sniffled.

Lauren took a box of tissue off the end table and placed it on the trunk in front of the girl. Makayla plucked two out.

"I don't care if you were also doing drugs, that's not why I'm asking. I'm *only* interested in Ruby," said Sam.

At that statement Makayla narrowed her eyes at Sam. "I don't use drugs."

Sam raised his hand, palm out. "I'm just saying, this is not about you."

Makayla remained quiet, eyes focused on the steamer trunk.

She's debating how much to divulge, thought Lauren.

Makayla drew a breath, exhaled, and spoke. "I know Ruby smoked weed once in a while but that was all. She didn't start using meth until after she and Carson hooked up. That's when she began to change. Like I said, after she moved in with him we quit hanging out like we used to. I saw her at school but I could tell a lot of times she was on … something. I'm not sure what. I tried to tell her she shouldn't be using anything, it could hurt the baby." Makayla concentrated on stroking Maverik's soft ears. "That's one of the reasons why she quit hanging with me. She didn't say it to my face, but whenever I told her she should quit using, she'd roll her eyes and tell me I didn't know anything. That I should just leave her alone. That I didn't understand."

"Carson graduated last spring, right?"

Makayla nodded. "But he dropped Ruby off and picked her up after school."

Sam consulted his notes. "And you said Ruby didn't use after Evie was born?"

"Yes. Ruby texted me the day after she had the baby. She was freaking out, saying the police took her baby away from her. They kept Evie in the hospital because she had drugs in her body. And not the kind they give you when you're having a baby. The doctor … or hospital, I don't know who, called the police. The doctors or whoever said Evie was born addicted to meth."

Makayla met Sam's gaze. "Is that true? Can a baby be born addicted to drugs?"

Sam nodded with resignation. "Unfortunately, Makayla, yes, they can. It happens a lot these days."

So far everything Makayla said confirmed Ruby's drug use. Lauren wondered where the story could be going. She got up and, without asking if anyone wanted anything to drink, brought back two glasses of water. She set them on the steamer trunk that served as a coffee table, one in front of Makayla and one for Sam.

"Thanks." Makayla picked up the glass and took a small sip. "Ruby talked with a social services worker. That lady said Ruby had to go to court. They would be having a — I'm not sure what kind of thing it was but it's where a judge decides if someone gets their baby back. How could they keep Evie from Ruby? That's so messed up." Makayla sniffled. "Anyway, Ruby was really scared. She didn't know what to do. After she was released from the hospital she went back to Carson's house. Later Ruby told me his mom was acting all weird, like she really didn't want her there anymore."

Sam took a large gulp of water, then continued to jot down notes. "Do you know if Carson attended the birth?"

Makayla shrugged. "Probably not. He's such a loser. But a day or so after the police took Evie, Ruby did go to court. She had her own lawyer and everything. Not like she hired her own but there was one there for her, she said. The judge told Ruby she couldn't have her baby back. Not then anyway. Right after the court hearing, Ruby started working with that DFS lady. I'm not sure what she does but she was in charge of everything. She told Ruby all the things she would have to do before she could get Evie back. She had to get drug tested like every other day that first week. And she had to have a place to live."

"Did Ruby continue living with the Millwoods during that time? Did she try to go back home?"

"She was staying at Carson's before she got Evie back. I think it was like a week." Makayla pushed her thick hair off her face where it immediately fell forward again. "I don't know what happened but she moved out of Carson's house the day she got Evie back. Or it might have been the next day. I don't remember for sure. I just know she texted me. She was at Carson's house and asked if I could come get her. When I got there she told me she wanted to get away from all of his family's drama."

"Drama meaning Carson's drug use?" When Makayla didn't respond, Sam added, "Again, I'm just gathering information, Makayla. I need to know any and all surrounding circumstances, to give me a better picture of Ruby."

Makayla used her thumbnail and scratched at the aqua-blue nail polish on her index finger.

Sam dipped his head, caught her eye and gave an encouraging nod.

"Yeah. Carson was making it hard for her to stay clean, she said 'cause he was still using. Plus, his mom was being really weird about the baby."

Lauren watched as Sam scribbled something down.

"Ruby had already asked her grandma if she could move in with her. So that day, that's where I took her."

The teen tilted her head in the direction of Ms. Nash's house. "Ruby told me when she first asked her that Ms. Nash said no. But she finally gave in and agreed to let her move in."

Maverik, apparently bored with all the talking, and/or needing a potty break, jumped off the couch, went into the kitchen and slapped the doorknob with his paw. Lauren let him out. Torn between waiting for her dog to return after doing his business and missing out on Sam's questioning Makayla, her curiosity won out and she returned to the living room.

"A few days later Ruby texted me, asked me if I could take her back to Carson's house to get some of her stuff." Makayla slowly shook her head. "That did not go good. Not good at all."

"Explain what you mean," Sam said.

"When we got to Carson's house it was awkward, you know, but he just told her to go get whatever. Then he left, went somewhere, out to the garage, I think. So we went to his room and started grabbing her things. Ruby didn't have much, just some clothes and, you know, baby stuff. Carson's mom had thrown Ruby a baby shower, so she had a bunch of things for Evie."

Makayla's words came faster now. "As we were putting them in my car, Carson's mom came home and went like all … I don't even know how to describe it … crazy-bitch on Ruby. She got out of her car and slammed the door really hard. Asked Ruby what the hell was going on. And when Ruby told her she was just taking her things, Ms. Millwood started screaming. I mean literally screaming. Said Ruby was nothing but a gold digger. Told us to get off her property before she called the cops. She was yelling so loud some of the neighbors came outside to see what was going on. It was super embarrassing. Mostly for her though." The words having all tumbled out, Makayla inhaled deeply.

"So how long, again, after Evie was born was she in contact with Carson?"

Makayla thought about the question. "Two weeks maybe. Ruby was staying with him when Evie went to a foster home but as soon as she got Evie back she moved out."

"So Ruby went from living with Carson to living with her grandmother, Ms. Nash?"

"Um-hum."

"No other place in between?"

"No. And I was there when her grandma told her if she found out she was using drugs, even once, or drinking or doing anything stupid, like having boys staying over" — Makayla rolled her eyes as she said this — "Ms. Nash would throw her out. And Ruby believed it. I did too. That old lady can be kinda scary."

The girl's recitation of events sounded reasonable. Ruby wanted to stay clean but not everyone can. Lauren knew that for a fact. She'd seen it too often in court. Drugs won. Sobriety lost. Maybe Ruby had a relapse?

"Detective, once Ruby started doing her ... I don't know what they call it with that social worker person ..."

"A case plan?" Lauren piped in.

Sam shot a look at Lauren. His expression said, *Please, don't help.*

"Yeah, a case plan. Once she had that, I don't think she ever used again. We texted all the time, and she told me how great she was doing. How nice Evie's foster parents had been. They even picked Ruby up so she could have visits with Evie in their home. I mean, it seemed like they went out of their way to help Ruby."

Makayla smiled at some memory she just conjured up. "She sent me tons of pictures of Evie when she finally got to bring her home. And I saw it with my own eyes when I visited Ruby at her grandma's house. She acted more like herself, like she used to be before she met dumbass Carson."

Lauren watched Makayla, whose gray eyes shone, excited, hopeful, that sharing what she knew would make it perfectly clear to Sam that Ruby had stayed clean.

"Makayla, I'll continue looking into this, of course. It's very early in our investigation. You have my word that the police are taking this seriously."

Dots of anger rose in Makayla's cheeks. "But you still don't believe me?"

"It's not really a matter of believing you. At the moment there is *nothing* that makes your friend's death suspicious."

"Why? Just because you didn't find a knife sticking out of her heart doesn't mean someone didn't kill her." The girl's voice held a mixture of pleading and anger.

Sam reached out to place a hand on the teen's forearm but she yanked it back and crossed her arms over her chest.

"We'll know more soon. And all this information you've shared is very helpful," Sam said.

Over the course of the interview, Makayla had become more confident in her answers, like a turtle daring to stick its head out of its shell. Makayla rose from the sofa, walked to the front door and opened it. Before she stepped outside she turned and narrowed her eyes at Sam. "You need to find out what really happened to my friend."

Chapter Nineteen

"**D**o you have time for a cup of coffee?" Lauren asked.

"I do. Thanks. Thought you weren't going to ask and I'd be forced to drink what's back at the station." Sam followed Lauren into her kitchen where the afternoon sunlight made the small kitchen warm and inviting.

While Lauren rinsed out the carafe and filled it with fresh water, Sam walked to the window and glanced out. "Uh, I think Maverik's up to something."

"What? Oh, crap, I forgot he was still out there." Lauren joined Sam at the window. Maverik lay on the deck clutching something in his paws, intently chewing. When she stepped outside to take a closer look, Maverik rose, ran past her into the living room and lay down on the rug next to the fireplace.

Lauren raced in after him. "What is that?" Maverik chewed

faster. She bent to get a closer look. A half-eaten to-go coffee cup hung from his lower lip. With one quick movement she swiped it out of his mouth. Lauren waved it in front of his nose. "Bad dog." Lauren tossed the remains of the now soggy paper cup into the trash can under the sink. She shivered with exaggeration. "At least it wasn't a rabbit. Eww."

"What was it?"

"An extra-large or grande or whatever cup from High Altitude Roast. Wind must have blown it into the yard. That's the only bad thing about having the greenway so close. I have to pick up trash that makes its way here." Lauren dipped her chin toward Maverik. "Otherwise he'd be eating all kinds of crap people throw away and then make himself sick. Thanks for catching that, Sam."

"Sure."

Lauren wrinkled her nose. "Though he did eat half of it." She went into the living room, where Maverik still lay on the rug. "And I'll be paying the price later on, won't I, when you barf that back up?" In response, Maverik rested his muzzle on his paws and closed his eyes.

Lauren washed the slobber off her hands in the sink, dried her hands on a dish towel, and poured them each a cup of coffee. She placed the mugs down and sat next to him at the round oak table. "What did you think about what Makayla said?"

Would Sam think the information Makayla shared with him was any help to his investigation? If the police thought the death accidental, there wouldn't even be an investigation. From his responses to the distraught teen, it sounded like he still leaned toward accidental death. But Lauren also knew from personal experience how thorough he would be.

"You know as well as I do — maybe even more so with what you hear in court — that people fall back into that lifestyle *all* the time. They don't mean to but they do."

"I know, you're right. I did hear it a lot when I was in court. I mean, *a lot*. I certainly don't miss that part of the job." Lauren blew on her coffee, the steam rising, warming her nose and cheeks. "They all say the same thing. 'I'm done with drugs, I'm tired of that life.' Or 'If you give me one more chance, judge, I'll never be back in front of you again.'" Lauren slowly shook her head. The majority of addicts that said those words probably meant it at the time they were spoken. Lauren herself wished, for them, that it were true, but it rarely happened. In the few years she had been an official court reporter, she had a front row seat to the revolving door of drug addicts who couldn't stay clean. They were back in court again and again, with charges of either possessing illegal drugs, selling illegal drugs, or stealing so they could support their habit to use.

Sam interrupted her thoughts. "They did the autopsy on Ruby this morning. They'll be releasing the body back to her family any day now."

How quickly we lose our identity. One moment we're someone with a name. And the next, we're "the body."

Sam didn't mean it that way. He'd often said everyone deserved to be treated with respect, even after death. He was just doing his job. Stating a fact.

"They did the autopsy already?"

"Yes. Roads opened up yesterday, late afternoon. Of course, it'll be a while before we have the results." He took a sip of coffee, then smacked his lips with exaggeration. "Almost as good as Dominick's."

With a raised eyebrow she said, "I'll settle for the 'almost.'" She dipped her head and smiled, raising her eyes to his. "Becoming a regular at Dominick's, are you?"

"What can I say? It's not a bad place."

"Not a bad place? It's a great place." She watched Sam as he suppressed a grin.

"Can't argue with you about that."

They sat in silence for a moment, each in their own thoughts. Sam finally said, "I'm going to be speaking with Blaine."

"Who's Blaine?"

"He's one of our officers now assigned to the Southeast Drug Enforcement team. He's going to update me on what kind of shit's spreading through town."

Sam rubbed the stubble on his cheek. In Lauren's eyes the five o'clock shadow made him look rugged and handsome, more interesting than being clean-shaven. She often wondered how he'd look with a full beard. Her mouth twitched with a smile at the image.

"We've got to get a handle on this, shut down the suppliers. The chief's been on me for answers." He shook his head. "I mean, I want answers too but it's not that easy."

"Sam, he's got to know that, right?"

"He does but he's the new guy in town. He wants to assure the mayor that he picked the right candidate for the position."

"So how has the new chief been to work with so far? You haven't really talked about him."

"He likes to micromanage, but other than that I don't really have a problem with him."

"So he's better than Ray Asshole Newell was? Wait,

why am I asking that? Anybody would be better than him."

"Newell had some good qualities."

Lauren coughed on the sip of coffee she had just taken.

"Careful, Lauren. And don't look at me like that."

Lauren's eyes went wide in mock surprise. "Like what?"

"Like I'm crazy for saying that. He knew how to run the department, that's all I'm saying."

"Well, you worked under him, you would know."

Maverik came in and placed his head on Lauren's thigh. She rubbed him behind his ears before speaking again. "Let's not go there."

He nodded. "I agree. Let's not."

"I'll just say one more thing and then I'm done. I promise."

"Of course." Sam arched a thick dark eyebrow, a smile playing at one corner of his mouth. "And what's that *one* more thing?"

Lauren narrowed her eyes. "Seriously."

Sam straightened in his seat. "No, really, go ahead."

"He's … he's reprehensible. Just the thought of Ray Newell makes me want to hurl. Plus, he's dishonest. And in case you forgot, he was going to let his wife get away with murder."

Sam opened his mouth to respond but Lauren cut him off. "Sure, that guy, Alden Bates had been sleeping with the chief's wife, so the chief was probably happy to have him out of her life, but still, he knew she killed him and *never* said a word." Lauren hadn't told Sam the whole history, of Ray Newell's relationship with her mother decades ago. Lauren hadn't completely processed the newly learned information. Maybe someday she would share it with Sam.

Sam raised his hands in surrender. "I'm not sticking up for the guy but I'll just end by saying, when it came down to it, he stepped up and saved your life."

I just ranted for nothing. Lauren sighed loudly. "Yes, he did. You got me there." She tightened her grip around her mug. Lauren did not want to talk or think about Ray Newell.

"Is something else on your mind?"

Lauren concentrated on the cup in her hand, debating if she should answer his question. After a long moment she said, "Well, I've been wondering ..."

"*Yes?*"

Chapter Twenty

Lauren swallowed hard. "The other day when Taryn came to get Evie, it seemed like the two of you knew each other." Lauren quickly added, "And I don't mean just professionally."

"You're right, I do know her." He waited a beat. "And you should know I know her."

Lauren's eyebrows pinched together.

He tapped his temple with his index finger. "Think, Lauren."

She tilted her head to one side and thought for a moment.

"She's Taryn Biggs now but she used to go by Taryn Biggs-Overstreet." He waited a beat before continuing. "She's my ex-sister-in-law."

How could I have not remembered that? So not an ex-girlfriend. Why am I always freakin' jumping to conclusions like that? "Right, right. I vaguely remember her using that long hyphenated name. Of course, I didn't know you back then. That's probably why I didn't make the connection."

"And she obviously dropped the *Overstreet* right after their divorce. I always thought Biggs-Overstreet was a mouthful."

"Well, that explains the tension I saw between you," Lauren said.

"I think it was just the usual ex kind of thing. On friendly terms, close even, when they're part of the family. Then when the divorce happens, awkwardness sort of creeps in. Kind of like you witnessed the other day."

"I did forget her last name was Biggs-Overstreet."

Sam grinned. "How could you forget a name like that?"

"Good question. But it sounds like you didn't like her."

"No, it's not that. It's more that she changed after their divorce. We got along well enough when she was married to my brother Kyle." He raised one shoulder. "But back then he and I weren't as close as we once were, and I didn't see much of Taryn other than in our professional capacities, and that wasn't very often really."

Lauren, elbows on the table, watched as Sam conjured the memories.

"I hate to say" — Sam used air quotes — "it's complicated, but it started when my younger brother felt it was his duty to warn me against marrying Ashley, my second wife. And I felt it was my duty to tell him to stay the hell out of my personal life."

"Oh." *What was wrong with Ashley?*

"Why didn't your brother like her?"

92

"It wasn't that he didn't like her. He just thought it was too soon for me to get involved with anyone, that I hadn't grieved over the loss of Abby." Sam shook his head and spoke into the mug in his hands. "He was probably just saying what a lot of people thought. And when Ashley and I got divorced, I realized that my brother was right." More to himself he added, "Somewhere along the way Kyle grew up. Who knew he'd become a sensitive, thoughtful guy."

Sam let out a deep breath. "Anyway, after my divorce from Ashley, him and I reconnected, you might say, grew close again."

Lauren nodded her understanding. Sam had told her he'd been divorced from someone named Ashley. And a few months ago he'd explained he'd been a widower before Ashley. His first wife Abby died in a car accident, the result of a drunk driver driving on the wrong side of the road. Lauren didn't know the details of her death, but hoped as their relationship grew Sam would feel comfortable sharing his past. Another thought crept in. One that had nothing to do with being open with her. Lauren feared when he did finally open up, she might learn that Abby and Sam were soulmates, and he'd never be able to love another woman the way he loved Abby. Maybe that was the real reason why it didn't work out with Ashley. Lauren turned her attention back to Sam.

"Kyle was still married to Taryn when he and I reconnected. By then he was having his own marital issues. He said their relationship was strained. He wouldn't tell me why other than he thought they were growing apart. And since their divorce he's mentioned that Taryn has been acting a little weird, harassing him and his new wife."

"Really? That doesn't sound like the Taryn I know. Like how?"

"Well, Kyle met his wife Joni after he and Taryn separated. It was my turn to suggest they take things a little slower. They were separated but his divorce wasn't even final. Of course, just like me, he told me where I could go, and take my advice with me." Sam raised one shoulder. "Kyle and Joni are married now … another thing I told him to hold off on … and they're expecting a baby. Joni seems like a good fit for Kyle. But when Taryn found out, she was not happy, not happy at all."

Well, duh.

Can't say as I'd be happy if I were Taryn, thought Lauren. Sam mentioned Kyle and Taryn were separated when he met Joni. But was that really true? That's what men say to make themselves look better in the eyes of everyone around them. It made Lauren think of Tony's lies. She shoved down the thought, not wanting to feel the familiar anger bubble up in her stomach.

"You said Taryn was harassing them. What do you mean?" Lauren asked.

"Little things. Driving by their house multiple times a day. Joni saw her parked a couple of houses down from their place a couple of times. Kyle had to threaten to call the police before she finally stopped doing that. And she texted him all the time. He finally blocked her number."

"That's too bad."

"It is. She needs to move on. Kyle has."

"It's not always that easy, Sam."

"No, but maybe she should at least try."

"We've become friends. I got to know her from kick-boxing class. She is strong."

94

"Strong, huh?"

"Yeah. After kickboxing she spends time in the weight room. I don't know how much she lifts or presses or whatever but she's in great shape. If only I were that dedicated."

"I'll remember not to mess with her then." Sam's gaze swept over Lauren with exaggeration. "And you look great just the way you are." He set his cup down. "But like I said, Taryn and I got along fine. She just caught me by surprise, seeing her at Ms. Nash's house that morning."

"I get it." Lauren refilled her cup and gestured with the glass carafe at Sam.

"No, I better not." Sam put his cup in the sink and stood next to Lauren. "I appreciate you setting up the meeting with Makayla." He gestured with his head to Maverik, who still lay by Lauren's chair. "He helped put her at ease."

Lauren smiled. "He's good that way. But it's got to be hard at that age to lose your best friend," said Lauren. "It's such a hard time as it is, being a teen. I can't imagine what it's like losing a close friend when you're that young. You must think your whole world is coming to an end."

"If it gets to be too much, hopefully she'll ask for help." Sam placed his hands on Lauren's shoulders. Her lips parted in a half smile. He leaned in and kissed her. Lauren draped her arms around Sam's neck as he slid his hands around her waist, pulling her against him. He pressed his full lips on hers. They stood in the small kitchen, bodies entwined, the reason for his being in her home pushed to the side.

Sam reluctantly released her. He cleared his throat. "I have to get back to the station. I'll text you later."

Thoughts of Ruby and feelings of sadness were momentarily forgotten. Lauren inhaled deeply as he walked past her and savored the scent of cologne, traces of cedarwood and verbena mixed with something citrusy.

He let himself out and she watched him as he got into his SUV and drove away.

Chapter Twenty-One

Sam added his empty cereal bowl and empty coffee cup to his already full sink of dirty dishes. He debated whether to load the dishwasher before leaving. A glance at the clock on the microwave told him it would have to be later. But this was the third day of *later*. A busy caseload always equated to a messy house.

He patted his coat pocket and felt the familiar shape of the key fob and headed to his police-issued SUV. As the vehicle warmed, Sam reached in the console for his aviator sunglasses, slid them on. They immediately fogged up. He waited a few seconds for the lenses to clear. The sunglasses might be a cliché of what cops wore but they did a good job of protecting his eyes from the combination of blinding snow and the morning's cloudless sky. The gauge on his dash read three degrees, finally climbing out of the subzero temperature from the night before. The arctic air that had taken up residence over southeastern Wyoming for the past week finally abandoned its icy grip and slowly began moving eastward.

Sam pulled out of his long gravel driveway and onto the snow-packed road, the SUV's four-wheel drive capability and high ground clearance a necessity in Crawford. Nonessential roads were always last to see a snowplow, the road he lived on being one of them.

The station's parking lot came into view. The sidewalk snow removal crew must have come the night before. The walkways were clear, and the snow that had pressed against the garden-level windows for days, finally gone. The sun would warm or at the very least brighten his workspace and his mood.

Inside, Sam walked over to Officer Fuentes, who was hanging up her coat. "Lola, I'm doing an interview this morning. I'd like you to observe and take notes."

The officer's dark eyes shone with excitement. "Yeah? Who are we interrogating?"

Sam arched an eyebrow. "We're not interrogating anyone."

"I mean you. Who are you interviewing?"

"Carson Millwood. He should be here at eleven thirty. And ..." A smile tugged at the corner of Sam's mouth "If I forget to ask an important question, I expect you to remind me."

Officer Fuentes nodded. "You got it."

* * *

"Thanks for coming in, Carson." Sam had gone out to greet the young man who sat in a chair in the lobby.

"Come on back." Sam turned. Carson stood and followed him down a long bare-walled corridor.

They reached Interview Room One and Sam stepped to the side so the young man could enter. Carson Millwood stalled at the door.

"Yes, right in here. Have a seat right over there," gestured Sam.

The painfully thin teen, with his hands shoved in his pants pockets, hesitated a moment more, then walked into the room and sat in the hard plastic chair.

"I'll be right back," Sam said. "Can I get you something? Coffee? Water? A soda?"

"Uh, no. I'm good." Carson looked around the gray windowless room, his eyes settling on the clear plastic bubble protruding from the ceiling in the far corner.

"I'll be right back." Sam left, leaving the door open. Sam wanted to get as much information as he could out of the young man. Carson Millwood's name had come up during previous drug investigations. If the young man said anything incriminating, he didn't want Carson's father's lawyer to have any possible reason to try to suppress what he said, including the argument that young Mr. Millwood had been detained in the room against his will and couldn't get up and walk out any time he wanted. The open door was proof positive he could. And, technically, all they were doing right now was having a conversation and Carson could leave if he chose to. Sam hoped he wouldn't, and instead offer some useful information into what Ruby had in her system that could have led to her death.

Sam returned carrying a blue folder under one arm and a bottled water in the other. Officer Fuentes stood by his side, phone in hand. Carson stood, head down, his slender fingers on the back of the plastic chair. He eyed Officer Fuentes as she and Sam took their seats.

Sam gestured for Carson to sit. "This is Officer Lola Fuentes. She's here to observe and take notes so I can concentrate on what you have to say."

Carson sat. He scooted the chair in, its legs scraping along the scuffed linoleum floor. Officer Fuentes, alert and ready, had her phone's note-taking app open.

Sam motioned with his head to the plastic bubble in the ceiling. "We're also recording our conversation, Carson."

Carson's gaze followed Sam's movement, revealing bloodshot eyes.

"The recording is routine." Sam checked the time, stating it out loud for the benefit of the recording equipment.

"Thank you for coming in and talking with us, Carson."

"You said it had to do with Ruby. Have you learned what happened to her?" Carson asked, his voice scratchy, as if he'd just woken up.

Sam placed the folder on the table and opened it. "Yes, this does have to do with Ruby. I'm investigating her death."

The young man nodded. He placed his hands on the metal tabletop. "I can't believe she's gone. I — I ..." He raked his hair back. "I just saw her a few days ago."

"What day was that?"

"It was the day before she died."

"So on Saturday?"

Carson nodded.

"Where did you see her?"

"At her house — her grandma's house, I mean."

"Why were you there? What did you two talk about?"

"We mostly just talked about, you know, how she was doing. How Evie was doing. I don't know, just to see how we each was doing."

"And how was she doing?"

"Good. Evie was living with her. Ruby returned to school. She told me she was on track to graduate. Seemed happy." Carson dipped his head, looking into his lap. "Doing fine without me."

Officer Fuentes stole a sideways glance at Sam and then added something on her phone.

"I understand Ruby used drugs when the two of you lived together at your house."

Carson shook his head. "No. She maybe smoked weed once or twice."

"Anything else that you know she used?"

Carson shook his head. "Nah."

"I know you and she used to be in a dating relationship. That she even lived with you for a time." Sam rested one ankle on top of his opposite knee and laid the blue folder in his lap. "I'm just trying to get a sense of Ruby. Who she was. What she was like. I'm hoping you can help me with that." Sam held Carson's gaze. "Ruby used more than marijuana, didn't she?"

Carson broke eye contact. "She might have used meth once or twice. I'm not sure."

"Do you know where she got the meth from?"

"No." Carson answered too fast and too loud, shouting the one-syllable word.

"Did you ever supply her with any drugs?"

Carson kept his gaze on his clasped hands. "No."

"Did she ever tell you where she got the drugs that she did use?"

"No."

"Ruby ever give you drugs?"

Carson snorted. "No."

Sam leafed through the pages in front of him. "Ruby and Evie, they both tested positive for meth at the time Ruby gave birth. Do you have any idea at all where she got the drugs?"

Carson lifted his gaze and met Sam's eyes. "I don't know nothin' about that. We had a fight a couple of days before she had the baby."

"You probably know it takes time for the drug to get out of your system."

The teen lifted his thin shoulders. "Yeah, I guess."

Officer Fuentes typed something on her phone.

"What did you two fight about?" asked Sam.

"Who knows. That was a long time ago." Carson let out an exasperated breath. "By then that's all we were doing was fighting. Ruby was always tired. Didn't want to go anywhere, and got mad at me for going out, hanging with my friends."

Sam tilted his head to the left. "Were you at the hospital for the birth?"

"No."

"Why not?"

"I was in Colorado." Carson fidgeted in the chair, avoiding eye contact with Officer Fuentes, who gave him a hard stare.

"Look, she wasn't due for another two months. I planned to be there with her but the baby came way early."

"What were you doing in Colorado?"

"What was I doing in Colorado?"

"Yes. It's a simple question," said Sam.

"Can't a guy just go to Colorado?" Carson's leg jiggled as he spoke. "I don't remember why I went down. Like I said, that was a long time ago."

Sam slowly nodded while maintaining eye contact with Carson. "Well, here's the thing, Carson. Word on the street is you were her supplier."

Chapter Twenty-Two

"No, unh-unh. Wasn't me. I don't supply nobody nothin'. Who told you that?"

Sam replied by asking another question. "I have to ask. The day Ruby died, did you give Ruby West methamphetamine or fentanyl or heroin? Maybe in the hopes of you two getting back together? You know, kinda sweeten the pot?"

Carson shook his head again, vigorously this time. Strands of greasy blond hair fell over his eyes. "No. She told me she wanted to stay clean, she really wanted to keep Evie and she wasn't going to do anything to ruin that."

"Does that mean you offered her drugs and she refused?"

The young man glared at Sam through the curtain of hair that still hung over his eyes. His voice rose. "I didn't offer her nothin'."

Sam shook his head. "Carson, preliminary toxicology results show Ruby had something in her system. And whatever it was was enough to kill her. I'm not saying you gave Ruby enough to kill her on purpose. What happened could have been an accidental overdose."

"I told you, I didn't give her nothin' that day. Or …" Carson sputtered. "Or anything for a long time."

Thank you. You just admitted to giving her drugs in the past. "You couldn't have known it was enough to kill Ruby. If you offered her the meth, it may have been laced with fentanyl and you didn't even know it."

Carson shook his head and slouched in his seat. "I already told you, she wanted to stay clean." He raised his eyes to Sam. "I admired her for that."

The room fell quiet. Sam waited to see if Carson would say anything more but he didn't. He returned his gaze to his lap.

Sam asked again. "Is there anything else, anything at all you can tell us?"

The room remained silent.

When Carson finally spoke his voice cracked. "When we first hooked up we did smoke meth together, but, man, that was ages ago. And I believed Ruby when she said she was clean ever since Evie was born. But, hey, I wasn't around her a lot then. And if Ruby died from an overdose, it *wasn't* because of me." He bit his lower lip. "I wanted to get back together with her."

"And did you tell her that?"

Carson nodded. "Yeah. I told her we should give us another shot."

"And Ruby's response?"

Carson's gaze went to his folded hands. "Ruby said she wasn't sure if that was such a good idea but she'd think about it. And she said we'd only get back together if I …"

Sam waited for him to continue but Carson sat quiet, clasping and unclasping his hands. "But only if you what?"

He pressed the heels of his hands into his eyes and slowly shook his head. "Nothing."

Sam cocked his head at Officer Fuentes and stood. "We'll be right back, Carson. Are you sure I can't get you anything to drink?"

Carson placed his head in his hands. "No."

Sam and Fuentes walked down the hall until they were out of earshot of the interrogation room. Sam said, "Can you think of anything else to ask?"

"No. I think you covered it. But maybe you can press him why Ruby was hesitant to move back in with him. Was it because he was still using?"

"I could ask but I don't think he's going to admit to even using at this point."

"Are you going to ask him if he's the dad?"

"Yes, I will."

When the two returned, Carson was still in the same position as when they left. He didn't bother to look up when they returned. They retook their seats. "Just a couple more questions, Carson, and we'll have you out of here," said Sam. "Did Ruby say why it might not be a good idea to move back in with you?"

Carson raked his hair back off his face. "I guess it doesn't matter now but I think she might have started seeing someone else."

Officer Fuentes's eyes widened. She got ready for Sam's next question.

"Who do you think she was seeing?" Sam asked.

"Some dude named Levi."

"What makes you think she was seeing Levi?"

"I don't know. Rumor, I guess. And back when we lived together I — I happened to see texts from him on her phone."

So you had trust issues and went through her text messages. "Did any of his texts mention supplying her with drugs?"

"I don't remember."

"Wouldn't that be something you would remember? I mean, if someone was giving my girlfriend drugs, I'd sure remember that."

"I never saw anything on her phone that said he was. And Ruby said they were just friends. He was in a couple of her classes." Carson's blue eyes darkened. "But the texts didn't sound like he just wanted to be friends. You know, if she died from an overdose, maybe he was her supplier."

"Any reason to think she was in touch with Levi recently?"

"I've talked to a couple of guys I know that still go to school there, if they seen Ruby hanging around anybody, you know, just checking up on her. Levi's name came up."

"How do you know he's involved with drugs?"

"My buddies heard that he could hook you up with some good shit."

"Do you know Levi's last name?"

Carson tilted his head. "Cress I think. Or Cross. Or — I'm not sure, something that starts with a C."

"Do you know when he texted Ruby last?"

"No. But listen, I don't believe Ruby would have used again, but if she was, ask this Levi dude about it." Carson pulled his phone out of the pocket of his hoodie and checked the screen. "I need to get to work."

"One more question. Have you taken a paternity test to determine if you're Evie's father?"

Chapter Twenty-Three

Carson's mouth hung open. "Yes — No. I mean no, I haven't taken a paternity test."

"Why not?"

"I didn't think I needed to. We were together the whole time."

"But your name's not on the birth certificate. Did you know that?"

"Yeah, I knew. But that's because we weren't married."

"Has Department of Family Services contacted you about taking a test?" asked Sam.

"Yeah. Some woman left me a couple voicemails."

"So when are you scheduled to take the test?"

"I — I haven't returned her call. I mean I will, I just haven't had time, not with work and everything."

"Where do you work?"

"At the quarry."

The teen didn't have to name the quarry, there being only one in the county. And it was owned by Carson's family. "And you haven't had time, you said?"

"Yeah. I work ten-hour days."

Bullshit answer. You work for your father. You could get all the time off you want.

Sam glanced at Officer Fuentes, who shook her head.

"Thank you for coming in and talking to us, Carson. We appreciate it." Sam pulled a business card from his shirt pocket and handed it to the young man. "If you think of anything else that might help us, don't hesitate to contact me."

Carson took the card without looking at it and gave a small nod. Sam and Fuentes escorted him back to the front area and watched as he ran up the steps and disappeared. Sam turned to Lola. "So what's your impression of Carson Millwood?"

"Besides the fact he's lying about supplying Ruby with drugs?" Lola pocketed her phone. "I think he was still in love with her."

"Really? What makes you think that?"

"Call it a woman's intuition."

"Gotta give me more than that, Lola."

"They broke up when the baby was born. That's, what, three months ago? And still he said he wanted to get back together. They're still in contact. And who knows, maybe that's why he's been putting off the paternity test. As long as he can believe he's the father, he can still live in his little fantasy world, where the three of them are one little happy family." Lola shrugged. "Like I said, just a woman's intuition."

When they reached Sam's office, Lola asked, "What do you think?"

"You might be right about him still being in love. One thing I'm sure about ..." Sam paused "He won't be coming back for another chat any time soon. At least not without his daddy or his daddy's lawyer in tow." Sam could see the question in the young officer's eyes.

"Mr. Brooks Millwood is a big man in our little corner of Wyoming. When he finds out his son came and talked to us without a lawyer being present, I'm betting he won't be too happy."

Officer Fuentes smirked. "Important men never are. What do you think about this Levi?"

"We didn't find anything useful on Ruby's phone. Makayla was right, it was new. Peterson uploaded a print-out of the call and text message log. It's in the file. Why don't you go through that, find out which one is Levi's number, check their message history. Either way, we need to talk to him."

"Ben? Our Ben works with cellphone software?"

"Yes. He's our in-house IT guy. We use him first. If he can't find anything on a phone, we send them to Cheyenne. Sam saw the look of confusion on Officer Fuentes's face. "DCI. The crime lab, it's in Cheyenne."

"Oh, right, right. Sorry." Fuentes's cheeks reddened. "My mind blanked for a moment."

"You'll be all too familiar with Cheyenne and DCI when you've got your own caseload. But like I said, it was a new phone and didn't tell us anything. We contacted Ruby's father but he said he got rid of her old phone months ago when he kicked her out. He didn't want anything to remind him of his daughter."

Lola shook her head in disgust. "And I thought my dad was bad. He's a saint compared to that jerk."

Chapter Twenty-Four

After locating Ben and explaining what he needed him to do, Sam returned to his office. A Tupperware container sat in the middle of his desk, warm to the touch. Sam smiled, knowing the contents inside. Chili. Nancy's red chili. How did she know he forgot to pack a lunch today?

Nancy had also placed a yellow sticky note next to the deep bowl. He picked it up and read through it. It had to do with the case he had been working on before Ruby's death. The thefts at the retirement center. The director of the center needed to speak to him immediately. The director must have used the word *urgent*, as Nancy underlined it three times.

He reached for the receiver on his desk, ready to tap in the number, when Nancy stuck her head in. "Eat first. That man can wait another fifteen minutes."

Sam pointed to the bowl. "Thanks, Nancy. But you do know you don't have to feed me."

"No, I don't. But you know I can't help it. I always make too much. There's no such thing as a small pot of chili. And, you know ..."

Nancy didn't have to finish her sentence. Her husband Carl passed away the same year as Abby. The difference between their losses being that Nancy and Carl had been married for thirty-one years, while he and Abby were married for five. Ever since he became a widower the woman had made it her mission to keep him well fed. At least at work. He considered it a bonus that everything she made tasted delicious. He inhaled the aroma of cumin, coriander and jalapenos. "Ahh. Smells great."

"It turned out really good this time. Not too hot, like the last batch." Nancy waved her hand in front of her mouth for emphasis.

*   *   *

After lunch Sam spoke with the director of the retirement center, then added some notes to that case file. Shafts of afternoon sunlight streamed into the office, illuminating the dust particles in the air. The sight always took him back to his English class, the last class of the day his senior year in high school and Ms. Schuster, "Come back down to earth, Mr. Overstreet."

Sam shook off the nostalgia. He thought about Carson's interview and what he said about the guy Levi. Sam needed to gauge Carson's story, so he decided to reach out to the one high school teacher he knew. He scrolled to the contacts on his phone, pressed the call button and was only a little surprised when it was answered on the third ring.

"Hey, Sam."

"I thought I was going to have to leave a voicemail."

"Hello to you too, big brother."

"Excuse me. Hello, Kyle. Got a minute?"

"I've got about five of them. I'm meeting with a very upset parent before my next class. They're going to tell me why I must've been mistaken when I gave their son an out-of-school suspension for starting a fight in the hall. What's up?"

"You heard about what happened to one of the students, Ruby West?"

"Oh, yes. It's all anyone's talking about around here."

"Was she in any of your classes recently?"

"Not this year, no. Why?"

"Do you know a Carson Millwood?"

"Ah, Carson. Yes, I knew him. He graduated last year."

"Well, I just got done talking to him. He and Ruby were in a relationship."

"Okay. I don't keep tabs on the kids' social life here. That alone would be a full-time job, Sam." Kyle chuckled at his own remark.

"I wasn't asking for confirmation."

"Good."

"Tell me what you know … or knew about Carson."

The line was silent for a few seconds. "Word was if you wanted marijuana, spice, meth, anything really, Carson was your man. Smart too. Never found him with any drugs on school grounds. And he did graduate, so he managed to get passing grades. I don't know how he did that if he was using as well as selling." Kyle added, "Though I remember he got a D-plus in my class."

"That is interesting." Sam heard his brother's muffled voice. "Thanks. I'll be right there."

Kyle cleared his throat. "I gotta get going. Mr. Not-My-Son is here."

"Just one more thing and I'll let you go. Do you know a student by the name of Levi? Last name Cross or Cress. He'd be a senior."

Kyle's response was immediate. "Oh, sure, I know Levi. It's Cress. He was in my calculus class last semester. Nice kid."

"Was he also selling drugs in school?"

"Levi? No. No way." Kyle snorted. "He's squeaky clean. Keeps to himself." Kyle quickly added, "Not in a serial-killer kind of way. I know he belongs to a couple of clubs."

"What kind of clubs?" asked Sam.

"Math club for one. The kids use my classroom once a week to meet. And I believe he's part of an anime club that was started last year. Why are you asking about him?"

"According to Carson Millwood, Levi was also involved in drugs at school."

"Knowing Carson's reputation, I'd say he was doing a little deflecting from himself."

Sam huffed out a small breath. "I thought that might be the case." He went around the desk and sank into his chair. "Thanks, bro. This helps."

"I'm here to serve. In my own academic way, that is. Let me know if I can help you with anything else. I was shocked to hear about Ruby overdosing. Pretty sad event."

"It is. Hey, I may have more questions for you later."

"And as you know I've got my finger on the pulse of the teen scene here at Crawford High."

Sam pictured his brother's crooked grin. "Of course you do," said Sam before hanging up. He thought about what Kyle said about Levi. Like himself, his brother was intuitive and often spot on about people.

Carson, I've yet to prove you're a drug dealer, but I'm pretty sure you're a liar. The question in Sam's mind was the why. Why did he lie about Levi? Was it like Kyle said, to distance himself from drug involvement in school? Or did it have to do with Ruby and her feelings for someone else? Was Carson jealous of Levi, and it was his immature way of hoping to get the guy in trouble?

Chapter Twenty-Five

Maverik barked and ran to the living room window, whining with excitement. Lauren opened her front door as Taryn jogged up the front steps. "Do you mind if I use your bathroom before we go?" Taryn asked, bouncing from foot to foot.

"Of course not. Come on in." Lauren pointed. "It's just around the corner there."

Maverik inserted himself between the two women as he sniffed the new visitor's boots and pant legs while accepting her pats on the head. "Aww, what a cute dog you are."

"I'm just going to let him out and then I'm ready to go." Lauren went to the kitchen and opened the back door. "Maverik, come." He kept his attention on Taryn as she walked to the bathroom. Lauren knew he wanted to sniff the visitor more or at least get a few more pats on the head. "Maverik," barked Lauren, "go do your business."

He trotted past her, then ran into the yard. Lauren shut the door and did a quick check to make sure the stove had been turned off. Then she went upstairs, making sure there were no lights on, all the windows locked, though she hadn't opened any in months, with it still being winter.

Downstairs she stuck her head out the door and whistled for her dog. He ran in, raced around her, then ran into the living room and started a second loop of the same. "Take a seat," Lauren commanded. Maverik stopped and sat, black nose up, eyes expectant. "Good dog." Lauren had been trying out new phrases on Maverik. He seemed to be taking to this new one. She gave him a training-size treat, along with instructions to be good for Tess, his pet sitter. The treat disappeared in one bite.

Taryn stood in the living room, surveying the area. "I like your place. Nice and cozy."

"Thanks. We like it."

Taryn's penciled-in brown eyebrows raised into a question. "We?"

"Me and Maverik. Right, Maverik?"

At the mention of his name, the dog jumped on Lauren, his front legs reaching her chest. "Off. Off." Maverik put his paws on the floor, his body shaking with uncontrolled enthusiasm. Lauren pointed to him. "As you can see, he's easily excitable. I have to be careful what I say. I still consider him a work in progress."

Lauren reached for the tote she'd placed by the front door earlier, and followed Taryn, locking her front door and jiggling the knob, a habit she couldn't shake. She walked to Taryn's car and slid into the passenger seat of the older-model Prius. "Taryn, thanks again for inviting me."

"No, no. You don't have to thank me. I'm excited to have someone to go with."

"I haven't seen you at kickboxing lately. Did you drop the class?" Lauren asked.

"No, I've just been so busy with work. The job is all-consuming. Haven't been able to get to the gym as often as I'd like. After dealing with unhappy parents all day long, by the time I get home all I want to do is curl up on the sofa and binge-watch *The Office*, even though that's exactly when I should get my ass to the gym. Get rid of all my frustration of having to listen and deal with stupid all day long."

"I hear ya," said Lauren.

"We'll have plenty of time to catch up on the drive. And it shouldn't be too busy. Sundays are always less crowded. People heading home after skiing all day Saturday."

Lauren fastened her seatbelt. "I've been looking forward to this. It's been such a long winter. I now have to travel for work, which I didn't when I worked as the official, but don't go anywhere for fun. I just hope I don't hold you back. It's been forever since I skied."

"That's okay, you won't. And we can go our separate ways once we've done a few runs together. I should be thanking you for agreeing to come with me. It's more fun having someone to ski with. I haven't been to Keystone this season. Kyle and I used to go a lot. And ... since I got custody of this season's ski passes, heck, I wasn't going to let them go to waste." Taryn forced a laugh and then her face turned solemn. "Kyle wanted out of the marriage so bad I'm pretty sure he would have given me custody of one of his kidneys just to get me to sign the divorce papers."

"That sucks." Lauren knew how Taryn must feel. It had taken Lauren years to stop badmouthing Tony. Even now, the occasional slight rolled off Lauren's tongue.

"It did. It *does*." Taryn put the car in reverse, backed out of the driveway and put the car in drive. She punched the gas pedal hard and Lauren's head pressed into the headrest. She saw a stop sign ahead but the car continued to pick up speed. Lauren reflexively pressed her right foot into the floorboard.

Chapter Twenty-Six

They lurched forward in the Prius as Taryn slammed on the brakes.

"I'm *so* sorry, Lauren. I don't know what came over me. I didn't mean to do that. Oh, God, I'm such an idiot. Are you okay?"

"Uh, I'm fine. Really, I am." Lauren forced a small laugh. "I just thought you were trying to show me how much power your electric car has."

"I'm still having a hard time adjusting, Lauren. And ... and ... never mind." Taryn inhaled and slowly exhaled, then proceeded through the stop sign.

"I do know how hard it is. Hey, maybe we should stop at the gym and do a little kickboxing before we head out," Lauren joked, wanting to lighten the mood.

Taryn let out a laugh. "Yeah, maybe. I never told anyone this but" — Taryn stole a quick glance at Lauren —

"sometimes when I punch that bag, I pretend its Joni's face."

Lauren's eyes widened. *Wow.*

"But no, a few runs down some fresh powder will take my mind off the terrible week I've had. And let me forget about Kyle for a while." She drove out of Lauren's street.

Lauren twisted in the seat to face Taryn. "Until you showed up at Twila's house, I didn't realize what a hard job you have. I mean, in court I listened to you guys testify all the time, but to see it … to see you in action, it gave me a new appreciation for what a caseworker really does."

"It's got its moments, that's for sure." Taryn kept her attention on the road and asked, "How did you end up at Ms. Nash's house that morning anyway? Did you see the lights from the police cars and ambulance out your window?"

Lauren cleared her throat and turned her eyes toward the road. "Actually … I found Ruby."

Taryn covered her mouth with her hand. "Oh, Lauren, I didn't know. I just assumed you saw all the commotion outside, and that's how you found out. That must have been awful. I can't imagine."

"It was awful. It's — I've started having nightmares again."

"Oh, no."

"Yes. That's another reason I've been looking forward to this weekend. I can't seem to stop thinking about what happened."

"I don't think I could either. So did you find Ruby? Where was she? Did Ms. Nash call you for help?"

"No, it was my dog, Maverik. When I let him out, he jumped the fence and wouldn't come back." Lauren continued, her voice quiet, almost as if talking to herself. "I went into their backyard, and Ruby … she was just lying there in the snow."

"Already dead?"

"Yes." Lauren adjusted the vent on the dash. The unwelcome but now familiar image appeared. Ruby with a look of surprise in those unblinking blue eyes of hers. Lauren squeezed her own eyes tight, willing the image to disappear.

Taryn kept her attention on the car in front of them. "I'm sorry, Lauren. That was thoughtless of me. I shouldn't have brought it up. I shouldn't be asking questions. I didn't mean to upset you."

Lauren opened her eyes and cleared her throat. "That's okay, but maybe we can change the subject to something else, something fun?"

"Of course. It's just I remember I was shocked to see you there at Ms. Nash's. That's all."

"Same here. I was surprised when I opened the door and saw you. But then it dawned on me why you were there."

Taryn gave a small nod.

"You had to take Evie. I didn't realize how fast you guys get notified. You were there pretty quick."

"Yes. We're notified immediately. We all have work cell phones for when we're on call. And lucky me, that was my weekend to be on call."

"So the job really can be twenty-four seven."

"When we're on call, yep, sure is."

"I couldn't do what you do, Taryn."

Taryn stopped at a stop sign, then turned onto the two-lane highway that would take them into Colorado.

"Lauren, there are days I tell myself I should find another profession. In fact …" Taryn stole a quick glance at her friend before returning her focus to the traffic in front of her. "I'm seriously considering leaving."

"Leaving DFS?" Lauren hoped that was what she meant. She liked Taryn and didn't want her friend to move away.

"Yes, quit being a caseworker. And also move away from Crawford, go back home."

"Where's home?"

"Buffalo … Wyoming that is, not New York." Taryn gave a small laugh. "I'm thinking about going to work for my family's ranch. I'd be on the business end of things." Taryn flipped the sun visor down. "When I went to the University of Wyoming, my father wanted me to take business courses, then come back and work with our family's cattle company. Of course I didn't listen to him. I had my own ideas." She snorted. "Now Buffalo looks good. How pathetic is that? But my father said the offer still stands."

"I've been to Buffalo a few times for depositions. That whole area is beautiful, with the Big Horn Mountains right there."

"It's really pretty. Plus this job can suck all the life out of you." Taryn let out an exaggerated breath. "If I'm honest with myself, it already has. I don't think I'm cut out for it anymore."

"Oh, Taryn, I'm sorry — I mean that you're thinking of leaving but I understand. You don't have an easy job, that's for sure. The abuse and neglect cases were the hardest ones to listen to when I was an official. And I only heard a fraction of what you must have dealt with on a daily basis, but that was more than enough for me."

"Yeah, well ..." Taryn's voice drifted off as if she were lost in some inner thoughts.

"Would you think about staying in Crawford and just doing something else?"

"I have no family here. Ever since Kyle and I broke up, I've been feeling ... I don't know ... lost, I guess is the best way to put it. There's nothing keeping me here except work, Lauren."

"I get it. Last fall I was thinking about moving back to Casper."

"Really? Is that where you grew up?"

Lauren nodded. "But I have an aunt here in town. And work has picked up — that was the main reason I was thinking of leaving. It's hard to freelance here. I traveled a lot to cover depositions. But now that more things are reported remotely, it's really helped." Lauren leaned back into the headrest, looking out the windshield, her gaze unfocused. Lauren enjoyed grabbing a bite to eat with Taryn after their kickboxing class. Or meeting on a Saturday morning for coffee, but Lauren understood their friendship wasn't enough to keep Taryn in Crawford.

If Taryn moves, who's going to motivate me to go to the gym?

"Oh, I didn't tell you the latest the other day at kickboxing."

Lauren turned in her seat, waiting for Taryn to continue.

"Kyle and his lovely new cow — I mean bride — are expecting a baby."

"Wow. Already?"

"Um-hum."

Sam told Lauren about the pregnancy, but for some reason Lauren didn't want to let on that she already knew, so she said, "You know Tony cheated on me and with who, right?"

Taryn nodded. "That explained why you were a suspect in Judge Murphy's murder." Taryn glanced at Lauren and gave a sheepish shrug "Sar-ree. You know how office gossip is." She took one hand off the steering wheel and pressed it to her chest. "But I never thought that."

"Thanks. But I should never have been a suspect. Their affair was over and done by the time she became a judge and I started working for her." Lauren shook her head at the memory. "Thankfully crazy Amanda confessed all." Lauren breathed in a shuddering breath. A familiar anxiousness rose in her chest, the one that always surfaced when she thought about the events of last fall. She was about to change the subject when Taryn did it for her.

"I know Kyle dumped me because I couldn't get pregnant. I just know it. The fact that he and his wife are already expecting is proof positive. Kyle and I were fresh out of college when we got married. We wanted to concentrate on our careers before starting a family. But when we finally did try … it never happened. It was me. I couldn't get pregnant. We talked about IVF but that's for people with money. It was way out of our budget." Taryn rolled her eyes. "And then Kyle moved on to someone else."

Lauren did a mental head shake. If a man really loved you, they wouldn't leave you because you couldn't have children. Then Lauren remembered she didn't have the best track record when it came to relationships. Maybe all men wanted ... or needed ... was an excuse to cheat, an excuse to leave.

"Taryn, you'll meet someone else soon. It just takes time." Lauren turned in her seat. "What about Leo?"

Taryn met Lauren's gaze before turning her attention back to the road. "Leo? You mean Leo from the gym?"

"Yes, Leo from the gym. And not just *from* the gym. He owns it. And he owns one in Cheyenne too. And I can tell, he's into you." Lauren nodded knowingly.

"Yeah — No, I don't think so." Taryn tilted her head as if thinking. "Nah."

"Yeah, I think he is. He always makes a point of being around when kickboxing class is over, asking you how the session went. He even asked me why you haven't been in lately." Lauren nodded and raised her eyebrows for emphasis.

"Oh, please. He's the owner of the place, he has to ask. Wants to keep his customers happy and all that good-business-owner crap."

"Well, I'm a member and he *never* asks me how the class went." Lauren didn't add that the reason Leo kept his distance likely had to do with the fact that by the end of a kickboxing class, sweat poured out of her body like she'd been sitting in a sauna for an hour. The kind of sweat where everyone gives you a wide berth until you've showered.

"Forget it, Lauren. With all those women at the gym to choose from, he'd probably cheat on me. Just like Kyle. Then he'd be having a baby with one of those women."

Lauren straightened in her seat, not knowing what else to say. The two were silent for a time. Lauren watched as the Prius passed mile marker after mile marker. After they'd traveled a few more miles, Taryn broke the quiet. "So you know Sam? I mean outside of his professional capacity as a detective?"

"Uh, we know each other. After Judge Murphy's murder was solved, we've … we've been sort of seeing each other." Lauren hadn't gotten around to announcing her relationship with Sam to many people. Anyone, really. She didn't know why. Or maybe she did. She wanted to wait and see if it worked out. Now Taryn knew. It shouldn't change their friendship. But if it did, it probably wouldn't matter with Taryn thinking of moving away.

Lauren twisted the cap off her bottled water and took a long drink. "I never mentioned it before because … well …" Lauren's voice trailed off.

"Who you date is really none of my business, Lauren, but…" Taryn flipped her turn signal on to go around a semi.

Chapter Twenty-Seven

"But what?" Lauren asked.

"Well, I'm sure you know he's been married before?"

Lauren nodded. "He told me about Ashley."

"Did he tell you about his first wife, Abby?"

Where is Taryn going with this?

"Yes. He … he told me a little bit about her, that she died in a car accident."

Taryn flexed her fingers around the steering wheel. "I'm sorry, Lauren. I should keep quiet but I can't. You're my friend, you deserve to know. Sam was cheating on Abby."

Lauren's stomach clenched. *Sam cheated on Abby?*

Taryn continued. "He married Ashley so soon after Abby died. I don't think he waited even a year."

Lauren sat quiet, as the weight of Taryn's words sank in.

"Did Ashley actually tell you she and Sam were seeing each other while he was married to Abby?"

"Well, no. I didn't even know Ashley before they got married. Lauren, I'm talking about Abby. I was friends with Abby."

"Oh. You and Abby, you were friends?"

"Yes. She went out of her way to make me feel welcome when I first moved to Crawford. I didn't know anyone in town … other than Kyle and his family."

Lauren didn't want to sound like she cared about Sam's past but couldn't stop herself from asking, "So Abby thought Sam was cheating on her?"

"No. But he must have been. Who does that? I mean, who gets married so soon after their wife dies?"

Lauren didn't have an answer to that question. She sucked in a slow breath and thought about what Sam had told her about his relationships. He had explained that his breakup with Ashley had been his fault. He should never have married her. He wasn't over his first wife. It was a terrible mistake, he'd said. To Lauren that sounded like he loved Abby a great deal. And after his divorce from Ashley, Sam said he started therapy. Or was it grief counseling? Either way, it didn't matter. The important thing, Sam finally began dealing with the loss of Abby.

Over the last few months Lauren and Sam spent a lot of time together. She felt like she was beginning to know him really well. But Lauren had to ask herself, how well does anyone know another person?

"Taryn, just because Sam married Ashley right away doesn't mean he'd been cheating on Abby."

With both hands still on the wheel, Taryn shrugged.

"That's true. But like I said, you're my friend, and I thought you should know. I don't want to see you get hurt."

"Thanks." *Thanks for planting that seed, the size of an avocado pit, in my head.* Suddenly Lauren didn't want to be talking about Sam. Or cheating husbands. Or past relationships. Lauren stared out the passenger window at the snow-capped mountains in the distant west, not sure of how she felt right now.

Sam, did you cheat on your first wife? Can I trust you?

A pang of dread gripped Lauren's stomach. She no longer wanted to be in this car, no longer wanted to go skiing.

Chapter Twenty-Eight

Sam eased his Dodge pickup into what he considered his spot just off the gravel lane. The heater on his old pickup struggled to push out warm air in the short drive over.

Another son-of-a-bitch cold morning.

He cut the engine. Abby's headstone sat just over a rise from where he parked. He pulled on his blue knit cap, braced himself for the cold and got out of the truck.

The wide footpath was deserted on this Sunday morning. He trudged further into the cemetery until he reached the newer plots. The morning sky mirrored the landscape of gravestones, anemic gray as far as the horizon. He had visited Abby every Sunday for the past three years. That is until recently. In the last two months he'd been here only twice.

Sam reached her spot, knelt and brushed away snow, his fingertips turning cold. When he reached the dormant brown grass, he reached in his coat pocket, pulled out a small seashell and set it next to the others that encircled the front of Abby's headstone.

Sam's brow furrowed. *I used to know exactly how many I'd placed here but I've lost track.* After breaking up with Ashley and moving into his new place, he was ready to let go of some memories. That was one of the things he and Ashley fought about, Abby's presence being all around them. Ashley had been right. Sam came up with this idea. A little silly maybe, seashells at her gravesite, but he hadn't been able to simply toss them in the trash.

"Your seashell collection is getting low, Abby. There's only a few more left and then you'll have them all with you. And I'm saving the biggest for last." Sam thought back to their honeymoon in Key West, Florida, and how Abby spent hours on the beach hunched over collecting shells. Sam exhaled, his breath visible for a second before quickly disappearing. Sam let out a small chuckle. "Yes, it's the one you just had to have after we stopped at that little outdoor bar on the beach, the one with the souvenir shop. It was the best conch chowder we ever had, not that we had anything to compare it to. Never even heard of conch chowder before." He shook his head. "Remember how I argued with you, that we didn't have room for one more souvenir, not even one conch shell. You, of course, proved me wrong by grabbing my toiletry bag, tossing out my deodorant, shaving cream, and razor and telling me, 'Now there's room.' You had an answer for everything."

Sam's mind flashed to Abby's wicked grin, mischievous blue eyes sparkling, and … for the first time, actually smiled at a memory. Before this moment he rarely let any

memories of their life together surface. They always reminded him of how much he missed her.

He took in a deep breath, noticing the sensation of the
cold air filling his lungs. He zipped his jacket all the way
up, folded his arms around himself, tucking his hands into
the warmth of his jacket armpits. "Abby, I know it's been
a while since I've been here. And I know you'd be the first
person to say, 'It's okay. Go, get on with your life.' And
you know I tried that before and it didn't go well."

Sam glanced up, feeling another's presence. A familiar
figure, a thin gray-haired man, slightly hunched, walked to
a cement bench several yards away. He sat and began having his own conversation in front of a stone angel, whose
wings were spread as if ready for an embrace.

Sam coughed and cleared his throat. "I've met someone.
Her name is Lauren. We met last fall during a murder investigation." He smiled at the memory. "For a short time, she was
a suspect." Sam kicked at the snow with the toe of his boot.
"I — I want you to know, I'm trying. I'm really trying to move
on with my life. It's just — it's just so hard sometimes."

He squeezed his eyes shut, took a steadying breath and
then continued. "I never said this to you before, Abby, but I
want you to know how sorry I am. I'm sorry you never had
the chance to become a mom. That was all my fault." Sam
sniffed, then wiped his nose on the sleeve of his jacket. "I was
scared. I didn't think I'd make a good father. That I'd be just
like my old man. You knew what he was like. And you heard
me bitch about him enough. I was — I was afraid to take the
chance. But you, you would have been a great mom. So I
wanted you to know how sorry I am for being so damn self-
ish."

Sam knelt on one knee, ignoring the frozen ground, and placed his hand on the cold granite headstone, letting the familiar feel of the words, *ABIGAIL RUTH OVERSTREET, Loving wife and daughter,* seep into his fingertips.

Back in his pickup truck, he turned the key, feeling the deep rumble of the engine come to life. He sat there for a minute. Finally he put the pickup in gear and drove out of the cemetery, heading toward the shafts of sunlight breaking through the clouds.

Chapter Twenty-Nine

The phrase "It's like riding a bike; once you learn how, you never forget" popped into Lauren's head on her first run. Excitement gathered in her chest the moment she pushed off the top of the mountain with her ski poles and picked up speed. She left all thoughts of Sam and his possible cheating at the top of the peak and concentrated on avoiding coming in contact with pine trees and other skiers in her path.

She'd joined Taryn on a couple of the medium runs but bowed out when Taryn suggested they go down one of the black diamond slopes. Lauren's skiing skills had never been that good. She let her friend go down those alone, though Taryn wasn't alone for long. Lauren caught sight of Taryn, laughing and smiling with a tall man in a black-and-yellow North Face jacket. Lauren saw the two of them together on the chairlifts several times that day.

Back in the Prius on the drive home, Taryn and Lauren talked about some of the men that hit on them while they relaxed in the lobby of the lodge ... hit on Taryn being the more accurate way to describe it. They categorized them in order of date-ability. One, I would date him in a heartbeat. Two, I would date him if I had no better offers. And, three, you couldn't pay me to go out on a date with him. They were acting like a couple of guys at a bar but the harmless topic had them snorting with laughter.

Lauren had asked, "What about North Face guy?" Taryn at first feigned ignorance as to who she meant, but then broke out into a wide smile. Rory was from Denver. She confided that he'd asked Taryn for her number.

They settled into a comfortable silence the last thirty minutes of the drive. When the first exit for Crawford came into view, Taryn said, "I'm going to get a coffee."

"Ooh, a latte does sound good," Lauren agreed.

Taryn pulled the Prius into the drive-thru of High Altitude Roast and stopped at the menu selection. "Have you ever had their sugar cookie latte?"

"No," Lauren admitted.

"You have got to try it. It's *the* best ever. And I kinda consider myself a connoisseur." Taryn chuckled at her own remark.

"It sounds good. I'll try it. And you have to let me buy. I was going to offer to pay for gas but" — Lauren glanced around, then at Taryn — "this is an electric car."

"Haha." Taryn raised a sly eyebrow. "But if you're buying, I'll get a large."

Lauren took a tentative sip of her latte as they pulled

into traffic. "Oh. My. Goodness. This is delicious. I think it's going to be my new favorite."

Taryn nodded. "Told you it was good."

The drive to Keystone started on a sour note when their conversations focused on exes and past relationships and cheating, thought Lauren. She watched her friend flirt and have fun. The skiing wore them both out, and the trip back to Crawford had been filled with a comfortable silence. Lauren smiled to herself as she savored the sweetness of her sugar cookie latte.

Chapter Thirty

Taryn pulled into Lauren's driveway. Lauren got out, waved goodbye to her friend and started to walk to her front door when she heard raised voices coming from Ms. Nash's front yard. A woman stood on Twila's porch, her hand gripping the screen door handle, and a look of exasperation on her face.

As Twila pulled the door shut, the last of her words drifted over to Lauren. "I will not."

The woman dressed in a wool coat and black leather heeled boots turned to leave. She caught Lauren staring. She tilted up her witch-like chin but not before giving Lauren a condescending look. The woman strode down the sidewalk, got into a white Cadillac SUV and drove off.

Lauren hesitated, trying to decide whether or not to check on her neighbor. *Twila will probably tell me it's none of my business*, thought Lauren as she walked to her neighbor's house. She knocked and the door immediately opened.

"I told you no. What are —"

Lauren waved hello with her fingers. "Is everything all right? I just saw … It looked like that woman was trying to get inside your house."

"Come in before Percy has himself a heart attack." Ms. Nash stood back and Lauren stepped inside. Lauren picked the Papillon up and squeezed him. He wriggled and squirmed with excitement. Lauren kissed the top of his head and then set him down.

"That was Stephanie Millwood, Carson Millwood's mother. Carson used to date Ruby. A pretty pushy lady if you ask me."

"What did she want?"

"She wanted to come into *my* house and have a look around. She gave some lame excuse about Carson leaving something here and her son wanted it back."

"What did she say he left here?"

"A ring."

A ring? An engagement ring?

"I told her there wasn't nothin' of his here. I ain't seen no ring. And I wasn't going to let her in my house no matter how insistent she was. And let me tell you she was pretty insistent, telling me she just wanted to look in Ruby's room to make sure." Twila let out a harsh laugh. "I was not going to let that woman step foot inside my home, not after what Ruby said about her, being so mean and all to her. Accusing my granddaughter of being dishonest, trying to get Carson to marry her just for his family's money. That woman said the baby wasn't Carson's." Twila narrowed her eyes at

Lauren. "Of course Evie was his baby. My granddaughter was no tramp."

"Of course she wasn't," Lauren added quickly, sensing Twila's agitation.

"Anyway, I told Ms. Millwood to get off my property and not to come back." Twila moved toward the door, signaling to Lauren it was time for her to leave as well.

"If you need anything, Twila —"

"Yes, I know, you're here if I need anything. But I'm okay." Ms. Nash smiled at Percy. "We're okay, aren't we?" In response, the Papillon danced on his hind legs, front paws swiping at air.

Lauren walked back to her house wondering why Stephanie Millwood tried to get into Twila's house. *What was she really looking for? And why did she say the baby wasn't Carson's?*

Chapter Thirty-One

The plan for this Monday morning was to work on the rash of burglary cases at the retirement center. Sam told the director he would be out there midmorning with an update. He walked out of the break room having just devoured one of Nancy's giant blueberry muffins, and headed to his office. Out of the corner of his eye he watched a tall woman throw open the door to the police station. Without waiting for Nancy to greet her, the woman jabbed a finger in Nancy's direction. Her artificially enhanced lips were moving, but being on the other side of the security glass, Sam couldn't make out her words. Her eyes, narrowed slits, expressed annoyance.

Instead of continuing down to his office, he walked over to Nancy's workstation. "Is everything okay here?"

Nancy peered over her reading glasses at Sam. Her facial expression, as well as her tone of voice, remained professional. "This is Stephanie Millwood. She's here to speak with you. It's regarding Ruby West."

Sam turned toward the security glass. He cocked his head. Ms. Millwood hadn't come alone. He could just make out Carson Millwood standing behind his mother. They were the same height, though his mother had the aid of three-inch heels. *That didn't take very long. Mommy here to rescue you?*

Sam opened the door to the lobby and gestured with his hand. "Please, come in."

"No. What I have to say won't take long," snapped Stephanie Millwood.

Sam took another step forward, letting the door close and click shut behind him. He shouldn't be having a conversation out here, but he'd listen to what she had to say before suggesting they go back to a more private area.

"Hello, Carson," Sam said.

Carson gave a small nod before shrinking back behind his mother.

Kid's probably embarrassed to be here.

The woman spoke over her shoulder. "Is this the detective you were talking with?"

Another small nod from her son.

"I'm Detective Overstreet. And you are Carson's mother I presume?"

"Yes, I am."

"What can I —"

"Let me cut to the chase, Detective. I came here to get a few things straight with you. One, Carson is not a drug dealer, so he is in no way involved in the death of Ruby West. And most importantly, he is *not* the father of her child."

That's the most important thing?

"And there's no need for him to prove that to you or the state welfare department, or whatever the name of that agency is." Ms. Millwood stood in front of Sam, hands now on her hips, her eyes locked on his. Her narrow chin tilted upward as if daring him to disagree.

Whether Carson Millwood gave a DNA sample to prove whether or not he was Evie's father didn't really concern Sam. His interest lay in finding out if Carson supplied the drugs that killed Ruby. The Department of Family Services, on the other hand, would surely like to be able to rule him in or out as the father of Evie.

Sam inhaled, and as he exhaled and spoke, his voice remained even, nonconfrontational. "Ms. Millwood, as far as the matter of paternity, we haven't asked your son to submit to a paternity test."

"That's good to know. But the other reason I came here is I want to share something with you that you may not be aware of."

Ms. Millwood tilted her head slightly, brushing her blonde-highlighted bangs off to one side. The practiced gesture exposed a smooth, unlined forehead. She was about to speak when a man entered the police station, toolbelt wrapped around his thick waist, and carrying a clipboard. Sam gave him a small nod as he walked over to the glass partition.

"Are you sure you want to talk out here?" Sam tilted his head toward the man.

Ms. Millwood considered the question. Before she could answer, the buzzer sounded, followed by a loud click of the door, and the man disappeared inside.

"My husband said I should let our lawyer handle this but Carson is my son. And so I'm here to tell you he's not the father of Ruby's baby."

"What makes you so sure he's not the dad?"

Carson turned away from the conversation, his focus on the illuminated exit sign.

"Because I've done the math. The baby was born full term ..." She turned to her son, shaking her head. "Not premature, like Ruby tried to convince you."

"And how do you know that, ma'am?"

"At first I didn't know. I went to visit Ruby and the baby at the hospital when she gave birth, but Evie was in the NICU."

Sam raised his eyebrows in a questioning look.

Ms. Millwood let out an exaggerated breath. "Neonatal intensive care unit. I'm a registered nurse. I used to work at the hospital, in labor and delivery as a matter of fact. Anyway, I just assumed Evie was there because she was born premature and wasn't well enough to go home. When Ruby arrived at my home without the baby, I didn't think it out of the ordinary."

Ms. Millwood turned to Carson and narrowed her eyes at him. His cheeks reddened.

She returned her focus on Sam and continued. "No one told me the baby was born addicted. I had no idea that Ruby had been using drugs while she was pregnant. I didn't learn that until Ruby arrived at our home a week later with Evie. As soon as I laid eyes on that baby, I demanded answers. Ruby admitted that Evie had to stay in the hospital to rid her body of the drugs. But she continued to insist the baby was premature." Ms. Millwood huffed a disgusted breath. "I'm very knowledgeable in the field of obstetrics. And even if I weren't, anyone with half a brain knows that a baby weighing eight and a half pounds is *not* premature. That's just simply unheard of."

"And that's how much Evie weighed at birth?" Sam asked.

"Yes. That's when I started to question whether Carson was the father." She glanced over her shoulder again and rolled her eyes. "This one wanted to believe it was his."

"Mom, stop," Carson said through gritted teeth.

Ms. Millwood continued, ignoring the plea in her son's voice. "Carson can't be the father. According to my rough calculations, the baby being full term, Ruby had to have gotten pregnant in March, and she and Carson didn't start dating until May. That's when you started dating, isn't it, Carson?"

Carson stayed silent, his eyes cast down at the scuffed floor tile.

She tugged at the sleeves of her winter white coat. "As I said, the day Ruby showed up with Evie, I told that girl she was no longer welcome in *my* home." Ms. Millwood tilted her head toward the ceiling and shook her head. "Here we were, opening up our home to Ruby, to her and my unborn grandchild … or who I thought was my grandchild. I let her live with us during her pregnancy. I even threw that girl a baby shower. But there was no way I was going to let *her* continue to take advantage of *my* son. She must have thought she had an easy out for herself, claiming Evie as his."

She pressed her lips together, then continued. "As I'm sure you know, our family's reputation is well known in

Crawford, throughout Wyoming actually." Stephanie Millwood let out a sigh. "She probably played Carson from the very beginning. Never had any real feelings for him."

"*Mom,*" Carson hissed.

"I'm sorry, Carson, but I'm afraid it's the truth. I told you before —"

Carson didn't wait for her to finish. He turned, gripped the handle of the glass door, threw it open, ran up the stairs and out of the building.

Ms. Millwood waited for the door to close before continuing. "Just so you know, Detective, Carson did take a paternity test. Brooks and I insisted." She patted her Prada handbag. "We couldn't have this ... this cloud hanging over our head. We're on our way to drop the results off to those DFS people, so we can prove once and for all that Carson is not the father."

Her sharp tone suddenly softened. "Then maybe my son can get on with his life. This whole ordeal really has taken its toll on him. I don't know what he saw in that girl, but he was so in love with her that he was willing to overlook the fact the child wasn't his." She raised her chin. "But I wasn't."

Stephanie Millwood cinched the belt tight on her cashmere coat. "I would prefer you not speak to my son again without our lawyer present."

Sam nodded politely. "Thank you for stopping by. If you don't mind, would you be willing to supply us with a copy of the paternity test?"

Stephanie Millwood pursed her deep red painted lips. She pulled an envelope out of her bag, removed a sheet of paper and handed it to Sam, who turned and passed the sheet under the glass divider. He spoke into the intercom system. "Nancy, would you please make a copy of this."

With a nod, Nancy took it to the printer at the far end of the room.

While they waited for the copy to be made, Sam asked, "You said you were a registered nurse?"

"*Am* a registered nurse. I co-own Blue Sage Day Spa. I'm sure you've heard of it."

Sam nodded. He reached for the piece of paper that Nancy pushed back through the opening.

Stephanie Millwood held her hand out, palm up. "I trust this will end Carson's involvement in your investigation."

"Ruby is dead. From an overdose." Sam lowered his voice, his dark eyes boring into Ms. Millwood's. "If we discover he was the one who supplied her with a lethal overdose, even your family's reputation won't be able to save him from charges."

Ms. Millwood responded by glancing at her open palm and then back at Sam.

He half expected her to tap her toe in impatience. Sam handed her the document. She turned on her heel and left, her exit as forceful as her son's moments ago.

Sam went back inside, making his way to his office. Nancy, who sat at her desk, stuck her arm out, waving the copy of the test results in his direction.

"Thanks." He would read the document back at his desk just to be sure, though he already knew what it would say.

Stephanie Millwood is a nurse. How far is Mom willing to go to protect you, Carson?

Chapter Thirty-Two

Lauren pulled to the curb and parked. The time on the dash read two forty-five. Her appointment was at three o'clock. The one-story bungalow-turned-office sat nestled between two equally small houses.

Lauren waited a full five minutes before getting out of her car. She walked to the door, placed her hand on the doorknob and swallowed hard. Cars drove up and down the street, their drivers oblivious to Lauren's internal struggle. She could still leave. She hadn't opened the door yet. Lauren inhaled and slowly let her breath out. A battle of wills had begun as soon as she backed out of her garage. One insisted: *You need to talk to a professional. They can help you with the nightmares that, once again, started up after finding Ruby's body. A therapist can help you with unresolved issues, with the fact that your mother up and deserted you as a child, something that's clearly made it hard to have successful personal relationships. You want things to work with Sam, right?*

The other part of her brain argued: *Hey, you did try therapy. How did that turn out for you? Your own therapist was a killer. And if her husband, the creepy chief of police, hadn't intervened, you would have been her next victim.*

Go home. Now.

Lauren swiveled and took a step off the porch. The sound of the door opening made her stop.

"Ms. Besoner?"

Too late.

Lauren turned and faced the older woman. "Yes. Hi."

"I thought maybe the door was locked. I sometimes forget to unlock it in between clients. Please, come in." She stood to the side to let Lauren pass and pointed to a room off to their left. The faint scent of vanilla greeted Lauren, relaxing the knot in her stomach.

Afternoon sunlight filtered into the quaint space.

"Have a seat," said Meredith Williams.

Lauren sat. The seating arrangement looked a lot like her last therapist's. Maybe there was a required class counselors take in college, Ambiance 101. Two club chairs with a low table in between them occupied one side of the room, with a desk on the opposite wall, facing into the room. The big difference between the two spaces was the multitude of plants everywhere. Ms. Williams had plants on the desk, on a Parsons table under the window, and spider plants hanging in baskets in two of the corners. *Maybe I should add some plants to my office space.*

"Let me quickly go over the online form you filled out, Lauren, and then we can discuss how I can help you." Ms.

Williams smiled, the lines around her green eyes deepening.

Lauren relaxed into the chair.

*   *   *

The hour had gone by fast. Lauren left the therapist's office with homework, an appointment for next Thursday, and a new sense of hope.

Chapter Thirty-Three

The printer outside Sam's office sputtered to life. After it had gone silent, he went and retrieved the pages, two reports, and set them on his desk. The names and faces of two women stared back at him. Cammie Johnson and Emily Hightower. Sam read each of their autopsy reports. They both had died within the last five months. At the moment nothing unusual stood out about each overdose victim. They shared a few common elements. Both young. Both single. Both left behind a young child or children. In today's world, not unusual. Cammie and Emily both died by the same lethal cocktail, fentanyl-laced methamphetamine. The two women were also known drug users, neither knowing their last injection of drugs would be their last … anything.

Sam shook his head as he wrote their names on a lined sheet of paper. When the final autopsy report came back on Ruby West, if she had the same drugs in her system he would add her name to this list.

Every day for the last three weeks … ever since Ruby's death … Chief Finch had been in Sam's office, asking for any new updates on the rash of drug overdoses in the city. This morning was no different. Chief Finch had left two minutes ago demanding a break in the overdose cases, as if all Sam had to do was snap his fingers to conjure one up. If only.

Ruby's death had been the latest one, but since Sam had yet to receive her final pathology report, he couldn't provide any new information, other than an update from Officer Blaine's work with the Southeast Drug Enforcement Administration. The team had narrowed down the source of where the drugs were coming from, and they were now working with the feds to secure warrants for wiretaps on several minor sellers and a couple of major ones. None of the major suppliers lived in Crawford. Carson Millwood's name came up as a minor player, in the sense that he sold drugs to support his habit.

Sam's phone vibrated on his desk. When he saw the notification, he groaned. A reminder from his walking app. He hadn't logged any steps in over two hours. A banner snaked across the small screen. *Don't lose momentum. Get up and go. You've got this.*

He glared at the screen. "It's ten fifteen in the morning. Give me a freakin' break." He placed the phone face down on his desk. Someone from the county HR department had the brilliant idea to hook up the police department with a Get Healthy Stay Healthy program. It was pushed by the city at the start of the new year to accept the challenge. He successfully avoided the challenge for more than a month but had grown weary of seeing Nancy's daily email reminder to sign up, and finally installed the app. He'd only had it on his phone for a couple of weeks. With its constant pop-up reminder notification pings, along with a health tip of the day landing in his inbox, he regretted having caved to Nancy's insistence.

He rotated his head in a slow circular motion and heard the familiar cracking in his neck. He'd been sitting at his desk working on the computer since seven thirty. The damn app was right, he needed to get out of this chair and move. He slipped into his coat and walked to the lobby.

Nancy's fingers paused on her keyboard. She must have felt his presence because she glanced over her shoulder. She raised her penciled-in eyebrows and asked, "Where are you off to?"

"Just going for a walk."

"In that cold?" Nancy shivered for added emphasis.

Sam smirked. "Get Healthy Stay Healthy says it's time to walk. I'll be back in a few."

"Oh, are you liking the new app?" Nancy asked.

"Like? No. That app has way too many notifications." He exhaled sharply. "Don't get me started."

"Sorry," Nancy said, looking sheepish. "So far no one's a fan."

"Shocker." Sam pulled on his blue knit cap, Carhartt insulated gloves, and left the building. He walked at a brisk pace, taking a walk around the courthouse/government complex. It took up one city block. After he'd completed one lap, his eyes were watering from the frigid air. He paused only a moment, considering whether to go around the complex one more time. He adjusted his cap, bowed his head into the wind and strode two blocks with purpose, landing on the doorstep of Dominick's Bakery.

He stepped inside and inhaled, letting the aroma of coffee and baked goods fill his nostrils.

Dominick came out of the kitchen holding a tray of warm scones. He placed the tray onto the top shelf of the glass-enclosed case. "Hello there, Detective. How is your day goin'?"

"It's going okay, Dominick. How about with you? How's business this morning?"

"Business is great. Had a run on scones this morning. Not sure why but I ain't complainin'." Dominick wiped his hands on the towel that stuck out from one of the pockets of his white apron. "What can I do ya for this morning?"

Sam placed his order, a black coffee and one of the freshly baked scones. He took a seat at a small table against the wall with a view of the sidewalk.

It felt odd sitting in here without Lauren. It wasn't that this was her place, but meeting her for coffee or lunch at least once a week for the past four months, he'd grown accustomed to her being there, smiling at him from across the table.

Sam dunked his chocolate chunk scone into his coffee. *When the hell did I become a scone dunker?* It wasn't like he was some stereotypical cop who only ate powdered donuts, the kind that the Maverik convenience store on the edge of town sold, but still, *scones?* Again, he thought of Lauren and her influence on his food choices. Dominick's was her favorite eatery. But what now made Sam a regular was Dominick's baking abilities. If everything he baked didn't taste so damned good, Sam wouldn't be dunking anything in his coffee.

Without any further analysis of his current pastry selection, he simply finished the scone with one last bite. He had begun to frequent the bakery after a brisk walk — the Get Healthy app be damned — and to think about whatever open case he had that was challenging. Plus, the coffee tasted way better than what the police department offered. He would never tell Nancy that since she was the one who always made a pot of coffee in the morning, then again in the afternoon, and she thought her coffeemaking rivaled Starbucks.

As he sat, his thoughts focused on the recent rash of deaths in town and how he hoped getting the feds involved would at least put an end to the batch of bad drugs that had hit the streets here in Crawford and in almost every other Wyoming town.

As he sipped on his coffee he saw Brooks Millwood, a man with a linebacker physique barely hidden inside a suit, enter the bakery. Sam had encountered Mr. Millwood in the not too distant past when Mr. Millwood's office and warehouse had been vandalized. He had come to the station to complain about the lack of progress being made in finding whoever broke in. The man's tone had been that of a very busy man who had no time for the ineptness of the Crawford Police Department. It didn't help that a suspect had never been identified in the case. Sam had his own ideas of who could have done the damage. He thought it might be someone in the family business, his brother perhaps, or one of his nephews. Mr. Millwood refused to answer certain questions or provide certain documents, leaving Sam no choice but to close the case without an arrest.

Mr. Millwood went to the counter and placed his order. He pulled a credit card out, tapped it on the reader, then pocketed it. While he waited, he turned to survey the patrons. When Mr. Millwood's eyes landed on Sam, he pushed off the counter, walked to Sam's table and sat without an invitation.

Sam straightened in the chair, body tensing as Brooks Millwood invaded his space. Sam spoke evenly, masking his annoyance. "Hello, Mr. Millwood. Care to join me? Oh, wait, you already have."

The tall man narrowed his blue eyes at Sam. "It's Overstreet, right?"

"Yes. Detective Overstreet."

"Yes, I remember you." Mr. Millwood scoffed. "One of Crawford's finest."

"What can I do for you, sir?"

"You had Carson come down to the police station. You talked to him without an attorney."

"Yes. I asked if he'd speak with me about Ruby West. He came in willingly."

"You need to stop telling people around town that *my* son is a possible suspect in your investigation into *that* girl's death."

Sam placed his elbows on the small table, clasped his hands and leaned into Mr. Millwood's space. "*That* girl has a name. It's Ruby. Ruby West. And I'm not sure where you're getting your information, but I haven't given away any details about anyone. Besides, the matter is in the very early stages." Sam took another sip of his coffee and waited to see if the man had more to say.

"Carson had nothing to do with that girl's — with Ms. West's death."

"That's good to know. But if it comes to my attention that someone in our community is selling drugs that are killing people, and your son is that someone, then I will most definitely be in contact with him again."

Mr. Millwood's hands balled into fists. He spoke through clenched teeth. "All my son did was try to help Ruby when she got pregnant. He is not a drug dealer, Detective. You are barking up the wrong tree and wasting your time viewing him as having anything to do with illegal drugs in Crawford. He's a Millwood and would never be involved in criminal activity."

Oh, a Millwood, is he? Well, that clears everything up. "If your son is not involved in anything, you have nothing to worry about. But word on the street is he is involved in selling illegal substances." Sam watched the large man's face turn crimson.

Mr. Millwood narrowed his eyes at Sam. "You better watch what you say."

"Or else?"

"Or else you and the police department will be looking at a lawsuit. Slander is no small matter."

Sam lowered his voice, not wanting any customers to overhear their conversation. "You and I both know your son has a juvenile record. He's eighteen now. No longer a kid. And granted, from what I hear he's a small-time dealer compared to others in our community, but if I find out he had anything at all to do with supplying the drugs that killed Ruby West … and I mean anything … I'll take the information to the county attorney and ask he be charged appropriately. That's just the procedure I follow, regardless of *anyone's* last name."

"You might want to rethink your position. If you harass my son, I can … and I will … make your life difficult."

"I can assure you, I don't *harass* people —"

Mr. Millwood cut him off. "That's not what I heard."

"Well then, all I can say is you heard wrong." Sam wasn't going to take the bait and ask him who he heard this from. Or even what he was talking about. Everyone who grew up in Crawford knew the Millwood name. Sam sensed the man's entitlement, wafting off him like a cloying cologne. Big house on the edge of town. Big donor to local charities. And sitting across from him, Sam saw the big ego to match. Mr. Millwood wouldn't tell him where he heard the rumor because Sam knew the man had to be blowing smoke, that no one had been spreading rumors. There was nothing to spread.

"Mr. Millwood, I will investigate this case like I do all my cases. And I will follow proper protocol. Which I also always do."

"Don't say I didn't warn you." Brooks Millwood scraped back his chair and stood.

"Am I interrupting anything?"

Chapter Thirty-Four

Brooks Millwood swung around to see Chief Finch standing in front of him. Mr. Millwood's eyes did a slow sweep of the chief, who stood in uniform mere inches away.

"Ah, you must be Harrison Fetch, the mayor's new hire," said Mr. Millwood.

"Harrison *Finch*. Indeed I am." The chief stuck his hand out. "And you are?"

Mr. Millwood waited a long beat before returning the handshake. "Brooks Millwood."

"Any relation to Mayor Millwood?" Chief Finch asked.

"How very astute of you. Yes, he's a second cousin of mine." Mr. Millwood cocked his head in Sam's direction. "I was just telling your underling here that he should be careful who he accuses of drug dealing. My son is not involved with the selling of narcotics. And Carson certainly didn't supply his ex-girlfriend with anything illegal." Mr.

Millwood puffed his broad chest out. "And I will not have my family's name dragged through the mud. I *will* have a talk with the mayor if I hear any more rumors flying."

"I assure you, sir, Detective Overstreet is doing his job and doing it properly, making sure we have a complete picture of the situation, as he's required to do. There's no need for you to get defensive."

Mr. Millwood's gaze took in Chief Finch, from his hat down to his thick-soled boots. An almost imperceptible sneer appeared on Mr. Millwood's lips. "See that he does, Chief." With those words, the large man brushed past an older woman on his way out of the bakery, leaving his order behind at the counter.

Chief Finch stepped back and caught the door before it rocked on its hinges. "What was that all about, Sam?"

"Well, you know his name. He's Carson Millwood's father, the young man we recently talked to. He was Ruby West's boyfriend."

Chief Finch slowly nodded. "From the looks of things I take it y'all had a few heated words?"

Sam watched as Brooks Millwood strode down the sidewalk and out of sight. "Is it that obvious?"

"I'd say so. And from what I hear around town, nobody should look that mad after visiting Dominick's Bakery." Chief Finch chuckled at his own remark before walking to the counter and placing his order. He returned to Sam's table carrying a coffee in one hand and a pastry in the other. "Mind if I join you?" He sat across from Sam, not waiting for a reply. The chief bit into a bear claw and chewed in silence. He swallowed, smiled and took another bite. "Best darn bear claw I've had in ... well, ever."

"Let me guess. You were looking for me, and Nancy suggested you come here?"

The chief smiled. "As a matter of fact I was. And she did."

Nancy knows me too well. "That new program, you know, the fitness app, was telling me I needed to get some steps in. And ..." Sam trailed off as he gestured toward the door of the bakery. "This is where I landed."

"I can understand why," Chief Finch said as he took another bite of the bear claw.

"If you ever want to get on her good side — not that you would need to, Chief — all you need to do is bring Nancy a raspberry danish. That'll do the trick." Sam gave him a knowing nod.

Chief Finch ripped open two packets of sugar and added them to his black coffee. "I came to find you because I just got off the phone with the mayor. He wants to know if we have any new information on the West case. And if we can connect her overdose with others we've had here in Crawford. He's got a conference this afternoon with some of the other mayors in the state. He wants an update on our progress trying to shut down the flow of drugs into our town. I told him I've been in contact with some of the other chiefs of police around the state. It seems we're not alone in this drug shit show. There's been a recent uptick in overdose fatalities throughout all of Wyoming, but the mayor's not satisfied with that answer. Have you heard back from the pathologist?"

"The autopsy's been performed but we don't have the report yet. I'll give Dr. Grant a call as soon as I get back to the station and find out when we can expect the results."

The chief nodded and took a sip of coffee. "Why don't you tell me about Mr. Millwood."

"Sure, but there's not really much to say about the man. Married to Stephanie Millwood, a nurse who's the owner of a day spa here in town." Sam took a sip of coffee. "Carson came in to answer a few questions. Willingly, I might add."

"I think I understand," Chief Finch said.

"Brooks Millwood comes from a long line of money. His family owns the rock quarry at the edge of town. He owns a ton of land north of Crawford. And" — Sam paused for effect — "I don't know if what I've heard is true, but there are rumors that the Millwoods are exploring the feasibility of mining for gold." Sam watched his boss's wiry salt-and-pepper eyebrows inch up at the mention of gold.

"I didn't know mining for gold was a thing. In Wyoming anyway."

"It is." Sam drained the last of his coffee and set the cup down. "Wyoming is a treasure trove of different minerals and metals, and here in our county there have been some potential gold … and even nickel veins located, all on Millwood's land. He's a very wealthy man. And if there is gold or nickel to be mined, he'll be that much richer."

"From what I overheard, it sounded like he was threatening you."

Sam pressed his lips together. "An empty threat, I'm sure. He's just having a hard time believing his son is involved in drugs."

"So this Millwood has got the not-my-child mentality?"

"Exactly, sir."

Chief Finch and Sam continued to talk while the chief ate his pastry and finished his coffee.

Sam pushed back his chair and stood. "I should be getting back. I'll let you know about the autopsy results." He stood, took his coat off the back of the chair and slipped into it.

"A piece of advice, Overstreet."

The tone in Chief Finch's voice made Sam stop zipping up his jacket. "Yes, sir?"

"I suggest you watch your back with that one. Men like him will try and make your life a living hell." The expression on Chief Finch's face read that he spoke from experience.

Chapter Thirty-Five

"Sam." Nancy, eyes not straying from her computer screen, stuck her hand out as Sam walked by.

"Sorry, Nancy. I didn't bring anything back for you, but I did let the chief know what your favorite pastry is from Dominick's."

"So I was right." She huffed. "Some healthy walk that was. And thank you for telling the chief what I like, but no, I wasn't expecting a handout from you." She raised her eyes at him. "Though that would have been a nice gesture." She waved the pink sticky note stuck to her fingertips. "Message for you. One you've been waiting for."

"Thanks." Sam read the name and number on the little square piece of paper as he walked to his office. He stuck the note on Ruby West's file, which sat on top of three other open case files. He reached for the receiver and punched in the number Nancy had written down. When the call connected, he identified himself, the case he was calling about, and was transferred to Dr. Grant, who picked up on the third ring.

"Hello, Detective. Thank you for returning my call."

"Of course, Doctor. I just got your message."

"Did you have any questions about the toxicology results?" Dr. Grant asked.

"Questions about the tox report? Do you mean it's come back?"

"Well, yes, Detective. I received the results last week. Frankly, I was a little surprised when I didn't hear from you. That's why I thought I'd follow up, make sure you got my message, see if you had any questions about it."

Sam stared at the phone in his hand as if it were a foreign object. "I'm a little confused, Doctor. Previous message?"

"Yes. Are you saying you didn't get a call or a message from my assistant?"

"Your assistant? No, I don't believe we did." Sam scanned his desk, rifled through a few sheets of paper in his inbox tray. No note, no message, but he already knew there wouldn't be.

"Are you sure? Is it possible the message never got passed on to you?"

"I'll check with the staff here when I get off this call. But, no, I don't have anything from your office."

"Well, that would explain why you haven't called me sooner. I thought you'd be in contact with me. I apologize. I should have followed up with the information myself when I didn't hear from you."

Out with it already, Doc.

167

"Ms. West's death, at first blush, appears to be from an overdose of methamphetamine laced with fentanyl. The large amount of drugs in her system caused her to have a heart attack, so in that sense it was due to an overdose but ..." There was a long pause. "Since I got the toxicology results back, I am no longer ruling her death as accidental."

Shit. "What does the report show?"

"We found flunitrazepam in her system."

Sam's pulse quickened. He hitched himself on the corner of his desk. He cradled the phone between his shoulder and ear as he grabbed a sticky note, reached for a pen and scribbled the word the doctor said.

"Also known in street jargon as roofie or forget-me-not," added the doctor. "I assume in your line of work you're familiar with the actual drug name."

Sam nodded even though he knew the doctor couldn't see his reaction. "A common date rape drug."

"Yes, exactly, Detective. Your victim was most likely sedated at some point prior to being injected with the methamphetamine."

Sam remained silent, processing this new information. "So you're saying methamphetamine was in her system but most likely administered after the effects of the roofie took place?"

"Yes, that is my opinion of the sequence of events."

"There would be no logical reason for her to take the sedative," Sam added, talking more to himself as he underlined the word flunitrazepam twice.

"Correct." The sound of rustling papers could be heard through the phone. "I thought you'd want to know this information before the hard copy of the report was sent to you. I assume it will have an impact on the direction your investigation takes."

"Yes, it certainly will. Doc, I appreciate you calling me again and making sure I received this information."

"It's also fortunate that the autopsy was performed without delay," added Dr. Grant. "I know for a while we weren't sure when the body would arrive here. I don't know if you're aware but drugs like flunitrazepam do not stay in the system very long. If we hadn't gotten her when we did, it wouldn't have shown up on the tox screens."

"That was fortunate for us."

"Oh, and just one more detail, Detective. It's in my report but it goes along with the needle puncture, thought you might be interested to know. Your victim was not an intravenous drug user. No sign of old tracks anywhere on her body. I did a thorough exam looking for that specifically."

"Thanks. Good to know."

"Again, I'm sorry if there was any mix-up on my end, preventing this information from getting to you sooner, Detective."

"Thank you for following up." Sam ended the call and cussed under his breath. *Who the hell messed up and dropped the ball on passing along the message?* Sam dragged his fingers through his dark hair while he paced.

Someone else had been at Ms. Nash's house that morning. They managed to give Ruby the sedative. Mixed into a drink most likely. Then once incapacitated, they shot Ruby up with enough methamphetamine to kill her. She did not accidentally kill herself.

With one phone call, Ruby's death went from unintentional overdose to murder.

Chapter Thirty-Six

Sam went out to the lobby. "Nancy, has the chief returned?"

Nancy's amber eyes didn't stray from her computer screen as she answered. "He just got in. I think he —"

Without waiting for her to continue, Sam strode down the hall and knocked on Chief Finch's door. "Sir."

"Come in." The chief, who had been looking at his cell phone, placed it on the desk. "What's up, Overstreet?"

"I just got off the phone with the pathologist on the West case." Sam stepped into Chief Finch's tidy space. "We have a homicide on our hands."

Chief Finch's head shot up, eyes wide.

"Ruby had roofies in her system." Sam relayed the conversation he'd just had with the pathologist.

Chief Finch let loose several expletives, then went quiet for a moment. Then he said, "It would have been nice to have known this sooner."

"Agreed, sir."

The chief shook his head. "Well, go find out who did this."

"I plan to, sir."

After Sam left the chief's office, he stopped at Officer Fuentes's desk. She held up her index finger as she talked on her phone. "Thank you for this information. Yes, I'll let you know if anything new develops." A pause, then, "Yes, yes. Good-bye." She placed the receiver in its cradle. "What's up, sir?"

Sam shared the details of his recent phone conversation with Dr. Grant.

Lola shook her head. "Shit. We've been going at this all wrong the whole time then."

"Shit is right. We've wasted valuable time. Now that we know, we'll need to reinterview everyone. And talk to Nash's neighbors. Fuentes, I want you to canvass the neighborhood. With so much time having gone by, it's probably a long shot but maybe someone will remember seeing or hearing something from that morning that will help us."

"I'll get right on it," said Officer Fuentes.

"Damn it." Sam's facial features were a portrait of anger mixed with frustration. Nancy wouldn't have forgotten to give him the message; he'd bet his life on that. The call from the pathologist's assistant must have come in when she was away from her desk. Her calls went to voicemail when she was on her breaks. He thought back over the last few weeks. The only time she had been absent was in the afternoon when all the clerical staff went to the safety center complex for training on the new phone system they would be using once the police department relocated to its new building. Sam remembered a temp filling in for Nancy for several hours that day.

"Lola, I'll talk to Nash and to Lauren."

Lola tilted her head left and raised her eyebrows.

"What?" asked Sam.

"I was just wondering if" — Officer Fuentes cleared her throat — "if you should be the one questioning your girl-friend?"

Sam raised his eyebrows, a protest forming on his lips.

"I sensed something between you two at Ms. Nash's house that morning," Officer Fuentes said.

"More of your woman's intuition, I suppose. Listen, she's not —" Sam stopped. He hadn't put a label on their relationship, but the time they had been spending together these last few months made it clear to him that he cared for her. A lot. And it wasn't just the usual physical attrac-tion reasons, although those feelings still surfaced at the mere sight of her entering a room.

Up until now he'd been satisfied with the way things were. Sam avoided spending much time analyzing what the two of them had. Just enjoyed it. They hung out. They had great sex. And while she had yet to spend the night with him, Sam enjoyed the view of her slipping out from under his sheets, admiring her ample curves as she gath-ered her clothes off the floor. But more and more he thought about what it would be like to wake up in the morning, Lauren's curves pressed against him, her bare skin warm to his touch.

Lauren herself never pressed him or hinted that she wasn't happy with how things were. If anything, she made it a point to drive herself to his house, always leaving before midnight, like some modern-day Cinderella, only Lauren claimed she had to go home to take care of Maverik.

From some of the counseling sessions Sam attended in the last six months, he knew the real reason he avoided bringing up the question of where their relationship was headed. It came down to two things. Afraid of what Lauren's response might be if he admitted he was falling in love with her. What if she didn't feel the same way about him? But the bigger reason was fear. Fear of opening his heart again, and losing her. Like he lost Abby.

Sam snapped back to the present, with Lola looking at him, waiting for him to say something. "Okay. You talk with Lauren. She's pretty observant. Now that we know Ruby's death wasn't accidental, see if she remembers anything out of the ordinary that morning, the night before, or days before. See if she remembers any cars, visitors at her neighbor's house. And we need to talk to Nash and Makayla again."

Officer Fuentes opened her phone and began tapping.

"What are you doing?"

"I'm adding the names to my notes app." Officer Fuentes held her phone out to Sam.

Sam stared at the screen. *I feel like a fucking dinosaur.*

"It's a great app. You should try it."

"Yeah, okay. Maybe I will." Sam paused. "And, Lola."

Officer Fuentes went back to tapping on her phone. "Yes?"

"Good catch. I know Lauren isn't involved but we always need to be careful about that, not let our feelings get in the way of being objective." Sam caught the fleeting smile on the officer's lips before she tucked her phone away.

"I want you to talk to Ruby's father. Update him on what we've learned. I know she hadn't lived at home for some time but maybe he can tell us who some of her other friends were, besides Makayla, when she was living at home. I'll contact Carson Millwood again, see if he'll come in without a lawyer." Sam rubbed the back of his neck. "I'm going to contact Taryn Biggs again too. See if she has any more information she can share."

Chapter Thirty-Seven

Twila agreed to see Sam that evening. When he phoned her, he offered to come first thing in the morning but he heard the eagerness in her voice when she said, "No, tonight is fine."

Sam heard Percy's muffled yips as he walked up the few steps to Ms. Nash's front porch. He saw the living room curtain flutter. A moment later Twila opened the door.

"Hush now," Twila said into the Papillon's large ear as she held him in her arms.

"Come on in." She turned and shuffled into her living room. Twila put her dog down and slowly lowered herself into her ancient recliner, the effort to settle in causing her to grunt. She motioned with her outstretched thin arm for Sam to take a seat on the equally aged sofa.

The death of her granddaughter had begun to take its

toll. Twila appeared more frail, more stooped when she had greeted him at the door.

"Thanks for agreeing to see me on such short notice, Ms. Nash."

She waved away his remark. "I figured it must be something important, so out with it."

She knows how to cut to the chase. He explained to her what the pathologist had discovered. "So we're looking at your granddaughter's death as suspicious."

"Didn't I tell you that from the beginning?" Twila's raspy voice held a note of triumph.

"Yes, ma'am, you did. And I'm sorry."

She narrowed her eyes at him. "You didn't listen to me because you young people think I'm just another old lady who doesn't know what the hell she's talking about." She started to cough, a deep rattle that started in her chest and racked her whole body.

Sam eyed her with concern. "Let me get you some water." He stood.

She shook her head, unable to speak. After what felt like a full minute, the coughing subsided enough for Twila to reach for the clear nasal cannula that snaked from her oxygen tank to her end table. She placed it in her nose and drew in long hungry breaths.

Sam waited until Ms. Nash's breathing returned to normal before saying, "Again, I'm sorry."

Twila nodded at Percy, who had jumped in her lap. "We knew she was a good girl, didn't we?" In response, the Papillon licked her papery, thin cheek.

"I'd like to ask you some more questions about Ruby. And about that morning."

"Go ahead."

He pulled out a pen and notepad from the inside pocket of his jacket. "Do you remember what time you got up that morning?"

"I think around eight thirty. Used to be an early bird but now I don't sleep good most nights. And if I have a bad night, I sleep in. If I remember, that was one of them nights."

"Had you seen Ruby that morning?"

Twila shook her head. "It was quiet — well, it's always quiet until I put in my hearing aids." She stroked Percy's head as she talked. "I used to have good ears up until recently. Just another thing old age has robbed me of." She heaved a sigh. "Where was I? Oh, the door to Ruby's room was open, so I stuck my head in. She wasn't there but Evie was. Still asleep. Then I came downstairs."

"And since you didn't see her at all that morning, I assume she wasn't downstairs?"

"Of course not." She let out an annoyed breath. "I thought she might be out shoveling snow, but more likely she was outside having a cigarette. I wouldn't let her smoke in my house."

Sam nodded his understanding.

"I told her she should quit. Look where smoking got me." Twila gestured to the oxygen tank beside her on the floor. "But, of course, she didn't listen. Why would she take advice from an old woman?"

"As far as you know, was there anyone here at the house that morning?"

"No. But like I said. I slept in that morning. If anyone was here, I probably wouldn't have heard them, not without my hearing aids."

Sam made a note and continued. "Was Ruby seeing Carson during this time?"

Twila pushed her glasses up the bridge of her nose. "Carson did come over a few times." She cocked her head. "But there was one time, maybe two weeks or so before she died, she asked me to watch Evie. I wasn't too keen on the idea but Ruby said she needed to talk to Carson. And the baby had just went down for a nap, so I said yes."

"Did she say what she needed to talk to Carson about?"

"No." The old woman absently stroked Percy's head. "I remember that Evie took a good long nap, almost three hours, but when she woke up, Ruby still wasn't home. Let me tell you, I lit into that girl when she finally did get herself home. Said I wasn't having none of that."

"How did she seem to you?"

"She was all apologetic, saying over and over and over again how she was sorry. She seemed … she wasn't herself. She looked nervous. Upset."

"Did you happen to notice if her pupils were dilated?"

"Her what? No. No, I didn't. Are you saying she might have been on drugs or something?"

"I'm just trying to ascertain —"

"I don't think she was on anything."

Sam heard the tone in Twila's words. His question had put her on the defensive.

"I think she was nervous because she knew how angry I got. Thought I might tell her to get out. After Carson left, we had us a talk. More like I talked and she listened. I reminded her I was doing her a favor letting her stay with me. That she needed to be responsible. She got herself into this mess. She needed to get herself out. Get an education so she could support herself and that baby of hers. And that meant studying hard. And when she wasn't doing that, she needed to be here to take care of Evie. She told me I was too old to understand, that I don't know what it's like raising a baby all by yourself, and sometimes she just needed a break."

"Had she left you taking care of Evie often?"

"Oh no." Twila shook her head emphatically. "I wouldn't have it. She did go out once with that friend of hers. What's her name again?" Twila snapped her fingers. "Makayla. That's it. I told Ruby straight away, 'I ain't no babysitting service.' I am too old for that. And even if I was younger, that was her child and her responsibility."

Percy, who had been listening intently to the conversation, curled up in Twila's lap, his nose settling into the crook of her arm.

"Did her friend Makayla come over often?"

"Oh, I don't know if you'd say often. A couple times a week maybe."

"What did the two of them do when they were together?"

"Mostly went upstairs, stayed in her room. Makayla seems like a nice girl. A little too chatty for my liking but she was always a polite thing."

"Did Ruby have other people come to the house?"

Twila tugged the threadbare blue cardigan closer to her neck before answering. "Only one other person. A boy … well, not a boy. He was around Ruby's age I'd guess."

"Do you know his name?"

"Said his name was Levi. I don't know a last name, so don't even ask. He was here" — Twila's gaze went to the ceiling — "maybe three times. He never came in. Ruby must have been expecting him because she was always on her way out the door when he pulled up. I asked her who he was but all she said was, 'Just a friend.' And they would leave."

"And leave you with Evie?"

"No. She took Evie with her."

Sam raised an eyebrow.

"I told you I made it clear I wasn't no babysitter." Twila rocked in the recliner and nodded at the same time. "The only other times I watched Evie was when Ruby had to go do one of them pee tests or whatever she had to do to prove she wasn't doing drugs, that she was following her case plan."

"Ruby didn't have her own car, did she?"

"Nah. She couldn't afford one. I let her use mine. I don't drive much anymore. She'd pick up groceries for us. She wanted to get a part-time job but I told her one thing at a time. Get used to being a mother first. Work on finishing your schooling. She was a smart girl. Good grades. A part-time job could come later."

"How long was she gone when she went out with Levi? Do you remember?"

"I didn't time it, but I don't think too long. An hour maybe."

Sam jotted down what she'd said, then asked, "Can you describe him?"

"Yes. I didn't get a good look at him, only saw him as he and Ruby would leave. Kinda on the short side. Clean cut. Dark hair."

Probably the same Levi that Carson mentioned.

"Can you describe his vehicle?"

"Older pickup. White. Louder than the dickens, I'll tell

ya. I don't know the make or model. I don't pay much attention to that kinda stuff."

Sam tapped his pen on his notepad. "And she didn't tell you anything about him?"

Twila shook her head. "No. Said he was a friend from school. But I think she liked him. Like maybe they were dating."

"What makes you think that?"

"Woman's intuition."

What is it with women and their intuition? Sam arched an eyebrow.

Twila glared at him. "That's right, intuition. I was her age once. A century ago maybe but I still remember what it was like to be sweet on a boy."

Sam made a note of the meager description of the vehicle next to Levi's name. He added an asterisk, a reminder to contact Levi Cress and find out what kind of relationship he and Ruby had. He slid the notebook and pen back into his jacket pocket.

"I'd like to take a look in Ruby's bedroom, if you don't mind. We didn't do a thorough search before but ..." His voice trailed off.

"Go ahead." Twila set Percy on the floor and eased herself out of the recliner. "It's the first room on the right, up them stairs." Percy sat on the floor, scratched behind one ear and then followed Sam.

"Ms. Nash, there's no need for you to come up. I don't want you to exert yourself."

"Don't you be telling me what to do in my own home, young man," Twila snapped, but she remained at the bottom of the steps.

Sam took the stairs two at a time. He walked into Ruby's room. The small bedroom appeared to be in a state of transition. Clean folded sheets were ready to be put on the twin-size mattress. Two piles of clothes lay neatly folded on the mattress. One presumably belonging to Ruby, the other to Evie.

Two empty cardboard boxes sat at the foot of the bed waiting to be filled. There were personal hygiene items on top of a white dresser, along with a pack of cigarettes and a lighter.

The bassinet was against one wall. Inside were an open pack of diapers, baby wipes and a couple of onesies.

He pulled a pair of latex gloves out of his coat pocket, slipped them on and went through the teen's meager belongings. He examined the few clothes still hanging in the closet. On the top shelf of the closet were a couple of notebooks. He opened them, flipped through the pages. They were notes Ruby had taken for different classes.

Sam moved on to the white dresser. He pushed aside her personal items; bras, panties, socks, checking underneath for something, anything significant. Sam found nothing. Nothing that explained why someone would want to kill Ruby.

"I need to pack their things up." Ms. Nash stopped in the doorway, her breathing labored. "I guess I'll take them to Goodwill." She picked up a giraffe-print onesie from the pile of clean laundry and placed it in one of the boxes on the floor. Her voice trembled as she spoke. "She didn't have much but I can't just throw it away."

Sam didn't say anything. He heard Ms. Nash's continued labored breaths and hoped she wouldn't have another coughing episode. He thought about asking her if she needed to sit down but remembered her indignant tone from downstairs.

When her breathing sounded normal, he asked, "The cigarettes and lighter, those are Ruby's?"

"Yes. They were on the kitchen counter that morning. Like I said, she wasn't allowed to smoke inside. I don't know why I kept them. Just one more thing to throw away."

"Has anything been removed from the room?"

Twila glanced around the room and shook her head. "No. Yesterday was the first time I've been in here. I washed the sheets is all. Every darn thing takes so much longer to do than it used to." She shook her head as if disappointed in herself for being old, her body betraying her with slowness and frailty.

"Oh, I did remember something. That's why I came up. I wanted to tell you before I forget again."

Sam scanned the bedroom one more time before turning his attention to Twila.

"One of Ruby's teachers came by to visit her."

A teacher visited Ruby? Sam's brow furrowed. "Do you happen to remember when this was?"

Twila placed a hand on the doorjamb as if to steady herself. "It was maybe a month and a half after she moved in. She was back in school by then, so it had to be after the Christmas break."

"And did Ruby and this teacher talk?"

"Yes, but they talked out on the front porch. Ruby was on her way out. Had to take one of them pee tests." She squinted at Sam through her thick lenses. "I mean, a teacher that makes house calls? Never heard of it. When Ruby came home, I asked what he wanted, why he stopped by."

"What did she say?"

"He wanted to make sure she was adjusting with being in school again, being a mom *and* a student." Twila raised a bony shoulder. "Kinda strange, if you ask me."

"What was his name?"

"Let me think." She put a gnarled finger to her chin. "Harper. No, not Harper. Harlan. Yeah, Harlan."

"Was that his first name?"

Twila shrugged. "Don't know. But you're the detective, so I'm sure you'll figure that one out."

Chapter Thirty-Eight

"Taryn, thank you for making time to see me on short notice."

"Sure. No problem."

Sam contacted Taryn first thing in the morning hoping she would have time to answer a few questions about Ruby's case. He sank into the chair across from his ex-sister-in-law and pulled out his pen and notepad.

"I assume it's important; otherwise we could have just done this over the phone."

Sam heard the clipped, overly professional tone in her voice. Taryn turned to her computer, tapped a few keys on her keyboard. Ruby's case file appeared on her screen.

"There have been some developments in Ms. West's case, so I'm really here to ask for your help."

"Developments? What kind of developments?"

"We're no longer looking at Ruby's death as accidental."

Taryn's eyebrows disappeared under her fringe of bangs. "Really? So not a drug overdose?"

"As you probably know, I can't go into details, but we're now ruling Ruby West's death as suspicious."

With an exaggerated breath, Taryn asked, "Then how can I help, Detective?"

Detective. So that's how it's going to be. Well, I am no longer her brother-in-law, so she does have a point. But I do have a first name. "First, do you know who Evie's father is yet?"

Taryn shook her head, eyes still on the screen. "We thought it might be Carson Millwood. I'm sure you know … with your great detecting skills … that the two had dated on and off."

I'm starting to see why my brother divorced you. Sam needed as much information as she could provide, so he chose to ignore Taryn's remark.

"But Stephanie Millwood brought us the results of Carson's paternity test. He's not the father, which I suspect you also know."

"What does the department do in a situation like that, where you don't have a father?"

"With Ruby dead we don't have many, if any, options for locating the father. We've put an ad in the legal section of the newspaper, but so far no response." Taryn rolled her eyes upward. "Shocker. There's probably several guys walking around out there that could be the dad."

"Several? What makes you say that?"

"Because, Detective, I've been doing this long enough that nothing surprises me. If Ruby was using before she got pregnant …" Taryn trailed off, then continued.

"Women like her — girls really — often sleep with a guy in exchange for drugs. So there could be lots of potential baby daddies out there." Taryn shook her head slowly. "Chances are we'll never know who the bio dad is."

Female voices, high and chattery outside the open door, grew louder. Sam glanced over his shoulder and waited for them to pass before continuing his questioning. "I understand. Let me ask you, the times you interacted with Ruby, did she ever say anything to you about anyone having a problem with her? Anyone she didn't get along with? Anyone who was bothering her? I know it's a long shot, but is there anything that you felt was off? You know, her being scared of someone?"

Taryn didn't answer right away. "No. She never confided in me, but no surprise there. I was her caseworker, not her friend."

"Right." Sam sat thinking what else he could ask. He tucked his notebook back into his coat pocket. "Taryn, thanks for your time."

"Sorry I couldn't be of more help." Taryn gave a tight-lipped smile.

Sam stood. "Look, I know that we're no longer related and I also know we're not ever going to be friends, but I'm sensing more than a few hostile vibes. We can be civil, can't we?"

Taryn snorted and gave a little shake of her head. "Civil? For a detective you really aren't very sharp. At least when it comes to personal matters."

He dipped his head and waited for her to continue.

"Sam, it's not about the breakup between Kyle and me. I'm over that. It was how you treated my best friend."

Sam cocked his head to one side like a German Shepherd hearing its owner speak but having no clue what the sound meant.

"I'm talking about Abby. Abby deserved better. She deserved someone that really loved her."

What the fuck are you talking about? Taryn's words were an unexpected gut punch. He took a moment before speaking. "Where is this coming from, Taryn? Of course I loved Abby."

"Really? You loved her so much that you turned around and married Ashley … what was it, less than a year after Abby died? Please." Taryn's words came out in a bitter stream. "I was devastated when Abby died. She was more than a sister-in-law to me. Abby had been a great friend. But you? No, you started dating Ashley — you — you …" She sucked in a breath and lowered her voice. "Abby deserved better."

Sam's teeth clenched together as he stared at this woman who he thought he knew, her torrent of words a verbal slap to his face. He wanted to argue with her. Explain how hard life had been after Abby passed away. For months after she died, Sam's first sensation when he woke, the empty spot beside him. And then remembering. *Abby is gone. Abby. Is. Gone.* The gut-wrenching realization made him wish he had never woken up.

Taryn's voice cut into his thoughts. "You and your brother are so alike. Must be an Overstreet thing."

Sam came here for information about a case, not expecting to hear Taryn rehash her life with his brother. And certainly not expecting her to question his love for Abby. He'd concentrate on his breathing and staying calm. Staying professional.

"Kyle told me how your dad treated your mom, always cheating on her." Even wearing makeup, red blotches formed on Taryn's cheeks. "I guess that's who Kyle got his moral compass from." With a final verbal jab, she added, "And you too, no doubt."

He couldn't argue with what Taryn said about his father. That much had been true. His mother put up with his father's cheating until they became empty nesters and she finally divorced him.

Neither he nor his brother were anything like their dad, and Sam didn't believe his brother had cheated on Taryn, but Sam couldn't know that for a fact. He didn't have time to try to reason with this woman who clearly, at the moment, and perhaps for a long time, had despised him. She wouldn't believe a word he said.

Sam inhaled. When he exhaled, he released enough anger to speak without raising his voice. "Sorry you think that way, Taryn." When she didn't reply, he added, "Listen, I have a job to do. Please let me know if you think of anything that might help Ruby's case."

"Of course." Taryn turned and faced her monitor, chin raised. "Please close the door when you leave."

Chapter Thirty-Nine

"Right this way," Officer Fuentes said.

Lauren walked side by side with the officer, Lauren's breath quickening with each footfall. She commanded herself to inhale slowly and not think about the last time she sat here, the time Sam interviewed her — No, the correct word would be *interrogated*. All the questions, accusations about Judge Murphy's death came back to her, as she knew it would. Lauren wondered if it had been a mistake to offer to come to the station. *Don't be ridiculous. This time you're not a suspect. Yeah, but you didn't think you were a suspect last time you were here, did you?* Lauren smiled nervously as Officer Fuentes opened the door and gestured for Lauren to step inside.

When Lauren and Sam met for coffee at Dominick's two days ago, he told her about the pathologist's results and that Officer Fuentes would be questioning Twila's neighbors, and Lauren specifically. Lauren asked Sam why he didn't just ask her and be done with it. Sam explained it made more sense to have someone, not her boyfriend, interview her. Sam's use of the word *boyfriend* made him blush, which made Lauren smile inside. So she wasn't surprised when she returned home from work the following afternoon to find a business card with Officer Fuentes's name on it wedged between her front door and the doorjamb. On the back of the card she had handwritten a message to call or text her as soon as possible. Lauren texted the officer and offered to come to the police station the following day. Lauren would be subbing in court the next two days for the official court reporter, who had a sick baby at home. With the police station located in the basement of the courthouse, it couldn't have been more convenient.

"Have a seat." Officer Fuentes gestured to the chair at the far end of the table. "I'm going to grab some coffee. Would you like a cup? Or tea, water?"

"No thanks."

"Be right back then."

Lauren wrinkled her nose at the overpowering smell of disinfectant in the room. *Hopefully this won't take long.* The walls were a pale blue, not gray like the one she sat in six months ago when Sam bombarded her with questions. Instead of letting the memories surface, Lauren concentrated on why she was here and the observations she could offer to help with the investigation. Ever since Sam told her Ruby's death was suspicious, Lauren replayed the events of that morning on a continuous loop in her mind.

Officer Fuentes entered, phone in hand, and sat opposite Lauren, giving her a curt, all-business smile. She stated the date, time and Lauren's name for the record, and began.

"Lauren, thank you for coming down. I'm sure Detective Overstreet told you we're digging a little deeper into what happened to Ms. West."

"Yes, he did."

"I'd like you to think back to that morning and tell me if there's anything that stands out. Start with before you found her." Officer Fuentes took a sip of coffee and waited for Lauren's response.

"I've been going over that morning in my mind for the last couple of days. The only thing — and I don't know if it's important or not but I do remember seeing Ruby earlier that morning. She was entering the backyard from the side gate. I only noticed because my dog went to the fence and started barking as soon as I let him out. And that's when I saw her coming in."

"You said she was coming in from the side gate. Did you see her enter that way before?"

Lauren shook her head. "No."

"What can you tell me about that morning and seeing her? What time was that, by the way?"

"Early. A little past six thirty, I think." Lauren's nose twitched from the antiseptic smell in the room. "There's not much I can add to my first statement. I don't remember if I told Sam what she was wearing the first time I saw her outside. She had on a thin hoodie, plaid pajama pants, and a knit hat. She wasn't wearing the hoodie when I found her in the snow, but she was still wearing the same pajama bottoms. And the hat was hanging from a branch when I found her." Lauren's mind went to the image that now haunted her dreams, of Ruby's frosted lashes and cloudy eyes. She shook her head, sending the images scattering. "I think she may have met up with someone out in the front of her house." Lauren watched as Officer Fuentes tapped on her phone.

"Ruby saw me. She waved. I thought she looked a little embarrassed, like she was caught doing something she shouldn't. When I went back inside, I heard an engine start and a vehicle drive away."

"Can you describe the vehicle?"

"No, I didn't see it. I just heard it leaving. Whatever it was, it had a diesel engine."

"I know you wrote out a statement that morning. Did you include this information, about hearing a truck driving away?"

Did I? Lauren didn't think she had. Was this an important piece of information she shouldn't have left out? She felt her cheeks redden at the thought. "No, I don't think I did. But that truck had been there very early. I remember Ruby going inside, and a minute later I heard it drive off. So she was alive and I … I guess I didn't think it was important. I'm sorry."

Officer Fuentes thumbed a note into the phone's app. "No worries. You're telling me now. Anything else you remember about that morning?"

Lauren shook her head. "I can't think of anything."

"What about the night before?"

"I've been thinking about that night, and there was someone parked outside the night before. A pickup, an older truck. Light color, maybe white or silver."

"What time was this?"

Lauren thought back to that night. "I had just let Maverik

back in. I usually let him out around ten-ish to do his business. It must have been there for a while because I could smell diesel fumes when I opened the back door. It might have been the same vehicle I heard that morning." *So is this how turning into a nosy neighbor starts? Have I subconsciously been taking lessons from Twila Nash?*

"Was the vehicle there overnight?"

"No. I check all my windows before I go to bed, make sure they're locked." Lauren caught the raised eyebrows of Officer Fuentes. "It's a habit of mine. The vehicle was gone when I went to bed."

"What time was this?"

"Around eleven thirty." *I really am turning into Twila.* Lauren glanced at Officer Fuentes as the officer checked something on her phone. No wedding band on her finger. Her black hair fell past her shoulders, smooth and shiny even under the unflattering fluorescent lighting. *She must be working with Sam if she's questioning me. How closely are they working?* Lauren swallowed the bitter taste of jealousy that rose in her throat.

"Did you notice if Ruby had a lot of visitors? Or were there different cars parked in front of her house in the days, or weeks, before her death?"

Lauren closed her eyes while she thought. When she opened them, she said, "I don't remember anything unusual. I mean, before Ruby moved in with Twila, there were never any cars in front of the house. I did see different vehicles occasionally but I didn't pay much attention. I'm sorry. It's winter and I pull straight into my garage when I get home, so if they weren't there when I pulled in, chances are I wouldn't notice anyone."

"I understand. I think that's all the questions I have. Thank you for coming down." Officer Fuentes stood and opened the door, waiting for Lauren to join her. They walked to the lobby side by side. Lauren couldn't help but notice how tall and trim the officer looked compared to her own short, less-than-toned body.

"If you think of anything else, please call or text me. Do you still have my card?" Officer Fuentes asked.

"I do. I'll let you know if I think of anything else." Knowing her eye for small details, she didn't think she'd be seeing Officer Fuentes again. And she definitely didn't want to think about the attractive woman who worked so closely with Sam.

The officer held the door open for Lauren as she exited the lobby. She trotted up the stairs and out into the cold air. Inside the Volvo, she inhaled deeply, held the breath for a beat, then let it out slowly. She did this a few more times. As the car warmed, Lauren looked at the granite façade of the government complex with its wide staircase leading down to the police department. Lauren had answered Officer Fuentes's questions. And Officer Fuentes hadn't come across as aggressive. Merely professional and thorough. *Why am I sweating?*

Chapter Forty

It was late afternoon the next day when Sam found the time to reach out to the teacher Twila spoke of. It had been easy enough to track down the man who made "house calls," as Ms. Nash put it. A quick text to his brother and Sam had the man's name and the classes he taught. Only one Harlan worked there. Drake Harlan. Sam thought a trip to his old high school was in order. Find out the reason Mr. Harlan had gone to see Ruby. He couldn't picture a former teacher of Ruby's having any reason to pay her a visit at home.

He called his detective-in-training. "Lola, I'm going to speak to one of Ruby's teachers. If you're not in the middle of something important, I want you to be there." He listened to her response and said, "Great. Let's leave in about ten. Oh, and put in a call to the school, see if you can get Ruby's class schedules for this semester, last semester, and last year's as well."

As they drove to the high school, Sam repeated what Twila had said about Mr. Harlan visiting Ruby. Lola filled Sam in on her interview with Lauren. When she got to the part about Lauren hearing a diesel engine that morning, Sam interrupted her. "It must be this Levi kid. Twila mentioned him, that he had a loud truck. He'd come to the house on a few occasions. Lola, why don't you locate him and ask him to come to the station. We need to nail down when he saw Ruby and —"

"— why was he there so early on the morning she died?"

"Exactly," Sam said.

Sam pulled the SUV to the curb and cut the engine. Crawford High School sat across the street. The staff parking lot had a handful of cars, one of which belonged to Drake Harlan, a faded white Kia SUV, another thing Sam had checked on prior to leaving the station. Sam had also called the school and asked if Mr. Harlan was available. Sam had been informed he was with his science tutoring students, and could they take a message. Sam declined. He didn't want to talk to the teacher over the phone, Sam just wanted to know if he showed up at the school whether he'd catch Mr. Harlan there.

"So how are we playing this? Good cop, bad cop?" Lola held her hands out as if they were the scales of justice and were weighing their options.

"Since you're in uniform, I'll let you be the bad cop," Sam joked. "But really, we're here to see if Mr. Harlan can enlighten us."

"Right. That's what I meant." Officer Fuentes gripped the passenger handle tight as she opened the car door, preventing the wind from testing the strength of its hinges.

The two hurried across the street and up to the entryway. Sam pressed a buzzer above an intercom system, head tucked into his shoulders against the wind that blew directly at their backs.

A high-pitched nasal female voice came through a speaker, asking them the reason for their visit. Sam displayed his badge to the small lens at eye level, after which came a loud click, and the double doors unlocked. Once inside he asked the receptionist for the classroom number, declining her offer to have Mr. Harlan paged.

Lola shuddered, shaking off the biting wind. She smoothed down a few loose strands of her hair. "Do we know where we're going?"

"As a matter of fact we do. Unless the classrooms have changed — which I seriously doubt — I know the way." It only took Sam a moment to reorient himself in the ancient and dimly lit building. "This way," he said with a chin nod, and walked straight ahead with Officer Fuentes at his side.

"So you went to this high school back in the day?"

Sam nodded. "Yes." They strode past dented gray lockers, some adorned with graffiti. "So far it hasn't changed a bit." Sam's time in high school did ... and at the same time didn't ... seem all that long ago. *Coming up on twenty years next year. Twenty.* He tucked the thought away as he turned left, Officer Fuentes following his lead.

They reached the science lab, which was at the end of a long hallway. Before Sam could reach for the doorknob, the door swung open and a young female barreled out. "Oh, I'm sorry," said the thin teenager in front of him. Two girls behind her giggled. Sam and Officer Fuentes stepped sideways, making room for the students to pass. As the trio made their way into the hallway, backpacks slung across their shoulders, they turned curious eyes on Officer Fuentes, her uniform making her stand out to any high school student. They spoke in hushed voices as they walked away.

"What, did you not get enough of me?" A tall man turned from a stainless steel sink at the far end of the room, a mischievous smile slipping from his face when he saw the two strangers approach him. "Oh, sorry. I thought my students were coming back with a question."

They walked over to the man, Sam's badge displayed in his outstretched hand. "Are you Drake Harlan?"

"Yes, that's me."

"I'm Detective Overstreet. This is Officer Fuentes. We'd like to ask you a few questions." Sam watched the teacher's blue eyes take in Officer Fuentes before returning his attention to Sam.

"I've only got a couple of minutes to spare."

Sam followed Mr. Harlan's gaze to the clock on the wall.

"I have to pick up my son from daycare. They charge by the minute once you're five minutes late."

"We'll get you out of here quickly," said Sam.

"What can I do for you?" Mr. Harlan asked.

Sam reached in his coat pocket and pulled out his pen and notepad, Officer Fuentes pulling out her phone.

"It's about Ruby West," said Sam.

The science teacher blinked a few times. "Oh, Ruby. Yes, yes. It's terrible what happened to her. Everyone at school was shocked to learn that she passed away."

"Since you're short on time, we'll cut to the chase. I understand you visited Ruby at her home a week or so before her death. Why?"

The chemistry teacher gathered small vials containing a green liquid from the students' desks. "I knew she had only recently returned to school. I knew about her" — he did an exaggerated clearing of his throat — "situation, you know, her having a baby, and I wanted to check on her, see if there was anything I could do to make the transition back to school easier for her." He placed the vials in a tray and set them in the sink.

"And how did she seem to you?"

"She wasn't home, so I never got the chance to ask her."

"Ms. Nash said Ruby was just leaving and the two of you walked out together."

The teacher tilted his head to one side. "Oh, right, right. I did see her but only for a moment. She was running late for an appointment I think."

"Was she in any of your classes this semester?"

"No. No, she wasn't."

"Did you see her at all when she came back?" Sam waited a beat. "To school I mean."

Drake Harlan pushed the sleeves up on his blue-and-gray sweater, exposing a partial tattoo on his right forearm, and turned on the tap. He spoke over the sound of the water running. Mr. Harlan quickly rinsed the vials and placed them upside down on a mat next to the sink to dry.

"I might have seen her in the halls, but, no, we didn't have any interaction." Mr. Harlan pulled a couple of sheets of paper towel from a dispenser, dried his hands, then glanced at the clock again.

"Did you have Ruby in any of your classes last semester?" Sam asked.

"No. I tutored her last spring semester. So almost a year ago. She was struggling with chemistry, and as you can see" — he cocked his head in the direction of the door — "I tutor students after class. That's what I did for her."

"We understand you also coach the girls' track team."

"I do — or I did. My schedule has changed. I'm not going to be coaching this season."

Sam waited to see if the teacher would elaborate.

"My wife went back to work recently. She was on maternity leave. She's a nurse at the hospital. With her new hours, I'm responsible for picking up our son from daycare." Again Mr. Harlan checked the time. "Listen, I really need to get going."

"Just one or two more questions. "Did Ruby go out for track last year?"

Mr. Harlan furrowed his brow. After a few seconds, he said, "Yes, she did, but if I remember, she quit within the first week or two."

"Did she tell you why she quit?"

"No, she just stopped coming to practice. I didn't see her after that. But track isn't for everyone. It's a huge commitment." He began putting sheets of paper in a folder. "Or maybe her social life got in the way." Mr. Harlan stuffed the folder into a black backpack.

"Why do you say that?" Sam asked.

201

Another shrug. "You know how it is, teens, hormones, dating." Drake Harlan turned his attention to Officer Fuentes. "You must remember what it was like to be in high school. You barely look old enough to be a cop."

Officer Fuentes tapped something on her screen before raising her chin, looking at him through her dark lashes. She hinted at a smile with her lips and said, "You could pass for a high school student yourself."

Drake Harlan tilted his head to the side and ran a hand through his sandy-blond hair, a gesture Sam could picture him doing often.

"Yeah, I hear that a lot."

"And how old are you?" Sam asked.

The teacher straightened, pulling his gaze away from Officer Fuentes. "I'm thirty-two." He grabbed his phone off his desk and stuck it in a side pocket of his backpack. "I'm sorry, but I *really* need to go."

"Thank you for your time," said Sam. Officer Fuentes and Sam left the building and headed to Sam's vehicle, neither in a hurry, as the wind had died down during the brief time they'd talked to the teacher. Once seated inside, Sam started the engine. "I like how you handled Mr. Harlan's remark about you being so young."

"Thanks. Did we get anything useful from that?" Officer Fuentes asked.

"What does your gut say?"

Officer Fuentes cocked an eyebrow. "Besides I'm hungry?"

Sam rolled his eyes but smiled. "Yes, besides that."

She buckled her seatbelt. "There's something he's not telling us."

Sam nodded. "I agree."

"At first he denied having spoken to Ruby until you jogged his memory."

Sam cocked his head in the direction of the school. Officer Fuentes followed his gaze. The two watched as Drake Harlan emerged from the school, head down, shoulders hunched against the cold. He got in his SUV and sped away.

Lola smirked. "Someone's in a hurry."

Chapter Forty-One

Sam opened his front door. Lauren held out a bakery box. "A little something for dessert. Oh, and Dominick says hi."

"I didn't know his bakery was open Sundays."

"It is. I think he's a workaholic. Lucky for Crawford." When he invited her for dinner, Sam said he had everything he needed, but she didn't want to show up empty-handed.

He grinned as he took the box from her. "Thanks."

She removed her parka and Sam hung it on a hook next to a white down-filled jacket. He dipped his head and kissed her, his warm lips pressed against her cold ones.

Sam isn't a cheater. Is he? Ever since Taryn practically accused Sam of being unfaithful, Lauren found it hard to concentrate on work. She'd obsessed over Taryn's disclosure. Lauren even picked up her phone a couple of times, started to text Sam to say she was sorry but something came up and couldn't make dinner, only to delete the unsent message. When they first started dating, Sam explained why his second marriage didn't work out. He hadn't grieved the loss of his first wife. Lauren told him she understood. And Lauren did understand, as much as she could, never having experienced such a loss herself. But Sam hadn't spoken much about Abby or her death. Lauren hadn't pressed him for details, assuming he would open up when ready.

He draped his arm across her shoulder and pulled her into him. "I'm glad you made it."

He's not a cheater. Sam's kiss and embrace relaxed her mind. "No way was I going to turn down one of your famous elk steaks." She rubbed her hands together for emphasis. "That's all Uncle Jack talked about for days, that time you invited Aunt Kate and him over for dinner." Lauren lowered her voice. "I was a little surprised you invited me tonight."

He pulled away so he could look at her. "What do you mean?"

"I thought you'd be too busy with … you know … Ruby's case and all."

"The case won't get solved any quicker if I eat fast food. And … it's the weekend. I get to relax once in a while. Besides, I wanted you to meet my brother and" — Sam smiled and lowered his voice — "his very pregnant wife."

"I've been looking forward to meeting him." *Relax, Lauren.* She was always uncomfortable the first time she met someone new, wanting to make a good first impression. Tonight was no different, except after listening to

Taryn badmouth her ex-husband, Lauren assumed she'd be the one not liking Sam's brother. Or his new wife. Kyle sounded like an ass. Lauren reminded herself to keep an open mind. To remember what she heard in litigation, the two sides to every story.

They walked through the living room into the kitchen, passing a stone fireplace with logs burning, throwing out warmth.

Two people, one sitting and one standing, were at a small kitchen island, deep in conversation. They stopped talking as Sam and Lauren entered the room.

"Lauren, this is my brother Kyle. And this is Joni, his wife," Sam said.

Kyle extended his hand. "Nice to meet you, Lauren."

"Same here." Lauren returned his firm handshake, momentarily caught off guard at how much the two brothers resembled one another. The same dark brown eyes, square jaw. If Kyle had darker hair, or if Sam's were lighter, they could pass for twins.

Sam placed the bakery box on the kitchen counter and reached in the refrigerator, pulling out a bottled iced tea for Lauren. "Thanks," Lauren said.

Joni let out a little squeal. "Ooh, Dominick's. I love that place."

"I'm going to check on the steaks." Sam grabbed a platter and a large fork and headed out the back door.

Don't leave me here alone to make small talk. Lauren smiled at the couple. "So, you're Sam's younger brother."

The three exchanged pleasantries, followed by some perfunctory conversation about the barrage of snowstorms Crawford had so far this year.

"My brother tells me you're a court reporter," Kyle said, leaning against the island, a can of soda in his hand.

"Yes, I am."

"So you type on one of those little machines," Joni asked as she typed on an imaginary keyboard.

Lauren smiled. "Yes, one of those."

Joni twisted her long ash-blonde hair and swept it over one shoulder. "Wow. I've never known anyone that did that. You must be a fast typer."

"It's a little different than typing, but you do have to be able to write fast, at least 225 words a minute to graduate from school. And most people talk faster than that." Lauren stopped before going into any greater detail. Unless Joni or Kyle were genuinely interested to know more, she didn't want to risk boring them so soon after meeting the couple. She left it with the reaction Joni had, the mimicked typing on an imaginary keyboard.

Lauren couldn't help herself. She had to say one more thing about her profession. Then she would change the subject. "It's an interesting profession. You learn about a lot of different things. And every day you hear something new. Not always exciting, but I do like what I do."

"I testified in court once," Kyle said. "It was a long time ago. I was a witness to a car accident. This old lady — she must have been the court reporter because she was using that little machine — stopped me, like, three times, telling me I needed to slow down, that I was talking too fast." He let out a small laugh at the memory. "I was thinking maybe she needed to retire if she couldn't keep up."

Lauren had been mentally writing his words in her

head. "Just listening to you now, I'd have to agree with that *old lady.*"

Kyle chugged the last of his soda.

Lauren smiled tightly. "You're a court reporter's least favorite type of witness."

Kyle had the decency to look sheepish. "Oh, I never thought of how fast I talk."

"It's not something most people think about," Lauren admitted.

"In my defense, I was nervous."

"Come to think of it, you do talk fast." Joni nodded her agreement with Lauren. "But I still love you." She squeezed his arm and smiled.

"What do you like to do when you're not writing on that little machine?" Kyle asked.

Lauren thought for a moment. "I hike. And I do a little woodworking."

"Oh, yeah, that's right." Kyle nodded. "Sam showed me the shelf you made. He said it's made from beetle-killed pine."

Lauren nodded. "There's no shortage of that kind of wood in Wyoming, unfortunately."

"It's a really nice-looking piece," Kyle said.

"Thank you. What about you? Other than skiing, what do you like to do?"

He furrowed his thick eyebrows. "I do like to ski, but how did you know that?"

Chapter Forty-Two

Good question. How do I know that? Should I bring up that I went skiing with Taryn, using his season ski pass? "Sam mentioned you're almost as good a skier as he is." Small lies don't count, reasoned Lauren.

Kyle cocked his head to the side. "Oh, did he now? Well, besides being almost as good a skier as Sam, I like to hunt and do a little fishing. But right now most of my free time is spent getting the baby's room ready. You know, painting the walls, new carpet." He smiled at his wife, his dark eyes warming. *Just like Sam's eyes,* thought Lauren.

Joni ran her hand in small circles around her baby bump. "It keeps us both busy." She dragged a tortilla chip through a bowl full of guacamole. "I'd love to know more about being a court reporter. I was thinking after the baby comes ... and he gets a little older ... I'm going to change careers," said Joni. She added with a shy laugh, "Or get a career. Being a receptionist at a dental office is not exactly a career."

"I'd be happy to give you a demonstration, show you how the writer works, and give you some literature about what it takes to become a stenographer."

Joni's deep-blue eyes widened with excitement. "Oh, I'd really like that. It sounds so interesting."

Lauren smiled. "Great. I'll text you and we can figure out a time."

Sam stepped inside, bringing cold air and the scent of grilled meat with him. He set a platter of elk steaks on the table. "Hope everyone's hungry."

"I'm starved," Kyle said.

"You always are," Sam quipped.

Kyle nodded his agreement, then took a seat at the dining room table next to his wife. He placed his hand lightly on Joni's stomach. "I'm sure he's hungry too."

Joni placed her hand over her husband's. "If he's anything like his dad, yes, he is." They both laughed.

"So you're having a boy. When are you due?" Lauren asked.

"Soon. March 21." Joni beamed at Kyle. "We can't wait." She hitched her thumb in the direction of her husband. "Well, maybe me a little more than him. I'm tired of being so huge. I can't believe how much weight I've put on."

"You look great, babe," Kyle said.

"You have to say that, but thanks for lying." Joni smiled at Kyle. "According to my doctor, she said I put on enough weight, and I could stop eating for two now." Joni speared one of the steaks with her fork. "That ain't happening tonight."

Sam reached for his beer and took a swallow. "And my little brother here always wanted kids." He tipped his bottle toward Joni. "Looks like it's finally happening."

As Lauren chewed her perfectly cooked steak, she remembered her conversation with Taryn, who had said pretty much the same thing, how much Kyle wanted a family, at the same time telling her he was okay if they didn't have kids.

"You'll be the first one to give mom a grandchild. Thank you for that, bro. Now she can quit asking me."

"Yeah, but I'll bet she stopped asking when you and Ashley split up."

Sam grudgingly lifted one shoulder.

"So, you're welcome," Kyle said.

Lauren listened to the two brothers talk. Their conversation flowed easily with no undercurrent of competition, jealousy, long-held animosity. Lauren also quietly observed Kyle and Joni through bites of steak, noting their natural banter.

Before arriving at Sam's house, Lauren reminded herself all she had to do was to *get through* the evening, and assumed she wouldn't like Joni, the "other woman" as Taryn described her, one of the least offensive terms she used to describe Joni. But listening to Joni and watching her interaction with Kyle, Lauren found it hard to dislike her. Lauren took a bite of what she thought were mashed potatoes but soon she realized they were mashed cauliflower. "Mmm. These are so good."

"I made them," Sam said.

Lauren's eyes widened.

"Don't look so surprised. I told you I know my way around a kitchen."

"Good to know." Lauren chuckled. She then turned to Joni. "How long have you two been together?" She hadn't planned on asking the question but her curiosity won out. She wanted to know if Taryn had been right, that Kyle had cheated on her while they were still married.

"Let's see. We got married at the end of August. Kyle, what's it been now, nine, ten months ago that we met?" Joni mock elbowed her husband. "Love at first sight."

Kyle, his mouth full of steak, gave an exaggerated nod.

If Joni had her dates right, she and Kyle started dating after Kyle and Taryn separated, not while they were married. Lauren knew her ideas on relationships and family didn't necessarily match anyone else's. Like getting to know one another before committing to the idea of having a child together. They couldn't have known each other more than a couple of months before Joni got pregnant. But as she observed the two of them, they seemed genuinely in love.

Lauren thought of her relationship with Tony. They had been married for more than a year when she brought up the subject of wanting to start a family, have a baby. He'd said they should wait until they were more financially secure. Lauren grudgingly agreed, but always wondered whether Tony just used money as an excuse, that he'd already begun to grow tired of her.

Sitting here now, a failed marriage in her rearview mirror, no children, Lauren was in no position to judge anyone. *Stop overthinking, Lauren. Just enjoy the evening.*

*   *   *

After dinner they all went to sit in the living room. Sam brought the bakery box over to the coffee table. Joni leaned forward and opened it, a grin forming on her lips. "Raspberry-filled cookies. My favorite." She plucked one from the box and sat back with a smile, snuggling against Kyle. Sam took a seat next to Lauren on the loveseat opposite his brother and Joni.

The furniture was grouped around the fireplace, warm and inviting. Lauren leaned her head on the sofa and bit into a cookie. The conversation between Kyle and Sam turned to college basketball. Joni added her opinion on who would make it to the Final Four, talking stats and coaches and players.

Lauren's body jerked. She blinked. *Did I fall asleep?* No one seemed to notice if she had.

"… you talked to Drake the other day," said Kyle.

"We did speak with him," Sam said. "How did you know?"

Kyle raised a shoulder. "Word gets around fast at school."

Sam nodded.

"So no suspects in Ruby's death so far," Kyle asked.

"No suspects yet. We're going to reinterview a few people here in the next day or two. Go from there."

Lauren learned a few things about Sam since they started seeing each other on a regular basis. One of them, he didn't share details of ongoing cases. Sam had told her the less he said about a case, the less chance of misinformation being spread.

Kyle nodded. He glanced over at his wife, who wore a sleepy smile. Joni patted his arm. "I think we're going to get going," Kyle said.

Everyone walked toward the front door, where they all said their goodbyes. After Sam closed the door, he turned to Lauren. He pulled her in for a hug, pressing his lips to her ear. "Alone at last."

Chapter Forty-Three

Sam spent most of the next day following up on interviews. Officer Fuentes spoke with Levi, and also confirmed his story, that he'd stopped by to see Ruby before his shift started at the Maverik convenience store. Sam also updated Chief Finch on the latest developments with the Southeast Drug Enforcement Team.

Late in the afternoon, Makayla entered the police station and raised a tentative hand when she saw Sam on the other side of the glass partition. He nodded at her, then spoke to Nancy, who buzzed open the door that led from the lobby to the bullpen of the Crawford Police Department.

Nancy smiled at the nervous-looking teen. "You can come right through the door here." Nancy pointed to her left.

"Hi, Makayla," said Sam as he approached. "Thanks for agreeing to come down and speak with me."

Makayla nodded, her hands shoved deep in her coat pockets. "My mom wanted to come with me but I convinced her not to."

"She would have been welcome to sit in. That wouldn't have been a problem."

"I told her I could do this on my own. That you wanted to ask me a few more questions about Ruby."

"And I do." Sam watched her look around the police station, her eyes wide behind her glasses.

"Have you ever been here before?" Sam asked.

"Oh, no. I've never been in any trouble."

He let out a small chuckle. "No, I didn't mean it like that. We have kids in junior high come through. We show them around, give them an idea of what we do when we're not out on the streets giving people tickets for speeding."

"I — I never speed."

Sam had been trying to make Makayla feel at ease but so far he hadn't succeeded. "We're going to head back to our interview room. It'll be quieter there."

The short teen nodded and fell in step with Sam as they walked down the dimly lit hall.

"Right in here," said Sam as he opened the door. "Why don't you have a seat over there." He pointed to a chair on the other side of a table. "Can I get you some water? Or would you like a soda?"

"Oh, no thank you."

"As you can see" — Sam pointed to a video camera in a corner of the ceiling — "this is a little more formal than when I met you at Ms. Besoner's house. I'll be recording this. It just helps me so I can concentrate on what you're telling me and I don't have to take so many notes."

Makayla glanced at the camera but didn't say anything.

Someone higher up the chain of command, maybe the old chief, Ray Newell, thought pale blue walls would have a more soothing or calming effect for an interview room. And the chairs were cushioned, which made for more comfortable seating, but it was still a space where questions were asked, and where answers, sometimes painful ones, were spoken.

Sam observed that Makayla kept her hands stuffed inside the pockets of her pink puffer jacket.

"Like I said on the phone, this shouldn't take long. I just have a few more questions for you."

Makayla nodded and straightened in the chair.

"We're taking a deeper look into your friend's death. We don't think Ruby died from an overdose." Sam watched as she processed the statement.

"So she wasn't using." She met his gaze. "Ruby said she wasn't. She'd been trying to stay clean."

"There were drugs in her system, so I can't know for sure. But there are some things we still need to investigate further."

Makayla took her hands out of her pockets and folded them on the table. "I — I don't understand. She was using or she wasn't?"

"We think something besides the methamphetamine may have caused her death, so we're treating her death as suspicious."

Makayla's eyes widened, and before she could speak, Sam asked, "When was the last time you spoke to Ruby?"

"That Friday before ... before, you know. At school. We had lunch together."

"And how did she seem to you?"

Makayla didn't answer right away. Finally she said, "Okay, I guess."

"Did she say anything to you at all about any disagreements she was having with anyone? Anything bothering her?"

"She seemed … fine."

"Are you sure nothing was bothering her?"

"Um …" The teen averted her eyes, looking instead at her lap, at the door, at the plastic bubble in the corner ceiling.

"Whatever you remember about that day, even a small detail, it could be important, Makayla."

"It's — well …" She pushed her frames up on her nose.

Sam watched as Makayla struggled with whether to say something or be a loyal friend, even after Ruby's death, and stay quiet.

"She was fine at lunch. I was going to give her a ride home after school. I'd been doing that a lot this semester. She didn't have a car. Anyway, when we walked out together, Carson was waiting for her. Right outside the door. Said he wanted to talk. She told me to go on ahead, she'd meet me at my car in a minute. So I waited. It was way longer than a minute. I thought she might have forgotten I was going to give her a ride and left with him."

When Makayla said the word *him*, her tone equated to someone talking about a venomous snake. "When Ruby finally did get in my car, I knew she was upset. I asked her what he wanted." Makayla shook her head. "She said it was nothing. Carson just offered to give her a ride home. I knew there was more to it but she kept saying she was fine."

Makayla looked again at the video camera.

"I won't be sharing your information with people that don't need to know. Is there something you want to tell me? Maybe about Carson?"

"Um, I heard he sells drugs." Makayla quickly added, "But that's just a rumor around school. But I've seen him in the student parking lot, and since he already graduated, like, what's he even doing there, right?" She glanced at the camera again, then added quickly, "But like I said, it's just a rumor."

The heat kicked on, and the sound of warm air being pushed through the ceiling vent interrupted the quiet that settled in the small room.

Sam added Carson's name to the list of people to interview again. He waited for Makayla to offer more information about Carson. He broke the silence when she simply sat across from him avoiding eye contact. "What can you tell me about Mr. Harlan?"

Makayla furrowed her brow, the expression on her face one of confusion. "Mr. Harlan?"

"Yes. He's a science teacher at Crawford High School, right?"

"Uh, yeah, he is."

"What can you tell me about him?"

Makayla raised a shoulder. "I don't know. I mean I had him for chemistry but that was last year."

"What about Ruby? Did she take chemistry as well?"

Makayla nodded. "We were in the same class." She pushed a few strands of her curly brown hair behind one ear. It immediately fell forward. "He was the one that helped her get a passing grade."

"What do you mean? How did he help her?"

"Ruby was having a really hard time, you know, with chemistry. She told me she was failing and was thinking of dropping his class, but knew if her dad found out he'd go all bat-shit crazy on her. Plus, she needed to pass chemistry to graduate." Makayla closed her eyes as if thinking back to the conversation. When she opened them she slowly nodded. "Ruby ended up with a B-plus. I asked her how that happened. She said Drake tutored her after class."

"Drake?"

"I mean Mr. Harlan. Everyone calls him Drake though."

Sam nodded. "Anything else you can tell me about Drake?"

"Um, I don't know. Oh, yeah. He's the girls' track coach. Or was."

"When was this?"

"Last spring. March or April. Whenever track starts."

"I understand Ruby went out for track."

"Um-hum." Makayla blew out an exaggerated breath. "She talked me into going out for it too, said it would be so much fun. Then she quits before we even had our first meet. I was mad at her when she did that."

"Did she tell you why she quit?" asked Sam.

"No. I asked her but all she said was she didn't want to do it anymore. I thought it was because of Carson. That's when they started hanging out. A lot. They were *always* together. Ruby didn't have time for anything. Or anyone. And I was stuck running relays without her." Makayla's lips pressed into a flat line with that last statement.

"And you didn't quit?"

"Unh-unh. I was going to. I really wanted to. I would

have never gone out for it if it hadn't been for Ruby. I mean it wasn't horrible but I'm — I'm not really into sports. When Ruby quit I was ready to do the same but my mom told me I should stick with it. I should finish what I started. 'We're not quitters,'" Makayla said in a high-pitched voice, then rolled her eyes. "One of my mom's favorite things to say. *Ugh.*"

Sam suppressed a smile, glad his teenage years were so far behind him that they couldn't be seen in a rearview mirror. "How was Mr. Harlan as a coach? Did you like him?"

Makayla shrugged. "He was nice. Made it kinda fun. Not super serious, never yelling at us to run faster or anything like that." She paused for a moment. "But I think some of the girls just joined the track team because *he* was the coach."

Sam stopped writing and cocked his head. "What do you mean?"

"A lot of the girls thought he was hot." Makayla's cheeks reddened at the comment.

Sam wondered if Makayla had also thought of him as hot.

"He's not bad looking for an old guy."

"Did Ruby ever describe him as hot?"

Makayla nodded. "Yes. When he was tutoring her in chemistry she kept going on about how cute he was, how super nice he was." She tilted her head. "Come to think of it, I bet that's the only reason she went out for track." She let out an exasperated puff of air. "Which is why I was so mad when she didn't stick with it."

"And you're sure she didn't give any specific reason why she quit?"

"No. She said she just wasn't into it."

Sam had asked the questions he needed to of Makayla. He took a moment to flip through his notepad to see if he needed to follow up on any of her answers.

"Just one more question, Makayla. I want to get you home in time for dinner. Did Ruby ever say who Evie's dad was?"

Makayla raised her eyebrows at the question. "It's Carson, isn't it?"

Sam didn't answer her question but instead asked another one of his own. "Did she specifically say it was Carson?"

"Yes, she told me it was his baby. But I didn't have to ask, I already knew. I mean, he was the only one she was seeing." Makayla pressed her fingertips together. "And when she found out she was pregnant, Ruby told me it was the worst thing that could have happened to her. And how stupid she was for letting it happen."

Sam nodded as he closed his notepad. "Thank you for talking to me again, Makayla."

Makayla's eyes searched his. "Are you going to find who killed Ruby?"

Sam saw her eyes shine with unshed tears. He wouldn't lie to her. "I'm going to do my very best to find out who killed your friend and make sure they spend a long time in prison."

* * *

Sam tapped on Officer Fuentes's cubicle. "When you've got a minute, come to my office. Let's update each other on the West case."

"I'm free now." Lola rose from her chair and followed Sam to his office.

"I just finished interviewing Makayla again. I think there was more to Ruby and the teacher's relationship than just tutoring and coaching. I want to talk to Drake Harlan again. Here. I'm going to see if he'll come in after school tomorrow."

"Okay. In the meantime, do you want me to do some online checking, see if there's anything that pops up? Anything that's in his past?"

"Yes. Lola, that's a good idea."

"I'll let you know what I find."

"Let's keep each other informed."

Lola nodded and disappeared down the hall.

Sam's lips curved into a small smile. *She's on her way to being one heck of a good detective.*

Chapter Forty-Four

"Drake, thank you for coming down." Sam extended his hand to the teacher, then gestured for him to take a seat. Sam had spoken to the chemistry teacher yesterday afternoon and Mr. Harlan reluctantly agreed to come to the station during his lunch hour.

Mr. Harlan's inspection of the room stopped at the camera that poked out from the ceiling in one corner.

"We always record what goes on. Saves me from having to write down every little detail," Sam said.

The teacher nodded, his Adam's apple bobbing beneath his pale skin.

"I need to get my file. Can I get you a cup of coffee?"

"No, I'm good."

"That's actually a smart choice. Coffee's pretty old by now. Can I get you some water?"

"No, thanks."

"Okay. I'll be right back." Sam returned moments later and settled himself in the chair opposite the teacher.

Before Sam could ask a question, Mr. Harlan spoke up. "You said you had a few more questions for me. What can I help you with?"

"Like I mentioned on the phone, there's been a new development in Ms. West's case. I was prepared to meet you at the school, save you a trip down here, so, again, thank you for coming in." Sam didn't mind telling a lie. He wanted this interview recorded. He knew having a police officer return a second time to the school might raise some eyebrows from school staff and hoped it had that effect on Mr. Harlan. Turned out Sam had been right.

Sam studied Mr. Harlan as he sat across from him, hands loosely clasped together on the table, relaxed posture. A man trying to look nonchalant but his blue eyes darting around the small room telling a different story.

"It was no problem. Besides, if you showed up at school, the front office people might wonder why the police were wanting to see me again. That's how rumors get started, right?" Mr. Harlan laughed but it came out forced. "So what are these new developments?"

"Drake, let me get a few preliminaries out of the way first and then we'll talk." After getting basic information about the man, his name, phone number, address, and occupation on the record, Sam opened the blue folder in front of him and pretended to study its contents. Sam remembered what Makayla and Ms. Nash had said in their previous statements and didn't need his notes to refresh his memory.

"I asked you here because I was hoping you could help us."

Mr. Harlan's eyes widened ever so slightly at the statement. "Help you how?"

Sam went over the visit he and Officer Fuentes had with him at the school not long ago. He had Mr. Harlan confirm the things he had told them earlier, the teacher nodding and agreeing as he spoke.

"Drake, we're no longer investigating Ruby's death as an accidental overdose. She died under suspicious circumstances." Sam watched Mr. Harlan's reaction. He had a genuine look of surprise on his face.

"What I'd like from you, Drake, is the real reason you went to see Ruby. At her home a couple of days before she died."

Mr. Harlan shifted in his seat. He avoided Sam's gaze, whose focus remained on the teacher sitting opposite him. Mr. Harlan finally met Sam's eyes. "As I said before, it was to see how she was doing. I knew she hadn't been on good terms with her father for some time, more or less ever since her mother's death. She now had a baby to contend with. I'm a parent. I know how stressful it can be, and that's with two of us taking care of our little guy. I'm sure doing it on her own, with little help, was extremely hard. I just wanted to see if she needed anything. Help her in any way I could."

"And did she? Need help, I mean."

"Uh, not really. She said things were going okay. Thanked me for coming by. She was on her way out, so we didn't visit long."

"How did you know she wasn't on good terms with her dad?"

"I talk with all my students, Detective. I'm there for

them. And not just for help with science. Sometimes they share things with me. Ruby mentioned her strained relationship with her father a few times when I tutored her in science. I'd simply asked if things had improved, if their relationship was any better now that he had a grandchild. Sometimes that brings people around."

Sam nodded and tapped his pen on his palm, then held it still. "I thought you said Ruby wasn't in any of your classes this semester. Or last fall."

"She's not. She wasn't. But I got to know her from my chemistry class last year and the tutoring I did with her. She was a nice girl going through a really rough patch, you know, with the loss of her mother. I wanted to offer my continued support."

"Where did the tutoring take place?"

"In the science lab."

"Anywhere else?"

"I don't think so."

Sam turned his head slightly and gave the teacher a long sideways glance.

"Oh, wait. We might have met at the library once."

"School library?"

Mr. Harlan licked his lips. "No, the public library."

"The public library. How often did you do that?"

"Like I said, once. Possibly twice."

"Any particular reason for tutoring Ruby there?"

"Uh, no, not really. I think I might have suggested some books she should check out for the chemistry test that was coming up."

"Were you tutoring anyone else besides Ruby?"

Mr. Harlan straightened in his chair. "It's been a while

but I believe there was another student I was tutoring at the same time as well."

"Did this student meet you at the public library as well?"

Mr. Harlan ran a hand through his blonde hair. "Uh, I don't remember. That was a long time ago, Detective."

"The student's name?"

Mr. Harlan thought for a moment. "I — I don't remember her name right offhand. I wish I could."

"Maybe you could check your records."

"I don't know if I have anything from that far back. I mean, it would be in the student's file, I'm sure, but without a name there's no way to know for certain."

"When you tutored Ruby did you talk about other things besides chemistry? You said students opened up to you. Was there anything going on in her life then? You mentioned you knew her mother had passed away a couple of years ago."

"She did confide in me about that. Mentioned her mom and how much she missed her. How her dad was having a hard time dealing with Mrs. West's passing. How he was distant even before she died. He had a hard time dealing with — with the whole cancer thing. Ruby didn't feel she could talk to him about ... you know, girl things. Certainly not like she had with her mother." Drake rested his clasped hands on the tabletop. "I tried to fill that gap, at least a little bit, said I was available if she ever needed to talk to someone."

Sam nodded. "So would you say you were kind of a mentor to her in some ways?"

"Right, right. I told her I was there for her. That life can be rough. That she could always come to me with a problem."

"That was nice of you."

Not hearing the note of sarcasm in Sam's voice, Mr. Harlan continued. "I try to be supportive to all my students, especially the ones going through a rough time."

"Very commendable of you, considering you are a father yourself and must have a busy life outside of school. Can be hard to juggle so much going on at once, I would imagine." Sam caught the slight rise in Mr. Harlan's eyebrows. Sam continued. "The last time we spoke you mentioned that Ruby went out for track."

"Yes, she did. That was in the spring of last year. I thought an extracurricular activity might be good for her."

"So you're the one that suggested she do that?"

"Uh, yeah. It's something I tell a lot of my students if I see them struggling with ... with life. Find an activity, an outlet of some kind."

"Harlan, remind me again, why did she quit?"

The teacher clasped and unclasped his hands. "Like I said before, she just stopped coming to the practices."

"Did you go to her home then and ask her why?"

"No, I didn't."

Sam flipped through a few pages in the folder in front of him. He met Mr. Harlan's gaze and spoke in a casual, friendly tone. "A young, good-looking teacher like yourself, I imagine you get the female students flirting with you from time to time." He watched as Mr. Harlan's cheeks reddened. "Don't get me wrong. I'm not saying you'd ever act on it." Sam leaned forward. Gave the teacher a conspiratorial nod. "But maybe you returned the flirting with a little good-natured bantering of your own?"

Mr. Harlan's Adam's apple bobbed as he swallowed.

"Hey, I understand. I do. Girls in high school, they're not kids. I deal with teens a lot in my line of work. I see what some of them look like. They certainly don't dress like kids. They don't act like kids. You know what I'm saying. And you get to watch all those young things strutting in and out of your classroom day in and day out." Sam raised his chin slightly as if to say he knew it were true. "Nice perk of the job is all I'm saying."

Mr. Harlan gave a nervous laugh. "Uh, well, no. I — I mean, sure, at their age they're pretty and all, and some do like to come on to you. I think they just do it out of a dare with their friends. Or they're going through a phase, you know, having a crush on a teacher. It happens. But I'm there to teach them, and that's what I do. That's *all* I do." Mr. Harlan straightened in the chair, flicked his wrist to see the time on his watch.

"We're almost done here, Drake. Just one or two more questions, I promise." Sam closed the file, then locked his gaze onto the teacher's. "Did Ruby confide in you that she was pregnant?"

Chapter Forty-Five

"**N**o, *she didn't.*" The teacher's response came too quick. "I had no idea." Mr. Harlan pulled at his shirt sleeves. "Not right away anyway. Of course it became obvious later on that she was."

"Right." Again, Sam watched as the red splotches across the man's cheeks deepened. "Here's the thing, Drake. We're trying to piece everything together. There's no name for the father on the birth certificate, so I'm just going to come out and ask. Did you ever have sexual intercourse with Ruby West?"

"No. No, I did not." Mr. Harlan's whole face flushed crimson. "No way."

"Then I assume you wouldn't mind giving a DNA sample?" Sam paused. "Just so we can rule you out, of course."

Mr. Harlan stood abruptly, the chair legs scraping the floor. "As a matter of fact I do mind, Detective. I came here wanting to help Ruby. Help a former student of mine. A student who seemed to be struggling. But this ..." He waved a hand around the room. "This is totally ridiculous. I'm a married man and would never —"

"I didn't mean —"

"I did not have anything to do with getting Ruby pregnant. So, no, I am not going to give a DNA sample. Not without a court order."

Sam slowly nodded at the teacher, whose lips were pressed in a tight line, face still flush. *You're angry. But you're also scared.* In a calm voice Sam said, "Okay. I hear you, Drake. Just thought you'd like to cooperate. We're trying to eliminate any possibility, no matter how remote." Sam raised a hand palm out. "Last question, I promise. Where were you Sunday morning, the morning Ruby was killed?"

Mr. Harlan crossed his arms over his chest and glared at Sam. "I was home. With my *wife* and *child*."

"Thank you. I may contact your wife to confirm that." Sam watched as the anger left Mr. Harlan's face, replaced by something less readable. Fear? Dread perhaps? Whatever the emotion, Sam was convinced the teacher was holding back on his relationship with Ruby.

"I'll walk you out." Sam accompanied Mr. Harlan past Nancy's workstation, all the way to the exit. "Again, Drake, thank you for talking with me."

Mr. Harlan didn't reply, simply hurried through the door, ran up the steps and out of the building. Sam trotted up the stairs and watched the teacher make his way to his Kia. When Mr. Harlan reached the vehicle, he reached into his coat pocket and pulled out a pack of cigarettes. He extracted one, lit it, and took several quick drags before throwing it on the ground. Mr. Harlan slid behind the wheel of his vehicle and drove away.

Sam went to his SUV, opened the back hatch where he kept several plastic-covered containers with what he considered essentials. He pulled on a pair of latex gloves, grabbed an evidence bag and crossed the street. Sam reached for the cold, barely smoked cigarette and placed it in the bag. *This will do until I get a search warrant for your DNA, Mr. Harlan.* Sam took in the deserted street, the teacher having already turned the corner and driven out of sight. *And trust me, I will get a warrant.*

Chapter Forty-Six

Before leaving for her job that morning, Lauren reread the Notice of Deposition one more time to refresh herself about the case. *Gerald Radcliffe on behalf of S.L.R., a minor, vs. Wyoming Department of Family Services, and Jane Doe 1.* She put the document in her computer bag. The deponent, who would be answering questions under oath, was a man named Gerald Radcliffe, the complaining party. From the looks of the caption, it wouldn't be full of technical jargon. Lauren smiled at Maverik. "Should be an easy morning." He wagged his tail, as if in agreement.

Lauren parked her car far enough down a side street where there were no parking meters. She'd been spending too much money on parking tickets lately. She rolled her equipment up the few steps to the law office of Eli Dresser, the location for this morning's deposition. The heavy front door swung open before Lauren could grab the door handle.

"Saw you coming, Lauren. And you know me, ever the gentleman." Eli grinned at his own humor. His smile softened his hard-edged features.

"Yes, you are a gentleman. Thanks."

He swept his arm wide. "Come in. You know where to set up."

As Lauren walked toward the conference room, she asked, "Are you involved in this case? I didn't see your name on the notice."

"I am. I entered my appearance as co-counsel for the plaintiff yesterday. Samantha Edwards will be defending the deposition today."

Lauren nodded. "And I see DFS is the defendant."

"That's the first hurdle we're going to have to overcome, being able to sue a governmental agency. Defense has filed a motion to dismiss the case based on that. It's set for hearing next week."

They entered the conference room. Lauren rolled her carrying case to the far end of the conference table.

"This morning will be interesting."

"Working with you always is, Eli."

"You flatter me. I think." He cocked his head. "That was meant as a compliment, wasn't it?"

Lauren raised her eyes to the ceiling, pretending to think. "Uh, yeah, it was."

"That's why I told the assistant attorney general to call you."

Lauren raised a questioning eyebrow. "Because I give compliments? Or because I'm the only freelance court reporter in Crawford?"

"You being the only one in town, there is that, but

Cheyenne's not that far away. Oliver could have called a firm in Cheyenne to cover his deposition, but I said, don't bother. Lauren Besoner is right here in Crawford. And ... she's the best."

"And so here I am." Lauren let out a snort.

"I'm not kidding."

"We're so both full of ... full of compliments today. What's up with that?" Lauren shook her head. "But, no, really, thank you for the referral. I appreciate it."

"Of course."

Lauren considered any job where Eli was present a bonus. There weren't many attorneys ... maybe none ... where she felt comfortable enough to banter with them. Their relationship began in a professional capacity two years ago when she hired him to help her with her divorce. He knew about her personal life as part of the divorce proceedings, and after he no longer represented her, they fell into a less professional, more casual friends relationship. Lauren enjoyed meeting him every so often for a quick lunch to catch up on courthouse gossip.

While Lauren set up her stenograph writer and laptop, the two talked about what they'd been doing since the last time they'd seen each other. She started to open her mouth and tell him about the death of her neighbor's granddaughter but stopped herself. It sounded too much like gossip. Besides, she didn't want to think about that morning. When her thoughts went to Ruby and her on the snow, eyes vacant, lips tinged blue, Lauren's stomach knotted.

"You're looking good."

Lauren raised a doubtful eyebrow.

"No, you really are," Eli said.

Lauren automatically touched her cheek. She smiled at him, knowing the meaning behind his kind words. "Thanks." His words rang true, she did look like her old self. She had physically healed from the events that happened only a few months ago. Eli had been the one to call Sam, knowing she must have been in danger. That call literally saved her life. The scar on Lauren's cheek, which foundation covered nicely, was the only physical reminder of the events of that evening. Emotionally, she still had a ways to go before she'd consider herself fully healed.

"You did play a large part in saving my life."

Eli smiled. "I can't take all the credit. If I remember right, your dog played a big part in rescuing you."

"Yes, Maverik is a good boy." She dipped her head slightly and raised her eyes to his "Most of the time."

"How about a cup of coffee?" Eli offered.

She glanced at the clock on the wall. Twenty minutes before nine. "Sure."

He left the conference room. When he returned, Ms. Edwards came out of Eli's office and approached them. Eli made introductions, then the two excused themselves and went into his office to visit with their client.

A few sips into her hot beverage, Lauren watched a man in a navy-blue suit, carrying a messenger bag, walk up the sidewalk and into the office. Lauren had never met Oliver Fowler but had no doubt he was the assistant attorney general representing the State of Wyoming and DFS. The attorney, who appeared to be close in age to her thirty years, stuck his head in the conference room and raised an eyebrow. "We must be in here?"

"Yes." Lauren smiled and introduced herself and offered him her business card.

He pulled his wallet out to do the same. He flipped through the folds. "I'm sorry, I'm all out." He gave her an embarrassed smile.

"No problem. Your information is on the notice. I'll just take it off of there."

Mr. Fowler pulled his laptop from his bag, and while he turned it on, Lauren took what she knew would be her last sip of hot coffee for the morning. Lauren placed the cup behind her on a small side table, where there would be no chance of an accidental spill.

Eli, Ms. Edwards, and their client emerged from Eli's office. With everyone seated, Lauren had Gerald Radcliffe raise his right hand to be sworn. Once under oath, the deposition began with Mr. Fowler asking the questions.

Chapter Forty-Seven

At ten minutes past twelve o'clock, Mr. Fowler said the words that Lauren equated to music to her ears. *No further questions.* With the deposition now over, Lauren knew exactly why Mr. Radcliffe filed suit against the state agency. The things Gerald Radcliffe told Mr. Fowler regarding the actions of the caseworker, if true, were not only unethical but illegal. The allegations were that the caseworker did all these things on purpose, making it impossible for Sasha, Mr. Radcliffe's teenage daughter, to reunite with her infant son. Mr. Radcliffe hadn't been allowed to see his grandchild since the state terminated Sasha's parental rights ten months ago. The next, and final step, would be adoption of Sasha's son.

Lauren also learned who Sasha's caseworker had been. The Jane Doe on the notice now had a name. Taryn Biggs. She had been identified through various documents that were now exhibits attached to the deposition. When Mr. Radcliffe first mentioned the name, Lauren did an internal jaw drop. Her mind told her maybe she'd heard wrong but Lauren knew she hadn't.

Throughout the course of questioning Mr. Radcliffe, he made accusations that Taryn had offered his daughter drugs. And it also came out during the testimony that Sasha, an admitted drug user, accepted them. This had supposedly happened three or four times. A couple of days after the last time Sasha accepted the methamphetamine from her caseworker, Taryn requested Sasha to come down and do a random drug test. And while it was part of the girl's case plan to test whenever she was told to, Sasha's dad insisted that his daughter had been set up to fail the test because the drugs Taryn offered would still be in her system. And Sasha did fail. She tested positive.

Sasha didn't tell anyone at the time, thinking no one would believe her. After a failed suicide attempt, and the start of counseling, Sasha finally confided in her therapist what really happened.

When Gerald Radcliffe accused Taryn of doing these things, Lauren had a hard time believing his accusation. Her actions were the very opposite of what her job entailed, which was to help mothers and fathers reunite with their children. That the ultimate goal of the agency was to return a child back into their parents' custody. Why would Taryn do that? What possible benefit could there be to sabotaging Sasha?

Of course, after all this time Mr. Radcliffe had no physical evidence to corroborate his story. It was all hearsay. Still, Lauren's gut said the man was telling the truth. From her years of taking down testimony, Lauren knew a lot of the tells people displayed when lying. She didn't think Gerald Radcliffe had lied. But did that mean what he testified to had been the truth?

Chapter Forty-Eight

Before Mr. Fowler left, he asked Lauren for a fast turn around to get the transcript. Lauren nodded while inwardly groaning, but then remembered what Eli had said earlier about a hearing next week. Lauren disconnected her writer, backed up the file to the cloud, then shut down her laptop, all the while thinking of the testimony she'd just heard.

As Lauren gathered the exhibits and put them in the side pocket of her laptop bag, Eli came and stood beside her. "I told you it would be interesting, didn't I?" Eli gave her an exaggerated knowing nod of his head.

"Yes, you did. And you were right." Lauren shook her head slowly. "I know Taryn. I'm friends with her. I can't … I can't believe she did that."

"Did you not think our client was telling the truth?"

Lauren met Eli's questioning look, his Arapaho heritage evident in his questioning dark eyes. "No, I believe your client. I'm just having a really hard time thinking Taryn could do something like that. And you know what they say, there's two sides to every story."

"I'm not sure there is this time, Lauren."

❊   ❊   ❊

Lauren drove home, her mind still replaying what she'd heard. After putting her equipment in her home office, she texted Sam, relaying she just took an interesting deposition, and Taryn Biggs's name came up. Three wavy dots showed up on her screen immediately, then a text suggesting they meet for lunch.

She looked at her phone thinking text messages were tricky. They were words on a small screen without the emotion unless you inserted an emoji. Sam was not an emoji kind of man. When they texted goodnight, he'd send a GIF but only if she sent one first, and even then he didn't always respond in kind.

Did Sam sense she needed to talk to him? In person? What Lauren had to tell him could wait until they saw each other, which they would the day after tomorrow. *Whether he sensed it or not, Lauren, you'll get to see him soon.* The knot in her stomach lessened at the thought.

Lauren changed into jeans and a sweater. Back downstairs, she let Maverik out to do his business. When he returned, she gave him a dog biscuit for being good and not chewing on anything he shouldn't have while she had been working. Lauren patted him on the head, locked up and drove to Dominick's Bakery.

Sam sat at a table in the back, his attention on his phone.

He set it down as Lauren entered the bakery, gave her a quick nod of acknowledgment and joined her at the counter. They both ordered the combo special on the chalkboard menu, creamy tomato soup and a cabbage burger.

Lauren eyed the lone Danish in the pastry case. Another busy day for Dominick. *Just as well*, she thought. It had been a long winter. Lauren hadn't walked Maverik near as much as she'd told herself she would, using all the snow Crawford received as an excuse. She didn't have an excuse for why she didn't make it to the gym more often than she had.

"What would you like to drink?" asked Dominick.

"A hot tea for me." Out of the corner of her eye, Lauren caught Sam raising an eyebrow. "Trying to cut back on all the caffeine." Sam didn't need to know she needed to cut back on all the sugar in the lattes she enjoyed so much.

"Coffee, black, with room." Sam pulled out his credit card, tapping it on the reader to pay.

Dominick handed them their drinks, which they carried to the table, then sat. Sam poured a packet of sugar and one creamer into his cup. "Tell me about this interesting deposition."

Lauren dunked the teabag in the cup of hot water while she recited the allegations made against Taryn. Some time during her explanation, Sam had begun taking notes. When Lauren had finished, Sam rhythmically tapped his pen on the palm of his hand. Lauren knew he was digesting the information. She sipped her tea, wishing it were a vanilla latte or a caramel latte, or almost any kind of latte. She thought about Gerald Radcliffe's allegations, how

Sasha had her baby taken from her. It made Lauren feel uneasy. *Was Taryn capable of doing such a terrible thing?*

"Lauren?" Sam gently placed his hand over hers.

"Huh? Oh. Sorry." She leaned back in her seat so Dominick could place a bowl of soup along with a cabbage burger in front of her. "This looks delicious, Dominick."

"Smells great," Sam added.

"You two enjoy now." Dominick set a plate with a cheese danish on the table between them. "A little something for my two favorite customas. On the house."

"Thanks," Sam and Lauren said in unison.

Sam bit into the round golden-brown pastry filled with sauteed ground beef, cabbage and spices. "Mmm. This is delicious." He wiped his mouth with his napkin. "Dominick is a genius."

"Um-hum," agreed Lauren, around a mouthful of food. "Everything he bakes is to die for."

"Do you believe what this man" — Sam went over his notes — "George Radcliffe said?"

Lauren slowly nodded. "I do. He's simple ... I mean, he's just a normal guy, a dad raising four kids by himself. His wife walked out on him years ago and left the children with him. He works at the post office."

"I understand DFS tries to place kids with family, with relatives first," Sam said.

"Mr. Fowler brought that up. Mr. Radcliffe said he was overwhelmed enough raising four kids. He didn't think he could take on one more. Especially not a baby. So he was never considered a viable placement." Lauren blew on a spoonful of soup before continuing. "The state is going to take Sasha's deposition next week. Make sure she wasn't lying to her father, you know, coming up with an excuse. But why would she after all this time? I'm sure Ms. Edwards talked to Sasha before bringing the lawsuit."

"You're probably right. Did Mr. Radcliffe say if he ever went to the police to file a criminal complaint against Taryn?"

"He hasn't. Mr. Fowler did ask about that, why he didn't, but Ms. Edwards claimed attorney-client privilege."

"Ms. Edwards is Radcliffe's attorney, right?"

"Yes. Eli Dresser is local counsel but he only entered his appearance yesterday. Samantha Edwards was making all the objections."

Sam sipped his coffee, then said, "Don't know her."

"She's out of Colorado."

"Why was it attorney-client privilege?"

Lauren shook her head. "I don't know. All I know is she wouldn't let her client answer."

Sam took another bite of his cabbage burger.

"I still can't believe Taryn would do that. The whole thing is so ... just so weird, right?"

"That's one way to put it," Sam agreed.

Lauren, elbows on the table, took a sip of her now lukewarm tea. "I'm not sure why I texted you. It ... it was just so upsetting to hear."

"I'm glad you did."

"And you did say Taryn was kind of obsessed with Kyle and his wife. I don't know what that has to do with anything. I just thought you might want to know." Lauren's eyebrows pinched together. "If it's true, she could be charged with something, right?"

"Yes. After all this time there won't be any physical evidence to back it up. I've got to give it some thought. In the meantime, maybe Mr. Radcliffe will come to the station and at least file a complaint. Maybe I'll give Eli a call. I would think the attorney for DFS will tell the agency they are obligated to open an internal investigation of their own. I'm not sure of their protocol but if they do investigate and it turns out what Mr. Radcliffe testified to is true, they will be obligated to report Taryn to law enforcement."

"Even if Taryn denies everything?"

Sam downed the last of his coffee. "Yes. They would have an obligation to report it to police. We would open an investigation and it would go from there. This" — he gave a quick shake of his notepad — "is interesting information."

Lauren studied Sam, who suddenly went quiet. "What? What are you thinking?"

"I was just … This has just got me wondering, that's all."

You're onto something, Sam. I can see it in your eyes.

Sam checked his watch. "I've got to get back to work." He squeezed her hand, then rose and slipped into his coat. "I'm glad you texted me." Sam flashed her a sly grin, his dark eyes mischievous. "It also gives me a chance to tell you how good you look in that sweater."

Lauren's hand went to her chest, feeling the softness of the pink sweater he'd given her for Christmas. "Thanks." She felt her cheeks warm, all thoughts of Taryn momentarily forgotten. "I think I'm going to stay and finish this." Lauren lifted her cup.

Sam dipped his head and kissed her. "Catch you later."

Lauren watched him go. She sipped the last of the now lukewarm tea, thinking about Taryn. If the accusations were true, Lauren wouldn't go on being friends with her. She couldn't. *There has to be a logical explanation.* Until she knew more, Lauren would hold back judgment. But it would be awkward hanging out with Taryn. Lauren remembered their conversation when they went skiing, Taryn planning to move away, relocate back home to Buffalo. Maybe the Radcliffe situation had something to do with it. In the meantime, Lauren would try to avoid Taryn. If that meant fewer trips to the gym, that's what she'd do. *I can skip kickboxing for a while. Of course you will. You'll use any excuse to not work out.*

"That Sam is one of the good ones," Dominick said, clearing away plates and mugs at a dirty table.

"I'm sorry, what?"

"I said, your boyfriend is one of the good ones."

"Oh, Sam, he's not —" She stopped herself from explaining their relationship, and simply replied, "Yes, he is a good guy."

The baker continued to speak as he wiped the table down. "I think he's worth holding on to. You two are happy together. I watch people. I can see it."

Lauren smiled.

Dominick placed the dirty dishes in a plastic tub and took it back into the kitchen, humming as he went.

Lauren checked her phone for the time. She put her coat on and started toward the door, then stopped and did an about-face. Lauren went to the counter where she studied the day's drink specials. When she walked out of the bakery she held a cinnamon dolce latte in her hand.

Chapter Forty-Nine

Maverik sat at the back door waiting to be let out when Lauren entered the kitchen from the garage. "I'm sorry, I should have let you have more than five minutes outside before running off to have lunch." She glanced around the kitchen floor. No puddles. Maverik could probably last all day without being let out but he deserved more run-around time. When Lauren rescued him a year ago from behind the Maverik gas station, she had taken him to the vet to see if he had a chip and his owners could be found. No chip, but the vet estimated his age to be three years old. That equated to energy, lots of energy for a large mixed-breed dog.

Lauren watched him bound off the back deck. She went and changed into yoga pants and her well-worn brown-and-gold University of Wyoming hoodie. She took a sip of the cinnamon dolce latte she'd succumbed to ordering, then checked the time on the microwave.

She slipped into her hiking shoes, then opened the door to check on Maverik. She spotted him at the back fence sniffing through the chain links, his way of doing perimeter patrol. Lauren closed the door. *I'll be right back.* Lauren went to Twila's house and rang the bell. She rubbed her arms and glanced around as she waited. The afternoon sun didn't provide much heat even as the calendar promised warmer days but she spotted blades of green grass poking through the ever-shrinking patches of snow.

Percy's high-pitched yips sounded deep inside the house. The curtain moved in the window. The Papillon stood on the sofa, tail moving back and forth like a conductor's baton in time with his barks.

Yesterday Lauren telephoned Twila to see if she needed any help with picking up groceries, prescriptions, anything that needed to be done around the house. Lauren's offers were sincere, but she had come to expect Twila to say no. Lauren kept the surprise out of her voice when the old woman took her up on the offer. She said when Lauren had time she could come and take the bassinet. Lauren didn't know why but she found herself excited to have the chance to finally be taken up on her numerous offers to help her elderly neighbor.

Twila opened the door. "Come on in." To Percy she said, "You stay." The dog sat, his body quivering.

Lauren bent and scooped the dog up for a quick hug. "What a good listener you are."

"You know where it is." Twila would never be one for small talk. The tragedy that recently happened would not change that. Nor did Twila like to be hugged. The only hugs she gave were to Percy.

Lauren handed Percy to Twila once the old woman had

eased herself into the recliner. Twila turned her attention to a game show on the TV screen. Lauren went upstairs into the bedroom Ruby and Evie once occupied. The twin bed had a worn but clean bedspread across it. Nothing hung on the walls, nothing sat on the small dresser under the window, the room devoid of any signs that a teenager … or anyone … recently occupied the space. The bassinet, which was on casters, sat just inside the door. Lauren took a quick look around and then maneuvered the portable crib out of the bedroom. It was light but bulky. Lauren winced as it scraped against the wall as she carried it down the stairs and into the living room.

"I'll make sure this gets to Goodwill, Twila."

The old woman kept her attention on the TV and grunted a raspy, "Thank you."

The sight of the bassinet is probably too much of a reminder of the losses she recently suffered, thought Lauren.

"Lock the door on your way out."

Lauren wheeled the crib out the door, down the sidewalk and into her garage. She stopped at the Volvo and opened the trunk. She lifted the bulky item to set it inside. It was too tall. No way the trunk will close. Lauren tried laying it on its side. That didn't work either. After another unsuccessful attempt of trying to place it in the vehicle, the only thing Lauren managed to accomplish was bending one of the aluminum legs. "Shit. I can't take it to Goodwill now." Lauren set the bassinet on the floor. It toppled over, landing upside down. She checked behind her, almost expecting Twila to be there, shaking her head in disapproval.

"Cheap piece of crap." Lauren bent to turn it upright. She spotted something taped to its underside. A Ziploc bag with a small notebook and photograph inside.

Lauren unzipped the bag and took out the photo. She turned it over. It appeared to be a selfie of Ruby and a man Lauren didn't recognize. Lauren reached back in and removed the notebook, fanning it open. Left-leaning block lettering filled its white pages. A journal.

The little crib now forgotten, Lauren took the flowery spiral-bound notebook inside and placed it on the kitchen table along with the picture. Lauren eyed the journal. Ruby's personal thoughts and feelings were inside that book. She shouldn't read it. *Just turn it over to Sam. He can determine if it sheds any light on what happened to her. No, it probably is just your typical diary of a teen and holds nothing important.*

Lauren tried to busy herself, refreshing Maverik's water bowl, emptying the dishwasher. As she put glasses and mugs in the cupboard, she kept glancing at the table. Lauren went over and let her fingers brush over the journal's cover. When Lauren turned thirteen, she'd started keeping a diary. She remembered coming home after school and immediately going to her room to write about her day.

Where are those diaries now? Did I take them when I moved out? Maybe they're still in my old bedroom. Lauren pushed those thoughts away and examined the intricate and detailed plants Ruby drew in the margins in blue ink. She'd even put their scientific names next to each one. An interest in botany? Was that Ruby's passion? Did she have a passion? Have any interests? Hobbies? Lauren didn't know Ruby at all other than to see her going in and out of Twila's home. Lauren inhaled deeply, then put the thought out of her mind.

Just one page, that's all she'd look at, Lauren told herself. Just to see what kind of things Ruby wrote down.

Maybe it's more a calendar, a reminder of things to do. But why keep it hidden? *Because that's what teenagers do.*

The latte had grown cold. Lauren placed it in the microwave to reheat. She inhaled the sweetness and took a sip. "Mmm. Good job, Dominick." Lauren sat at her kitchen table, and feeling a little guilty, opened the diary and began to read.

Chapter Fifty

Thursday, March 20.

I HATE HIM! I wish he were dead. I wish I were dead. He made me feel like I was special. He said he loved me. I believed him. LIES! All FUCKING LIES! We haven't been together in over two weeks. He told me to stop texting him, that his wife was getting suspicious. But he was supposed to be leaving her so who cares what she thinks. Fucking Liar!

It's Olivia who's special now, not me. I just know it. I see the way he looks at her during practice. How he stands so close to her and places his hand on her back when he thinks no one is looking. How he leans in to whisper something, his lips touching her ear. And then she giggles. That used to be me. A-hole!! I'm not going back. I'm quitting track. I'm never going back. I can't bear to look at the two of them. I can't bear to look at HIM. I'm so glad I'm done with chemistry. Sitting in class knowing he doesn't love me anymore would have been unbearable. I HATE YOU! I HATE YOU DRAKE HARLAN!

Drake Harlan. Ruby was seeing a married man? A teacher? That's crazy. Lauren took an absentminded sip of her latte before continuing her invasion into Ruby's life.

Monday, April 30.

I told Drake today that I'm pregnant. He got sooo mad. He called me awful names. Said how could I be so fucking stupid. Then he asked me how could I be sure it was his. He said maybe it was that new guy I've been seeing, Carson. He knows it's not. I'm too far along for it to be anyone else's but his. How could he say that to me? HOW COULD HE? He told me the best thing to do was get rid of it. I don't know what to do. There's no one I can talk to. I want to tell Makayla but I can't. She won't understand. And she's mad at me for quitting track. And she doesn't like that I started seeing Carson. Says I'll end up doing drugs with him. She's not wrong.

If you were still alive, Mom, you'd help me figure this mess out. I know you would. I miss you.

Lauren stopped reading and ran her fingertips over five spots where the ink smeared. Five dried droplets. Remnants of tears shed. Flipping through more pages, Lauren stopped at a November entry.

Monday, November 21.

I'm a mom. Me. A mom!! I have a baby. I named her Evie Cynthia. She was born November 15. She weighs eight pounds and three ounces. A nurse came in that morning and told me my baby had meth in her system. That they have to monitor her for a while. She's having withdrawals. I did that to her. They told me she can't go home with me. I HATE my fucking stupid self.

A lady from the state came to see me while I was in the hospital. She said the only way I can get Evie back is to prove I've quit using. And I have to have a place to live. I've tested clean twice already. Where am I going to live? Maybe grandma's? She's not as mean as she looks. My dad's a big fat no. I don't want to continue living with Carson but I have to until I can find somewhere else. That lady said I should think about what's best for my baby. That I should think about giving her up for adoption. She didn't say it mean-like. She was kind. I could see it in her eyes. She told me there are lots of women that can't have children and I would be doing something good for someone. Maybe I should. I don't know what to do. I'm so scared. I wish you were here, Mom.

There were a few more entries. Some to do with Carson, with being a new mother, and liking a guy named Levi. Lauren texted Sam. She hadn't even had a chance to set the phone down before three wavy dots appeared on the screen.

Chapter Fifty-One

Sam viewed each of the attachments he asked Lauren to send him via text. He could make out the essential words. He'd offered to come to her house to retrieve the pages but she said she'd drop them off. While he waited for her to bring the hard copies, he reread the diary entries. He picked up his phone and texted Officer Fuentes. Less than a minute later, she stood in front of his desk, a questioning look on her face. He handed her his cell.

Officer Fuentes read Lauren's text, then using her thumb and index finger made the images on the screen larger and studied them. Officer Fuentes shook her head as she handed the phone back to Sam. "What a piece of work that guy is."

"That's putting it mildly."

"I did get a creeper kind of vibe from him that day at the school."

"Always trust your gut, Lola. Trust your gut."

She nodded slowly. "So what now?"

"Now we get that asshole back here for another interview. Hopefully he'll open up and talk without a lawyer. In the meantime, I want you to prepare a couple of warrants. Have you applied for search warrants before?"

She nodded. "A few times."

"Good. I want you to apply for two. One for Mr. Harlan's DNA. Unless Ruby was totally delusional" — Sam cocked his head toward his phone — "Mr. Harlan is Evie's father. And one for a search of his ..." Sam stopped.

"What?" asked Lola.

"Trying to decide if we should search his home or his classroom."

"What would we be looking for?"

"Roofies. Illegal drugs. Something he could use to incapacitate someone. I'm thinking that's probably what he did. He drugged her first, then injected her with enough meth that an overdose was inevitable." Sam thought for a moment. "Put both locations in the second warrant."

"Will do."

"You start on that, and I'll see if I can get Harlan in here for more questioning." He tapped his pen absently on his desk, then stood. "On second thought ..." He checked the time. It was four o'clock. "I'll pay Drake a visit right now. Going to shake things up a little."

"You mean you're going to shake him up," Officer Fuentes said with a hint of a smile.

"Figuratively speaking, that is my plan. He said his wife works at the hospital, right?"

"He said she just returned from being on maternity leave." Officer Fuentes raised her eyes to the ceiling, squinting while in thought. "So he and his wife have a six-month-old baby. And he's also the baby daddy of a now four-month-old."

"He's been a busy man." Sam's jaw clenched. "But that's all about to stop."

"I'll go get those warrants." Officer Fuentes turned and practically ran out of Sam's office.

＊　　＊　　＊

Twenty minutes later, Nancy knocked on Sam's doorjamb, holding out two crisscrossed piles of paper. "Your girlfriend dropped —" Sam's arched eyebrow stopped her mid-sentence. Nancy cleared her throat. "Ms. Lauren Besoner, Ruby West's neighbor, stopped by and dropped this off for you, sir." Nancy raised her own eyebrow at Sam. "Better?"

"Yes." The corner of his mouth twitched with a smile. "And you're right, we are seeing each other. But this," he said, taking the papers from her hand, "is business."

"Of course. I also made a copy."

"Thanks, Nancy." He waved the papers in his hand. "This is good. Next best thing to cellphone data." He placed the copy of the diary entries into a fresh new folder, then grabbed his coat off a hook on the back of his door. He checked the time on his watch. "I'm going to the high school and pay Drake Harlan a visit."

Officer Fuentes stood in the doorway. "Don't forget to bring this." She handed him a signed search warrant.

"That was fast. Good job, Lola." He took the signed warrant, placed it in his inside coat pocket and hurried out of the station.

Chapter Fifty-Two

Drake Harlan opened his front door. Sam caught the expression of surprise in the man's eyes before the teacher replaced it with a look of mild curiosity.

"Hello, Detective. Uh, what are you doing here?"

"I have a warrant." Sam pulled the document from his inside pocket and held it out to Mr. Harlan.

The teacher's voice caught in his throat as he swallowed hard. Mr. Harlan stared at the piece of paper in Sam's hand as if it were a snake, ready to uncoil and bite. "A — a warrant? You're here to arrest me?" He glanced nervously behind him. Deep inside the house, Sam heard a baby crying.

"No, not for your arrest." *Not yet anyway, asshole.* "For your DNA. May I come in?"

The teacher unfolded the sheet of paper, his eyes scanning the warrant. "I — I don't understand. Why do you want my DNA? I've done nothing wrong. I already told you that."

Sam glanced to his left and then to his right. "These houses are pretty close together. Wouldn't you rather talk somewhere more private? Just in case one of your neighbors is outside?"

Instead of opening the door wider to let Sam in, the teacher stepped out in bare feet, leaving the door slightly ajar. Mr. Harlan spoke, the words coming out in a hiss. "You can't come in. My wife is home."

"Oh, I didn't realize that. I thought she worked the evening shift at the hospital."

"Today's her day off."

From somewhere inside the house a woman called out, "Drake, did you leave the door open? Can you shut it, please? You're letting in cold air." A moment later, a petite woman balancing a baby on one hip appeared at the door. "Oh, hello. I didn't realize someone was here."

"Sorry about the door, babe. I'll be right in." Before his wife could say anything more, Drake closed it behind him, shutting her out of the conversation.

"Looks like it might be easier if you came down to the station."

Mr. Harlan closed his eyes and inhaled a resigned breath. "I guess."

"I do have a few more questions for you. They shouldn't take long. I'm happy to give you a lift. You can tell your wife you're helping with the investigation."

"No, I'll … I'll drive myself."

"That's fine," Sam said. "I'll just wait for you to leave, then meet you at the station."

"Okay." Mr. Harlan wiped his palms on his pant legs and retreated inside.

Chapter Fifty-Three

S am led Mr. Harlan to the interrogation room. "Have a seat and I'll be right back." He closed the door behind him, went to the supply room and retrieved a swab packet. He returned, about to open the door when he heard footsteps. He glanced over his shoulder to see Officer Fuentes jogging toward him. She held up her hand, sheets of paper waving in the air. "I've got them." Lola huffed, slightly out of breath. "I've got the search warrants for Mr. Harlan's home *and* his classroom."

"Great. I've got him in there right now." Sam gestured behind him with his head.

"He's here?"

"Yep."

"I thought you were going to talk to him at his house."

"His wife was home. I'm being Mr. Nice Guy and having him talk here."

"Ohhh." Officer Fuentes dragged the one-syllable word out as far as it would go.

"While I'm talking with him, you execute the warrants. Take two officers with you."

Officer Fuentes nodded and turned to leave.

"And, Lola?"

She looked over her shoulder. "Yes?"

"Start with the house."

"Sure." She grinned at Sam.

"By the time he gets back home, he and his wife will have *lots* to talk about." Sam would have taken more enjoyment in this part of the investigation except for the fact that there was a Mrs. Harlan. And her world, as she knew it, was about to turn into something ugly and unwanted.

"On it, sir."

Chapter Fifty-Four

"**M**r. Harlan, before we begin, I want you to know you can leave at any time."

The teacher nodded slowly but said nothing.

"You've had a chance to read the search warrant. You know why you're here. Have you ever had this done before?"

Mr. Harlan shook his head, mouth clamped shut.

"It's very simple, very quick. All I'm going to do is swab the inside of your cheek for a few seconds." Sam pointed to the package containing the swab kit that lay on the table.

Mr. Harlan's eyes focused on Sam's movements as Sam snapped on a pair of latex gloves and picked up the kit. The cellophane crackled as Sam tore the packet open, the sound accentuated by the quiet of the room.

"If I can have you open your mouth, please."

Mr. Harlan swallowed, then opened his mouth.

Several seconds later, Sam put the completed buccal sample in its protective sheath. "I'll be right back." He left the room in search of Officer Peterson. Ben's height and bright red hair made him easy to spot. He found him at one of the computer terminals. He handed Ben the container with the swab. "See that this gets to the crime lab ASAP."

"Yes, sir."

Sam returned to the interrogation room with a bottle of water, placed it in front of Mr. Harlan, and sat across from him. Sam did a slow mental head shake, reining in his anger. He remembered the words Detective Scott, his mentor, drilled into him. "Don't let your emotions get the better of you, Overstreet. You lose your cool, the guilty bastard gets the upper hand."

"Drake, I'd like to cut to the chase. I know you'd like to get back home. Your wife, I'm sure, is curious about what's happening. Why don't you make it easy on yourself and come clean with me. When we get the results back from the DNA test, what is it going to show?"

"Nothing. Nothing that has to do with me anyway. I didn't do anything wrong."

Sam slowly shook his head as he reached into the folder in front of him. He lifted his gaze to Mr. Harlan. Sam removed Ruby's original diary pages that were now encased in a plastic sleeve. He slid them across the table in front of Mr. Harlan.

The teacher studied the pages. As the color drained from the man's face, a sense of satisfaction pulsed through Sam's veins. *I didn't do anything wrong? Let me see you talk yourself out of this.*

Mr. Harlan read the pages, then pushed them away. He placed his elbows on the table and covered his eyes with the heels of his hands.

Seconds ticked by. Sam sat still. This once popular chemistry teacher, the life he had been living was about to change. Forever. The scrape of the chair legs as Sam moved in his seat was the only sound in the room.

Mr. Harlan finally spoke. "I didn't mean for any of this to happen. You have to believe me. It was all just a big mistake." He shook his head. "Shit, shit, shit," he repeated under his breath. "I can't believe this is happening."

Oh, it's happening. "I'll need you to tell me exactly what happened." Sam clicked his pen, ready to note important points that he'd want to review later from the video recording.

Mr. Harlan dragged his hand across his mouth and took in several ragged breaths. "Ruby was in my chemistry class. I got to know her better when I began tutoring her. I knew her mom had passed away and she had been struggling with that ever since. After our tutoring sessions, we would talk."

"Talk? Talk about what?"

"Yes, talk. About what she was going through, about how hard it must be for her at this point in her life."

Sam dipped his head as if to say, *Continue.*

"Maybe I shouldn't have counseled her, because I could tell she was developing a little bit of a crush on me."

Here we go. Time to blame Ruby for this shit storm that's about to become his life. Good luck with that, dumbass.

"I tried to redirect her. I suggested she go out for an extracurricular activity. Staying active is good for your mental health. I told her I was coaching the girls' track team and she should come try out." Mr. Harlan twisted his wedding band, moving it up and down on his finger. He avoided Sam's eyes. "One day after practice she was helping me put away some of the equipment. It was getting late. I offered to give her a ride home. It … it just happened."

You don't get to say that. You don't get to say "it" just happened. "You're going to have to be specific, Drake. I need details." Sam kept his attention on Mr. Harlan's face, a mixture of horror and fright in his eyes.

"I know. I know this is hard for you, Drake. I understand that. Just tell me what happened, and then we can be past the hard part. Did you have sex with Ruby while you were tutoring her?"

With effort, Drake Harlan opened up and described the physical relationship he had with Ruby. It started during the timeframe he tutored her. The first time they had sex it happened in his SUV. They did it once in his classroom. The rest of the times it happened in his vehicle. Mr. Harlan couldn't remember how many times they'd had sex total. Maybe five. He hadn't been sure. The teacher emphasized Ruby initiated their sexual encounters, not him. Sam wanted to tell him he didn't give a flying fuck if she had. He had been her teacher. Ruby, sixteen. A minor.

Chapter Fifty-Five

"Thank you for telling me the truth, Drake. I know this must be a stressful time for you."

"Yeah, it has been. It was a terrible mistake that should never have happened." Mr. Harlan's gaze went to the camera in the ceiling, then at Sam. "Can I go now?" The interrogation had been going on for thirty minutes. Drake shared a lot of details. Sam assumed he had also held back things as well. After all, Ruby was no longer alive to contradict him on any facts.

"We do have more to talk about, Drake."

Mr. Harlan twisted the cap off the water bottle and took a long gulp.

"We obtained a warrant to search your house and your desk at school. Officers are at your house right now as we speak. You can make it easy on yourself if you tell us everything, starting with how you drugged Ruby the morning you killed her." Sam watched Mr. Harlan's expression go from anger at the thought of his home being searched to confusion.

"*What?* Are you out of your mind? I didn't kill Ruby. I didn't drug her. I didn't give her anything. Ever."

"Where were you Sunday morning between eight and nine o'clock?"

"I told you before, I was home." His eyes darted left and right. No. I was home but I went out for a run. I often run on the weekends."

"No matter the weather?"

"Pretty much."

"Do you run with anyone? Anyone that can vouch for this activity?"

"My wife saw me leave. But, no, I run alone."

"You could have very easily skipped your run and gone over to confront Ruby."

"But I didn't. And my car was at home the whole time."

"Why did you do it? Was she planning on exposing the relationship you two had?"

"No."

"Did she hit you up for money in exchange for keeping quiet?"

"No."

"Was she going to tell your wife? What made you kill her?"

"I *didn't* kill her." Mr. Harlan stood so quickly the chair tipped backward. "And I'm done talking to you. So either arrest me or let me go."

Sam didn't have enough evidence at the moment to arrest him for Ruby's murder. He didn't know what the results of Fuentes's search were. She hadn't texted him. If she did uncover physical evidence connecting him to Ruby's death, Sam would drag the man back here. Only this time in handcuffs.

He wanted to shout, "Yes, I'm arresting your sorry ass for sexually abusing a minor, a vulnerable young girl." But Ruby was dead. There was no longer a live victim of the crimes he committed. When his DNA test came back matching Evie's, which Sam had no doubt it would, it would be up to the county attorney to decide whether to charge him with molesting Ruby.

Sam exhaled and spoke in a calm voice. "As I said at the beginning of the interview, you're free to leave. You are not under arrest."

Mr. Harlan nodded toward the door. "Then I'm out of here."

Sam got up and opened the door. Mr. Harlan brushed past him. "We'll be in touch, Drake."

Chapter Fifty-Six

As Sam walked back to his office, he texted Fuentes, asking for an update on the search. He placed his phone face up on his desk and kept checking the screen for a response. Fifteen minutes later, he received a reply. "*Heading back to station.*"

That didn't bode well. If they had found something, she would have texted him right away. He busied himself until he heard Officer Fuentes's familiar footsteps approach. She sank into the chair opposite Sam and shook her head. "We didn't find anything. Anywhere. Not a damned thing. No illicit drugs of any kind. No prescription meds. Nothing stronger than Tylenol."

"Well, he did confess to having a relationship with Ruby."

Officer Fuentes arched an eyebrow. "Really?"

"He admitted to having sex. He threw out that he

wasn't the only one. That she had a boyfriend, and maybe the boyfriend was the dad."

"Wishful thinking on his part?" suggested Lola.

Sam nodded. "Right. He denied having anything to do with her death."

"Maybe he kept the date rape drug in a really good hiding place. He most likely got rid of it," Officer Fuentes offered with a shrug.

Sam leaned back in his chair, considering what she said. "Maybe." He straightened. "Look, it's been a long day. You should go home. We'll start fresh in the morning."

"No argument here." Officer Fuentes got up to leave. "Kind of a letdown that we didn't find anything."

"It happens. Don't always find what we're looking for, Lola. Doesn't mean we quit searching."

Chapter Fifty-Seven

Sam followed his own advice and went home. He changed into workout clothes and spent thirty minutes running on the treadmill in his home gym, located in his workshop out back.

After showering and putting on clean sweats, Sam fixed himself two ham and cheese sandwiches and ate them at the kitchen island. He washed them down with a glass of milk. He went to put the dish and dirty glass in the sink, but there was no room, so he loaded everything into the dishwasher, then scrubbed the sink clean.

The workout earlier accomplished two things. Besides getting in his cardio exercise, it got the damn Get Healthy app off his ass about neglecting to get his steps in over the past couple of weeks. It also gave him time to think about Ruby West's case.

He continued the line of thinking after dinner, sitting

on the sofa with a cold beer, open but untouched. Mr. Harlan had eventually come clean about having a relationship with Ruby. He insisted he had nothing to do with her death. Sam would need to dig deeper to determine if the man was telling the truth. Sam had no doubt that if Mr. Harlan wanted to kill Ruby, he could have easily gotten ahold of roofies to sedate her and then injected her with a lethal amount of meth. Being smart, Mr. Harlan would have disposed of any illegal drugs just in case he got served with a search warrant. He taught at the high school. He more than likely knew who he could reach out to and score what he needed.

Of course, Mr. Harlan would have to be careful who he bought from. He couldn't trust scoring from a student, the student could demand something in exchange for not letting it get out that the science teacher bought drugs. He would have no guarantee he wouldn't be found out.

Drake Harlan had plenty of motive. If his wife found out, it would ruin his marriage. If anyone else found out, he would have been brought up on charges of second-degree sexual abuse of a minor. He could have ended up in prison. At the very least his teaching career would be over. All good reasons to want to silence Ruby.

But if the teacher had been telling the truth and he didn't kill Ruby, who did? Carson Millwood? Carson's mother? Did either of them have enough reason to want her dead? Sam remembered how protective of Carson Stephanie Millwood was. How the Millwood name couldn't be tarnished by having some white trash girl leaching off them. When Stepanie Millwood realized the child couldn't be Carson's, that would have made her very angry. Angry enough to kill? In her line of work in a spa, she'd have access to needles, and who knew what kind of drugs.

According to Sam's investigation, Ruby had left the Millwoods' home without a fuss, without threats of coming after Carson for child support or anything else. Ruby had known all along Carson wasn't the real father, so she probably knew going after their money would have ended up a dead end.

Without realizing it, he'd sat on the sofa until the room had grown dark. Sam turned on the lamp on the end table and took a sip of his beer. Warm. The more Sam thought about the case, the more convinced he was that Carson didn't kill Ruby. What real motive did he have? From the Southeast Drug Enforcement's investigation, Carson had access to illicit drugs, which would include flunitrazepam. But Officer Fuentes's woman's intuition said he still loved Ruby. Sam had to agree. Carson wouldn't want her dead.

Sam absently shook his head as he thought. The only motive he could think of … a weak one in his mind … was the fact that she lied to him about being Evie's father. Once Carson got over the hurt of that fact, if anything, he should have been relieved.

He had done some checking after Stephanie Millwood claimed the baby didn't come early. Her timeline of events showed Carson couldn't be the father. The paternity test confirmed that, of course. And Ruby's diary entries revealed who the father really was.

Sam's phone vibrated. He turned it over. Lauren texted him a GIF of a sleeping cat. He smiled and replied with a heart emoji.

He poured the rest of the warm beer down the drain and headed for his bedroom. They needed a break in this case. Ruby needed justice. He would do everything he could to give it to her.

Chapter Fifty-Eight

At seven forty, Lauren went upstairs, Maverik at her heels. She went to her office and turned on her computer. The deposition scheduled for this morning was remote. Outside, snow fell in horizontal sheets, the cold frosting the corners of her window. "At least I didn't have to drive 220 miles to Lander yesterday to be ready for this job today, Maverik. Just think …" She pointed outside. "If I had to be there in person, I'd be driving home in this crap afterward. Or worse, stuck up there if the road closed."

In response to her comment, Maverik lay down and closed his eyes. "I know, all I do is complain."

At eight o'clock, Lauren adjusted her computer screen, asked the witness to raise their hand to be sworn. The deposition began, all thoughts of driving on snow-packed roads forgotten.

Lauren wrote EPBD/EPBD on her writer. The words "Proceedings concluded" appeared on her realtime screen, along with the time, eleven forty-five. She removed her headset, unmuted her mic to say goodbye to the attorneys at their respective locations. Once disconnected, Lauren let out a long breath. The audio quality hadn't been great. She had to interrupt the witness to have him repeat his answer a few times, making the morning stressful, and it also meant more time editing the transcript. Still better than the prospect of a long and possibly treacherous drive home.

After putting her writer and laptop in their cases, she changed into a chunky knit sweater. She always dressed semi-professionally for remote jobs, meaning a blazer over a blouse on top, and jeans or yoga pants on bottom, a mullet of style, only with clothing. Today she wore yoga pants.

Lauren made a tuna sandwich for lunch. She had been sitting in front of her writer for almost four hours, so she ate standing up. Maverik nudged the doorknob and she let him out. A few minutes later, Lauren let him back in. She smiled at the sun breaking free from the clouds. *Yes. No more snow.* She topped off Maverik's water bowl. Lauren would be back before dinnertime but always made sure her dog had water.

Joni texted Lauren twice in the last week about giving her a demonstration on how her stenograph machine works and what exactly a court reporter does. Lauren was always on the lookout for potential court reporting students. Someone Lauren could share her passion for the career with. They agreed to meet at Joni's house this afternoon. Lauren would bring her laptop and writer so Joni could get a feel for what it felt like to *write* on it. If Joni continued to show interest after the demonstration, Lauren would direct her to the National Court Reporters Association and to some online schools.

Even though Joni's baby should be coming any time now, she insisted on a demonstration. Once she became a mother, Lauren knew Joni's priorities would change. Lauren couldn't relate to having a newborn and going to school at the same time, but as long as Joni had an interest, Lauren would be a spokesperson about the importance of capturing the spoken word, being the guardian of the record.

With Maverik back inside, she gave him the usual be-a-good-boy speech. Lauren knew he didn't understand her ramblings, but liked to imagine that he did, which meant that someday he'd be like the surly teenager who shrugs or ignores his mother's requests, simply turns and walks away, his way of saying, *Duh, Mom.* Or, *Whatever.*

Maverik stuck his nose in his bowl and in one gulp swallowed the crust from her sandwich. He sat back on his haunches, his brown eyes searching Lauren's hazel ones.

"Sorry, that's all you get."

Chapter Fifty-Nine

Lauren pulled to the curb. She got out of the Volvo, reached into the back seat and retrieved the rolling case that held her writer and laptop. She made her way to the porch. This had been Kyle and Taryn's home. She remembered her friend saying as part of the divorce settlement he refinanced the house and paid her her half of the equity. Taryn didn't want to live there, not without Kyle she'd said. It would always be a reminder of her failed marriage.

The home, in an older neighborhood on the east side of Crawford, sat sandwiched between two similar-looking homes. Lauren loved the look of the craftsman-style house with its covered front porch and white railing in front. Mature cottonwoods with massive trunks lined both sides of the street, their roots buckling the sidewalk in a few places. Lauren could imagine how pretty it would be in late spring when the trees leafed out, and even prettier in the fall when the leaves would turn golden.

Lauren rang the doorbell but couldn't hear a chime from inside. She waited a moment, then knocked. She glanced to her left. A vehicle sat in the driveway. *Joni must be home.*

She stepped back. The house numbers hung vertically on the porch beam. Right house. Lauren pulled out her phone and checked the screen. Right time. No new texts. *Maybe Joni forgot?*

Lauren started to text Joni when a shout, followed by the sound of breaking glass, came from inside the house. Lauren turned the doorknob. The door was unlocked. If Sam saw that, Joni would be in for one heck of a lecture. Lauren stepped inside, closing the door behind her, her excitement to show Joni the workings of her writer forgotten as she called out, "Joni?"

No answer. An uneasiness gripped her stomach. "Hello?" Lauren called out again before leaving the carrying case in the entryway. The sound of a cry of pain came from deeper inside the house.

"Joni, are you all right?" Lauren passed through the living room, headed to an open archway, and came to a halt in the kitchen. Her breath caught in her chest as she took in the scene. Shards of glass from a broken coffee carafe lay scattered on the floor, along with its brown liquid. Joni stood near the sink, her head tilted back, tracks of mascara racing down her cheeks. Taryn stood behind Joni, a fistful of Joni's ash-blonde hair in one hand, a large kitchen knife in the other.

Taryn? What the... "Taryn, what's going on? Put that knife down."

Taryn stood next to Joni, whose eyes were wide, like that of a startled deer.

"She's trying to take my baby," Joni wailed.

No, no. This can't be happening. Please, no. Lauren stared at them, at a loss for words. *Don't just stand there, do something,* her brain screamed. *Do something.* She took a step forward. "Taryn, please put down the knife. Let Joni go. Tell me what's going on."

Instead of loosening her grip on Joni's hair, she twisted it harder. Joni let out a screech. "This is all *her* fault," Taryn growled. "She stole my husband. She stole *my* life. And I'm going to get what should be mine."

Oh, shit. Taryn's totally lost it. "You're — you're upset. I get it. I really do. You wanted a family. And it was supposed to be you having a baby, not her, right?" Lauren forced the words to come out soothing while her mind reeled. Lauren couldn't look away from the knife. "I — I'd be upset too, I would. But this? Taryn, this isn't the answer."

"She's ruining my life. Everywhere I go, there she is. *She* was the reason I had to quit going to the gym. I couldn't stand to see" — Taryn brought the tip of the knife against Joni's throat — "her and her fat belly waltzing in on her way to the yoga class, carrying Kyle's baby."

Taryn now pressed the blade so tight against Joni's neck if she took a deep breath the knife's tip would penetrate her pale skin.

"Taryn, please. Please put down the knife. You don't want to do this." Lauren didn't know what to say to make the woman drop the weapon. Should she risk grabbing it? It would take only a millisecond to slice Joni's throat. *This can't be happening.*

Lauren took a small step toward Taryn. "This won't end well. You know that. Please, Taryn. This isn't Joni's fault."

"Oh, so you're going to take this bitch's side? Some friend you are."

"We *are* friends. Of course we are." Lauren wanted to say the right thing, only she had no idea what that was. What do you say to someone who's lost touch with reality? How do you reason with crazy?

"If you're not her friend, why are you even here, Lauren?"

"I … I came over to let her see my writer, to see if she might be interested in becoming a court reporter. You know me, I'll talk to everyone and anyone about what a great profession it is." Lauren forced a laugh. "Remember how I talked nonstop in the lounge at Keystone about being a court reporter? I'm sure that's why those two guys got up and left." Again, Lauren let out a small laugh and took another step closer to Taryn. "And I didn't know that's why you stopped going to the gym. I missed you not being there."

"Sure you did. And now here you are, friends with *her*. Don't you see, she steals everything that's mine."

"That's not true, Taryn," said Lauren. "I was going to text you to see if you wanted to hang out this weekend."

"Don't bother lying. It's too late."

"You don't want to do this. Think of the baby. If you kill Joni, the baby will die." Lauren heard the pleading, the desperation in her voice as she spoke the words. "You won't be able to save it."

For a split second, it looked as though Taryn was considering Lauren's words. Then Taryn said, "I'll take my chances." She tightened her grip on Joni's hair, pulling her even closer, so close that her lips were touching Joni's ear. "You should have left *my* husband alone. If you hadn't come along, Kyle and I would still be together. *You* took him away from me." Taryn spat out the last words, then shoved Joni to the floor. Taryn knelt over Joni, blade raised, ready to slice into her belly.

Lauren hurled herself like a linebacker at Taryn, knocking her off balance. Taryn fell hard, her legs caught in Joni's.

Taryn screamed, thrashed around, legs kicking out, unable to get up.

Lauren stomped on Taryn's outstretched hand, her boot coming down hard. Taryn shouted in pain and released her grip on the knife. It skidded across the tiled floor and came to a stop in the middle of the kitchen.

Taryn unraveled herself from Joni, and on hands and knees scrambled to where the knife lay.

Lauren tried to grab it but even with an injured hand Taryn was quicker. She picked up the knife, rolled on her back, and swung the blade wildly at Lauren. At that first swipe, Lauren thought Taryn had only cut the air. Lauren hadn't felt any pain. It wasn't until she felt something warm trickle down her hand that she knew she'd been cut. Blood covered her fingers and palm. It began to drip onto Taryn, who still lay on her back.

"You bitch," hissed Taryn. She kicked her feet out, making contact with Lauren's kneecap. It knocked her off balance and Lauren fell, landing on her back. Pain shot through her legs and her spine. Taryn got to her feet and stood over Lauren, Taryn's chest heaving, her face contorted with rage.

"Hey, Taryn."

Taryn turned her head just in time to see Joni swinging a brass lamp. It connected to the side of Taryn's head. She crumpled to the floor.

Joni held the lamp over Taryn like a baseball bat, ready to swing again, but Taryn lay still, a trickle of crimson darkening her short blonde hair.

Joni's voice dropped to a whisper. "Is she … Did I…"

Lauren managed to sit up but left a streak of blood on the floor. She stared at Taryn, who lay beside her, unmoving. "I — I don't know. Call 911."

Joni grabbed her phone off the kitchen counter and dialed. While it rang, she reached out with her free hand to help Lauren to her feet. Joni let out a gasp. "Oh my God, Lauren. What happened to your hand?" With those words, Joni's eyes fluttered and she sank to the floor.

A distant voice came through Joni's phone. "911, what is the nature of your emergency?"

Chapter Sixty

The phone on Sam's desk rang, dragging his attention away from the computer screen. He blinked a few times to moisten his eyes, then looked at the caller ID. He lifted the receiver. "Yes, Nancy."

"Makayla Dixon is here. Says she has something important to show you."

A moment later, the teen stood in front of his desk.

"Hi, Makayla. I understand you have something you'd like me to take a look at." He eyed the folded sheets of paper held tightly in her hands.

Makayla nodded, and Sam pointed to the chair. The teen sat and handed him what she'd brought. Sam unfolded the sheets of paper. Makayla watched him as he read. When he finished, he set them down and met her gaze. "Thank you for coming down here with this. It is extremely helpful to my investigation."

"I thought you'd want to see it right away," Makayla said, eyes bright behind her large frames.

"I'm curious though, how did you come across this?"

"I found it in some of Ruby's stuff."

Sam raised a dark brow. "Ruby's stuff?"

"Yes, but it was pure luck that I even got it. A couple of weeks ago I was walking to my English class and saw the assistant principal at Ruby's locker with a trash can next to it. I ran over and asked her what she was doing. She explained they had to clean Ruby's locker out. I guess I kinda lost it," Makayla added a little sheepishly. "I started yelling, saying, 'How could you do that? Those are Ruby's things.' Ms. Bellasario told me to calm down. She explained that Ruby's father didn't want what was in the locker and told her she should just throw it all away."

Makayla let out a sound of disgust. "Ms. Bellasario asked if I wanted to take some of her stuff, her things, that maybe there would be something in there I'd want to keep. She knew we were friends. Of course I did. She couldn't just throw away Ruby's things, like they didn't matter ... like Ruby didn't matter." Makayla drew a breath. "So she went and found a box, and after she removed a couple of textbooks, she gave me what was left. I took it home but I couldn't bring myself to look inside. Until today." The girl bowed her head and spoke, her voice barely above a whisper. "I should have looked sooner."

"Makayla," Sam said, his voice gentle.

Makayla lifted her head and straightened her frames, not bothering to wipe away the tears in her eyes.

"Sometimes we just have to do things in our own time. Don't beat yourself up over this. You brought it today.

And I really appreciate you doing that." He stood. "Come on, I'll walk you out."

After he escorted her out, Sam returned to his desk and smoothed out the neatly folded paper and reread what Ruby wrote.

Saturday, February 14

Taryn Biggs is not nice. I thought she was. She Is Not!! She called me yesterday to tell me the paperwork was ready for me to sign. I told her I changed my mind and that I was going to keep Evie. I said I was really sorry. I told her I would give back the money she gave me for the adoption. I spent some of it but I didn't tell her that part.

She showed up at the house later in the day. Thankfully my grandma was taking a nap, but I was afraid all her yelling was going to wake her up. Taryn said I couldn't back out, that it was too late, that we had a deal. She told me she was going to give me the weekend to come to my senses. Do what's right for Evie. But I am doing what's right for her. Taryn said she'd be back. I don't want to see her EVER again.

I'm a terrible mom. I almost let that nasty bitch adopt Evie. I'm so so glad I didn't. But now I'm really scared. What if she tries to take her away from me? Take me to court and force me to give her up. Can she do that? Can she?

Chapter Sixty-One

Chief Finch turned from his computer as Sam walked into his office. "Sam?"

The conversation Sam relayed about Taryn Biggs and her involvement with Ruby West was a short one. Sam showed Chief Finch the letter. Sam also explained the allegations that were made against the DFS worker, about her giving drugs to one of her clients, and using that so the girl would lose custody of her child. Chief Finch agreed Sam had enough to bring her in for questioning in the death of Ruby.

Sam went to his office, opened a form on his computer and filled in the blanks to request a search warrant for Taryn's home. After pressing the print button, he phoned the circuit court. Judge Smith was still in his office, and, yes, he'd see him and look over the search warrant request.

After handing the document to the judge's assistant, Sam waited in the lobby. There were two chairs in the area but he couldn't sit. He stood, trying hard not to pace and come across as impatient, even though that's exactly how he felt. Times like this made Sam realize that he would miss being in this complex. Sure, the police department had outgrown their space long ago, but to be able to just run upstairs, being minutes, seconds even, away from either circuit or district court, he'd miss this convenience.

A few minutes later, Sam returned downstairs, a signed search warrant in hand. He texted Officer Fuentes to see if she wanted to ride along. She didn't reply but arrived at his office seconds later. She checked the time on her phone. "Do you think Ms. Biggs will still be in her office?"

"Most likely. That's where we're going to start." Sam grabbed his phone, coat and keys. As he reached the doorway Nancy came in, her usual calm demeanor absent.

"Sam, dispatch just contacted me. There's been a call out to your brother's address."

"What? Are you sure?"

"His name is registered to the address."

"Shit."

"It's for police and ambulance. Thought you'd want to know."

"Any other details?"

"An intruder." Nancy tried to catch her breath. "Possible injuries. That's all I know."

Lauren mentioned going there to see Joni today. Sam slapped the search warrant into Officer Fuentes's hand.

"I'll let you do the honors on this. Skip her office, go straight to her house. You know the drill, bring a couple of uniforms with you. I'm heading over to my brother's house."

"I hope everything's okay," said Nancy and Officer Fuentes in unison.

As Sam rushed to his vehicle, he phoned Kyle, who picked up on the second ring. "Sam, what's the occasion for this call? You usually text." Kyle sounded curious, not like Sam interrupted him while in the midst of a crisis.

"Where are you right now, Kyle?"

"Just leaving school. Why?"

"Dispatch just received a 911 call to your house."

"What? Why?"

"I'm not sure. I'm headed over there now. You should —" Sam still had the phone to his ear but his brother had already dropped the call.

Chapter Sixty-Two

Joni opened her eyes and let out a groan.

Lauren, who had been awkwardly trying to pat Joni's cheeks to wake her, stood and helped Joni to her feet. Lauren searched for a kitchen towel to cover her bloody fingers, trying not to let Joni see them. "Police are on their way. Are you okay?"

Joni gripped the edge of the kitchen counter and bent over, cradling her belly. She let out a guttural moan, her face draining of all color.

"Are you hurt? You landed pretty hard when you passed out."

Through gritted teeth, Joni pushed her words out. "No. I think … I'm going … into labor."

"Oh, crap," muttered Lauren under her breath. *No, don't go into labor. Not here. Not now.*

After several seconds, Joni's face relaxed. She heaved a

sigh and straightened. "Do you think Taryn —"

The sound of approaching sirens silenced Joni's words. The two women looked at one another, then down at Taryn, whose eyes were now open, darting from side to side. As she began to sit up, the front door burst open. Men and women in blue uniforms, police and EMTs, flooded the kitchen. A moment later, Lauren saw Sam and Kyle rush into the house, their faces filled with shock.

Chapter Sixty-Three

"We've put Ms. Biggs in the interrogation room," Officer Peterson said. He had followed the ambulance to the hospital with Taryn Biggs inside. The officer's presence at the hospital caused medical personnel to take Taryn out of turn. After being attended to and released by the physician, he took her into custody. She had been processed into the detention side of the station.

While Taryn was taken to the hospital, Sam returned to the station and made a phone call to the Department of Family Services to confirm a suspicion he had brewing in his mind. He also printed out information on two recent cases listed as overdose deaths. Two young women. Women that Sam would now bet good money on had been clients of Taryn's. He would need more time to piece everything together and be confident he knew the truth.

Sam placed the sheets of paper on his desk, grabbed his phone and walked toward the interrogation room. Officer Peterson, who had been about to go into the room, stopped and held out the plastic cup in his hand. "She requested tea. I've got the recording equipment set up. She said she wants to talk."

Sam nodded. "That's good for us." He opened the door to the interrogation room, about to walk in, when Officer Fuentes jogged toward him, a huge grin on her face.

Sam closed the door. "Your search found something?"

"Oh, yes, it did. Drugs. Presumptive test says it's methamphetamine. And there were syringes. And ... " Officer Fuentes waited a beat. "An open blister pack with what I'm pretty sure are roofies."

"Wow." Officer Peterson grinned at Officer Fuentes. "What didn't Taryn have in her house?"

"It's all just been logged in with the evidence tech." Officer Fuentes waved the chain of custody document in front of Sam.

"Great. You want to conduct this interrogation?"

Officer Fuentes's dark eyes widened. "You think I'm ready?"

Sam nodded.

"Then, hell yeah." She placed her hand on the door handle, the look in her eyes saying *I am so ready.*

"Hold up just a sec," Sam said.

Officer Fuentes stopped and glanced over her shoulder. Sam explained what he wanted to accomplish and how he wanted the interrogation to be conducted. She would take the lead on questioning, believing Taryn would open up more being questioned by a female officer. When Sam finished explaining, Officer Fuentes nodded.

The two walked into the small room. Officer Fuentes placed the cup of tea Sam had handed off to her in front of Taryn.

"Thank you," Taryn said in a tired voice.

Sam took in the sight of his ex-sister-in-law. She wore wrinkled orange detention attire, her clothing having been bagged and put in evidence. She had a small bandage on her forehead, the area around it beginning to bruise.

Even though Taryn stood at five-eight, her curved, bent posture registered defeat, as if she were trying to shrink in size and somehow distance herself from what she had just attempted, and failed, to do.

"Officer Peterson tells me you're willing to talk to us," Officer Fuentes said.

"Yes," answered Taryn, her voice and blue eyes vacant of emotion.

Sam gave an imperceptible nod to Officer Fuentes.

"Are you feeling well enough to do that now?"

Taryn nodded.

"I'm sorry but I need you to verbalize your answer."

"I'm fine."

"Okay then. Taryn, why don't you begin by telling me everything that happened earlier today, beginning when you arrived at the Overstreet home."

Taryn took a sip of her tea, cleared her throat, and turned her gaze toward Sam. "Before I say anything, you have to know I *never* meant to hurt Lauren. I hope she's okay." With those words spoken, Taryn adjusted herself in the seat to face Officer Fuentes, and told her version of what transpired a few hours ago at the home she once lived in.

Sam didn't yet have any information to compare Taryn's with. The EMTs had whisked Joni away, with Kyle at her side. Lauren also went to the ER to have her hand looked at. Kyle texted him, letting Sam know Joni had been taken to the labor and delivery ward. For now Lauren and Joni's statements would have to wait.

The more Sam listened to Taryn, the more he wanted to shake his head. She acted like almost every other guilty person who sat in this room and confessed to a crime. If they put enough reasons — more like excuses — into their story, perhaps the person sitting across from them would feel sympathy toward them. Understand why they *had* to do what they did. Even excuse what they did.

Listening to her, one would think the events that took place were one big misunderstanding. "I only went over to talk to Joni." *Why would you even need to talk to Joni?*

"Things just got out of hand. No one was supposed to get hurt."

When Taryn got to the part about the knife *just* being there in her hand, and Lauren somehow getting hurt, Sam sucked in a slow breath and thanked God for there not being more serious, even deadly injuries.

"And then you, the police and ambulance all showed up," Taryn finished. She sniffed and wiped at a lone tear.

"We'll be right back," said Sam. He rose and motioned for Officer Fuentes to follow.

"Are we almost done?" Taryn asked.

"Shouldn't be much longer," Sam said.

"Good. I really need to use the restroom."

Sam observed Taryn. Other than looking tired, she'd been coherent and obviously understood the questions asked of her. "Officer Fuentes will escort you to the restroom in a moment." He needed to tread lightly, make sure anything she admitted to now wouldn't be recanted in the future, using a head injury as an excuse for saying the things she said. "We'll be right back."

Once outside the interview room, Officer Fuentes asked, "Did I leave anything out? Is there something else you want me to ask?"

Sam didn't reply.

"Sam?"

"Huh?" He brought his attention back to Officer Fuentes.

"Did I forget anything? Is there something you want me to ask her?"

"No, you did a great job. Offer her more tea, water, maybe something from the vending machine. I've got another line of inquiry I want to go into. I want to make sure she's well enough to continue."

"What do you mean? What other line of inquiry," Officer Fuentes asked.

"While you were questioning her, I began thinking about the deposition that Lauren took the other day."

"And?"

Sam didn't answer right away, his thoughts racing. Finally he said, "She's confessed to attacking Joni. And injuring Lauren."

"Right."

"You found meth and roofies at her home. You know where I'm going with this."

Officer Fuentes stared at Sam a moment, then snapped her fingers. "You're going to see if she'll confess to killing Ruby."

"Exactly. You didn't get a chance to read some of Ruby's diary. You'll understand once you do. It's the missing piece of the puzzle. But I need to make sure we do everything right." Sam rubbed his hand across his stubbled cheek.

"Escort her to the bathroom. Ask her how she's feeling. I want to make sure she's in agreement that she's well enough to continue with further questioning."

"And if she says she's not feeling well?"

"Ask her if she thinks she wants to be seen again by a doctor. If she does, make arrangements to get her back to the hospital. If she doesn't and insists she's fine, I'll come in and finish questioning her."

"What if she changes her mind and wants a lawyer?" Officer Fuentes asked.

"Then we'll let her call one." Sam met Officer Fuentes's gaze. "But I'm really hoping she doesn't. I'm going to go grab a few files before I have a go at her. I have a feeling Ms. Biggs is the answer to a couple of other accidental overdose cases. And if my hunch is right, Taryn has some explaining to do. And not just about Ruby."

"What are you —" Officer Fuentes started to ask, but Sam had already started jogging down the hallway, leaving her to stare at his back.

Chapter Sixty-Four

Lauren repositioned herself in the plastic chair in the ER waiting room. She held her right hand across her chest, looking like she was ready to recite the Pledge of Allegiance. Her hand was still wrapped in the dish towel that Sam had taken from her in her clumsy attempt to stem the bleeding. He refastened it and his quick reaction had stopped the red tide but not before the towel turned a bruised maroon color. Lauren knew Sam had been torn between needing to interrogate Taryn at the police station and wanting to take her to the ER. In the end she agreed to wait for a second ambulance to come, with a promise from Sam that he would get to the hospital as soon as he could.

Lauren had briefly seen Kyle at the nurse's station while he filled out paperwork before disappearing, most likely to the labor and delivery wing.

When Lauren arrived at the ER two hours ago, the tired-looking nurse on duty informed her, unfortunately, there was a longer than normal wait time. The nurse fanned her arm out to the filled waiting area, then tilted her chin at Lauren's makeshift bandage. "Your hand will have to wait." The gray-haired woman's words carried a note of sympathy, but that did nothing to reduce the throbbing in Lauren's hand.

Maybe I should go home, come back later. And how are you going to get home, Lauren?

Lauren thought about calling Aunt Kate for a ride home. A call to her aunt would only worry her. And Lauren could imagine Aunt Kate telling her to stay put until a doctor examined her wound.

Lauren touched the blood-soaked towel with her free hand, then closed her eyes, knowing her fingers needed medical attention. A few well-placed Band-Aids were *not* going to do the trick.

Chapter Sixty-Five

Sam entered the interrogation room. Taryn rolled her eyes. "Oh, it's you."

"Lola has a few things to finish up with," Sam said.

"So it's *Lola*, is it?"

Sam ignored Taryn's inference and placed a bottle of water next to her empty cup of tea. He sat across from her. "I have a few more questions to ask you. Did you get a chance to use the restroom?"

Taryn nodded.

"How's your head? Are you feeling okay?"

"I'll live." Taryn rolled her eyes. "I'm fine." She twisted off the cap of the water bottle and put it to her lips.

"I'd like to talk to you about Ruby West."

Taryn set the bottle down untouched. "Ruby West? I thought we were talking about Joni. What about Ms. West?"

"I have some questions about how she died. To be honest, Taryn, I believe you have information that can help with that." When Taryn didn't respond, Sam continued. "You came clean about Joni, and we appreciate that very much. I'd like you to do the same regarding Ruby."

"I — I —" Taryn's voice faltered. Her expression held no clue as to whether she would ask to speak with a lawyer or continue talking to him. "You were already there that morning before I arrived, Sam. You know what happened to her." Taryn pursed her lips and shook her head.

Sam opened the folder on the table and pulled out the plastic sleeve that held the diary entries Makayla had given him. He slid it around to face Taryn. She straightened in the seat, not looking at the document.

"It's from Ruby's diary. Go ahead, Taryn, read it."

Taryn reached for the pages, pulling them closer. Sam watched as she read the diary entries. When she finished, she placed her hand on the clear sleeve that held the pages, fingers splayed, exposing ragged-edged fingernails. Taryn pushed the pages toward Sam.

The room grew silent. The only sound came from the rustling of the plastic sleeve as Sam returned it to the folder.

Sam waited for Taryn to say something. He was good at waiting. Taryn would be the first one to speak. His expression remained neutral. Bored almost.

She inhaled a deep breath and then slowly shook her head. When she exhaled, her words rode on the long breath she let out. "We had it all worked out. Ruby agreed to let me adopt Evie. I was going to sign off on the DFS paperwork that indicated she had completed her case plan.

She would regain legal custody of Evie. In the meantime, while that was happening, I hired a lawyer to draw up the adoption paperwork. It was all worked out except ..."

"Except Ruby changed her mind and decided to keep her baby."

Taryn nodded slowly. "Yes."

"And you couldn't adopt through DFS because of the Sasha Radcliffe matter."

A flicker of surprise crossed Taryn's face. She opened her mouth to speak but instead closed her eyes and nodded again.

"I'll need you to give me the details of what happened that morning, Taryn."

Taryn placed her hands in her lap, clasping and unclasping them. The room stayed quiet. Sam wondered whether Taryn regretted what she'd said and if her next words would be, "I want a lawyer." Again he waited.

This time when Taryn spoke, the words came out resigned. "Well, you did your homework, I'll give you that much. You managed to find out about Sasha. After her father complained, the department opened up an internal investigation. So you can probably guess there's no way I'd be able to adopt a child through DFS, much less have a job, not with the allegation that Sasha put out there." A flash of anger ignited in Taryn's blue eyes before being quickly extinguished.

"When I first met Ruby, she had just given birth. She was still in the maternity ward. I got to see Evie just briefly. As I'm sure you already know, Evie had tested positive for methamphetamine and fentanyl. Ruby and I spoke for a long time. I told her all the things she'd need to do to get

Evie back with her. All the testing, etcetera. Needing a stable home and the ability to care for her daughter's needs. The hospital was still observing Evie. She was having withdrawal symptoms and it was uncertain what continuing issues she might have from having been exposed to the drugs through the womb, for who knows how long." Taryn let out a disgusted sigh.

"As I was driving back to the office, it dawned on me that if she would just give up Evie for adoption maybe I could adopt her. You've seen Evie, haven't you?"

Sam nodded. "Briefly at the house that morning."

"Then you see that she looks a little like me. The same hair color. I think her eyes are going to be blue, like mine. I could easily pass for her mother."

Sam heard the uptick of excitement in Taryn's voice, almost a giddiness.

"Ruby worked her case plan for a while. She was living with her grandmother. Things weren't ideal. Ruby mentioned how difficult it was having to care for an infant and go to school. That's when I suggested a private adoption. I touched base with her regularly. She was on the fence about it. Couldn't decide. Then one day in mid-January, during one of my visits, she said yes, she wanted to give Evie up for adoption. I immediately made an appointment with an attorney to draw up the paperwork. I even paid Ruby some money ... almost like a down payment you could say."

Taryn exhaled, then gritted her teeth. "Only, on that Friday when I spoke to Ruby, she said that she changed her mind. Ruby said that her and her new boyfriend Levi were getting serious and were going to try to make a go of it together and wanted to keep Evie. I told her we had a contract. She couldn't back out. I told her I would give her time to come to her senses and I'd be back."

Taryn looked at the ceiling and she shook her head. "They wanted to make a go of it. Of all the stupid things."

"That was the Friday before her death?"

Taryn nodded.

Sam cocked his head at the camera in the ceiling.

"Oh, right. Yes," Taryn said.

"What happened after that," asked Sam.

Taryn continued, her eyes unfocused. "I showed up at her house Sunday morning."

"What time?"

"Early. I took a chance that her grandmother wouldn't be up yet. If she had been, I would have just made it out to be an unannounced visit. But Ms. Nash was still asleep. I asked Ruby if she changed her mind about keeping the baby. She said she hadn't."

Taryn shrugged. "I came prepared. I stopped at High Altitude Roast and bought a coffee for myself and a hot chocolate for Ruby. It was my peace offering to her. I pretended I was okay with her changing her mind, that I just wanted to make sure she was doing all right."

"Where did you get the Rohypnol?"

"I'd confiscated it from a client a long time ago." Taryn lifted a shoulder. "You never know when something like that will come in handy."

Taryn, you are all kinds of crazy.

"I told her we should go outside and talk so we didn't wake her grandmother up. Actually she made that part easy. Ruby said she needed a cigarette. She wasn't allowed to smoke in the house. While Ruby went upstairs to get her lighter, I put the roofie in her drink. We went out onto the back deck. It took a few minutes for the drug to work, but you pretty much know the rest. She got sleepy. I guided her down the steps into the backyard. She still had the drink in her hand and spilled what little was left in it. I tossed the cup into the yard. I eased her down to the ground. Then I injected her with a combination of meth and fentanyl that I'd brought with me." Her eyes flicked to Sam's. "I did what I had to do. It was a peaceful death, Sam. She never felt a thing."

What you had to do? The overdose caused her to have a heart attack. Sam jotted down a few notes on the inside of the folder, counting to ten in his mind, needing to maintain his professionalism.

Taryn straightened in her seat. "I know Ruby would have started using again and Evie would never have what every child deserves. A mother who cares for them. A mother who puts them first. A life without drugs. I would have given her that. *Me.* I wanted to be that parent." Taryn shook her head.

"But Ruby had been clean, none of her UAs came back dirty."

"Like I told you when you came to my office that day, she had missed a couple of tests. And she did have one positive UA early on in the case." Taryn folded her arms across her chest. "I wasn't wrong, so don't look so surprised." She huffed. "You just don't get it. I told you, Ruby was no different than all the rest. She would have started using again. It would have only been a matter of time." Taryn's voice grew shrill. "They *all* do. They *all* go back to using. I told you that's what happens. Haven't you been listening?"

Back when Ruby's death was thought to be accidental, Sam had reviewed the autopsy reports of the recent overdose victims in Crawford. He'd come across the name Cammie Johnson. Her death was one of several considered to be an accidental overdose. On a hunch, Sam contacted the Department of Family Services and learned Ms. Johnson had an open case with the department. He also learned Taryn Biggs was her caseworker.

"Sam, you have to understand."

Sam snapped out of his thoughts.

"I didn't set out to do this. This was not planned. You have to believe me. It's just — I was *so* angry with Kyle when we broke up. He said we needed our space. Said that I was getting too involved in my clients' lives. But how could I not be involved? We've been short-staffed for several months now, meaning I'm on call most weekends. Going out on welfare checks. Mothers constantly relapsing, putting their children at risk. The job was becoming all-consuming." Taryn rubbed the spot where her wedding band used to be. Talking more to herself, she added, "We'd been trying to have a baby for over two years, and … and it never happened."

Sam had heard Kyle's version of this subject, but the one with Taryn losing touch with reality, he hadn't heard that before. He found it hard to comprehend.

Taryn swiped at a tear as it ran down her cheek. "Kyle said he was okay with not being a dad. That I needed to stop obsessing about wanting a child. As soon as I moved out, he changed his profile to single on every freakin' social media site known to man." She slapped her hand on the table. "Then … then his profile said he was in a relationship. He started posting pictures of him and his new girlfriend. The *happy* couple." Taryn brought her eyes to Sam's, not bothering to wipe away the newly shed tears. "And now they're going to have a baby."

Sam had to agree with Taryn. He saw it every time he saw his brother and Joni together, how very much in love Kyle was.

"I lost it when I found out. It should have been *me*, not her. If I'd gotten pregnant, we'd be the happy couple. That's how it was supposed to be. All I wanted was a baby." Taryn covered her face with her hands, loud choking sobs escaping through her fingers.

Sam stayed quiet. A small part of him wanted to reach out and touch her, offer her some small comfort. He stood. "I'll be right back, Taryn." The sound of crying followed Sam as he closed the door and walked down the hallway. He returned carrying a box of tissues, placing it in front of the puffy-eyed Taryn. She plucked two out and blew her nose.

"You've told me a lot, Taryn. I appreciate you being open with me. I know it's been hard." He let a few beats of silence pass between them. "I sense you're still holding back. I sense there's more you have to tell me."

Taryn shook her head, her gaze on the clump of tissue balled up in her fist.

* * *

"As you now realize, I have learned about Sasha Radcliffe and what you're alleged to have done in her case."

Taryn cocked her head. "Yeah, how did you learn about that? Did you talk to my supervisor?"

Instead of answering, Sam continued. "Did you know her father filed a lawsuit against the Department of Family Services?"

Taryn nodded. "I had a meeting a couple of weeks ago with the director of DFS along with their attorney. I was put on administrative leave. *Without* pay." Under her breath she added, "Not that any of it matters now."

"So what Mr. Radcliffe alleges is true?"

"Pretty much. I saw failure written all over Sasha's face the first time I met her. I knew she wouldn't stay sober. I simply fast-tracked the process."

Sam turned his phone over and glanced at the screen. No news from Lauren. No updates about Joni. "So the state takes away Sasha's child but, what, that's not enough for you? You have to take it to the next level with the next client?"

"Next level? I'm not sure what you're talking about, Sam."

Chapter Sixty-Six

"Cammie Johnson. That's what I'm talking about." He needed confirmation from Taryn. He needed to sort out the accidental from deliberate. Cammie's death could still possibly be self-inflicted. But Cammie had been a client of Taryn's, and what he learned about the Radcliffe case changed his thinking, no longer convinced the young woman's death was accidental.

Sam had been hunting down known and unknown distributors of illegal narcotics in Crawford. He assumed the common denominator in the recent rash of deaths was the cocktail of fentanyl and meth in the obvious lethal amounts found in their systems. Officer Blaine was still working with the DEA to uncover the main source. He reported they were close to an arrest but Sam didn't know much more than that.

With Taryn's admission of killing Ruby, and her deliberate, and successful, attempt to cause Sasha Radcliffe to lose custody of her child, Sam needed to take a closer look at all the recent overdose cases in Crawford again, at least the ones fitting the profile of Ruby. Mothers, mostly young, involved with the system due to being a drug user.

The quiet in the room expanded, pressing against the flat gray walls. *Maybe now she'll ask for a lawyer*, Sam thought.

She didn't.

"I admit I killed Ruby, but I did not kill Cammie Johnson."

Sam opened the blue folder again and flipped it around for Taryn to look at. "Why don't you tell me what happened then. She was the first one."

A wariness crept into Taryn's red-rimmed eyes. "What do you mean, the *first* one? The first one what?"

"You just admitted to killing Ruby West. I believe there's more victims out there." At the moment, all Sam had was a gut feeling Taryn had a hand in Cammie Johnson's death. A confession would clear up any doubts.

Taryn continued to stare at him. Sam met her stare and held it until Taryn lowered her gaze to the table.

"Take your time." Sam had his pen at the ready, waiting, even though the video recording would capture everything Taryn said.

Taryn's eyes remained down. Sam heard the shuddering exhalation of her breath, as if bracing herself for the words that were about to come. She raised her head and met his gaze again. "What do you want to know?"

"Cammie Johnson, I know she was a client of yours. Died approximately four months ago from an overdose." Sam watched Taryn's expression.

When Taryn finally spoke, she held her chin up, voice

312

strong. "I already told you, I didn't kill her. I didn't have anything to do with Cammie Johnson's death."

Sam flipped the blue folder back around so he could look at the documents. When he found the police report, he turned it toward Taryn. "It says you were there when the paramedics arrived."

"I was. I called it in." Taryn leaned forward. "She was dead when I got there."

"Okay. Why don't you start from the beginning and explain what happened. First, why were you at her house?"

"Yes, Ms. Johnson was a client of DFS. Yes, she was part of my caseload." She nodded slowly. "Brayden was her son. I was there to retake custody of him. I had spoken to her earlier that day, in the morning sometime. I let her know I would be coming by to pick him up, that the department was going to remove him from her home and return him to foster care, and she would once again have supervised visitations, at least for a while. Ever since Brayden had been placed with Cammie on a trial home placement, she had begun to miss her regular drug testing."

Sam watched Taryn as she played out the events in her head.

"I remember she missed testing two weeks in a row and that's a bad sign. And I'd also been having a hard time getting in contact with her. I didn't know for sure if she'd started using again, but that was my assumption." Taryn took a sip of water. "Anyway, Cammie got really upset when I told her I had to take Brayden. She started shouting at me over the phone, saying that nothing she ever did was good enough. I tried to calm her down. Told her that it was important that she keep her appointments for the drug testing. And in the meantime, I needed to pick up her son." She shook her head. "Brayden is her second child, by the way. Her parental rights were terminated with her older child. For the same reason. Drugs."

"And what happened, Taryn?"

"I had a few things I had to do, you know, check and make sure the foster parents were lined up. I told Cammie I would be there in the next couple of hours. When I got to her mobile home, I knocked on her door. There was no answer but I could hear a baby crying inside. Brayden crying. I knocked again, harder this time. Still no answer. The front door was unlocked, so I went in. Cammie was in the living room, lying face down on the sofa. At first I just thought she was passed out. Brayden was in his crib crying. I told her to get up. I admit I was angry." Taryn heaved a sigh and slowly shook her head. "But she didn't respond."

Sam jotted down something in his notepad.

"I went over to her and shook her." Taryn's voice rose. "I shook her pretty hard. She rolled off the couch, but still she didn't move. That's when I checked for a pulse. I couldn't feel one. I think I went into shock."

"Did you call for an ambulance?"

Taryn tore at the tissue clutched in her hand. "Yes, but not ... not right away. Like I said, I think I was in shock."

"When did you call 911?"

"I don't know." Her voice ratcheted up in annoyance. "I wasn't keeping track of time. Five minutes maybe."

Sam watched Taryn carefully for any tells of her lying. It had been a long time since he'd spent any time around her but Sam thought he knew her well enough to know if

Taryn wasn't being truthful. Sam sat across from Taryn, thinking, *I don't know this woman anymore.*

"When the police got there, I explained the situation to them and why I was there. When the paramedics lifted her off the floor and onto the gurney, that's when I noticed the needle. It was wedged between the cushions of the couch." Taryn exhaled deeply. "She'd relapsed. She'd gone back to using. I did not kill her."

Sam decided to move on to another subject. Or another client of Taryn's. He'd circle back to Cammie later, ask her specifics and see if she'd stick with the same story, the same order of events. Maybe Taryn had nothing to do with Cammie's death. Maybe she did. At the very least she had been negligent for not calling 911 immediately.

"Can you tell me what happened to Emily Hightower?"

Taryn crossed her arms over her chest. "I didn't have anything to do with Emily Hightower's death either." Her answer came quick. No hesitation or confusion about who Emily was. Taryn leaned forward and placed her arms on the table. "I'm done talking. I want a lawyer."

"Okay, Taryn. Thank you for being honest and willing to talk to me about what you did do." Sam spoke loud for the recording. "The time is seven o'clock." He got up and walked toward the door.

"Sam?"

He stopped, hand on the doorknob, and waited.

"Would you do me a favor?"

You want me to do you a favor? Good one. He glanced over his shoulder.

"Would you tell Lauren I'm really, really sorry? I never meant to hurt her."

Sam pressed his lips together and simply nodded before walking out of the interrogation room.

A few moments later, he returned with Ben. "Officer Peterson will see to it that you can call your lawyer, and then he'll escort you to a cell. It's too late for dinner, but he'll see if he can find something for you to eat."

Back in his office, Sam woke his computer and typed up his report. He sent it to the printer and then set it on Chief Finch's desk for approval in the morning. It would then be taken to the county attorney so they could bring the formal charges.

He zipped his coat, pulled up the collar and stepped out into the night. Stars littered the sky. With the cloud cover gone, the temperature had dropped below freezing. Sam inhaled and the hairs in his nostrils tingled. *Will it ever warm up?* Sam hurried to his vehicle. It faced the detention side of the police department. He put the car in drive, looked toward the station and visualized where his ex-sister-in-law would now be settling in for the night, for the next several days, and possibly weeks to come. Sam couldn't quite remember when he had last seen Taryn with Kyle. Sam would never have believed this was where she would end up. Sam thought he knew Taryn. Apparently he didn't.

On some level, Sam understood Taryn's frustration with dealing with people who were addicts. It was her solution to the problem that Sam took issue with, leaving no room for empathy for her. She'd turned into a killer. Possibly Cammie Johnson and Emily Hightower, then Ruby West. And finally her attempt on Joni's life, all because Joni was living the life Taryn thought she deserved. The life that should have been hers. The life *stolen* from her.

He shook off those thoughts, pulled his phone out of his coat pocket and typed out a text before driving away.

Chapter Sixty-Seven

A buzzing sound from her phone startled Lauren. She blinked, surprised that she had dozed off in the uncomfortable chair. Lauren reached for the phone with her right hand before remembering it was out of commission. The movement made her fingers throb. With her left hand, Lauren clumsily unlocked the screen. Sam texted her, wanting to know if she got home safely and if he could bring her anything. She tapped out a reply, "*Still at ER.*"

Lauren debated whether to get up and walk around but knew sitting would be a better option. She had half watched two home improvement shows on the muted TV screen that hung on the wall. Sometime during the third one, Lauren had fallen asleep.

Now awake, Lauren began to browse the internet for anything that would take her mind off her pain. She gave up after a few minutes. The anxiousness in Lauren's chest gained traction. *What if my fingers are so damaged I can't work? My career as a court reporter will be over.* Lauren placed the phone face down, slumped in the plastic seat and closed her eyes. A few moments later, she heard footsteps. *Finally.* She shifted in her seat and opened her eyes.

"Hey." Sam bent and kissed the top of Lauren's head.

In spite of being disappointed that it wasn't hospital personnel, Lauren smiled at Sam. He was the next best thing. Sam took a seat beside her.

"What are you doing here?"

He leaned in and kissed her gently on the lips before answering. "I came to keep you company until they call you back." Sometime during the day, his five o'clock shadow sprouted into the beginnings of a modest beard.

With those dark circles under your eyes, you look as tired as I feel.

Lauren rested her head on his shoulder. "Aww, thanks."

"It was a pretty intense scene in that kitchen. I mean, I knew you were going to be all right but ..." Sam trailed off.

"I still can't believe what happened. Did you get a chance to interview Taryn? Or did she lawyer up?"

"She spoke with us. About several events."

"Several? You mean there's more besides what happened today?"

"Yes."

"Well, don't leave me in suspense, Sam."

Sam slowly shook his head. "She admitted to killing Ruby."

Lauren pressed her hand over her mouth. "Oh my goodness. Taryn killed her?"

"Yes. And there's another overdose victim out there that had also been her client. She denies having anything to do with that one. I'm not sure how that's going to play out. Everything's going to the county attorney tomorrow. He'll decide the charges."

Lauren swiveled in the chair to face him, still finding it hard to believe the words Sam just spoke. "She admitted to killing Ruby?"

"Yes." Sam gently put his arm around Lauren and she leaned into him, her body relaxing into his. "We can talk about Taryn later." He spoke low in her ear. "You scared the shit out of me back there at the house, Lauren. The thought of something bad happening to you when I saw that blood on the floor, I just … I just don't want to —"

"Lauren Besoner."

Lauren saw a nurse with a clipboard in hand walking in their direction.

Sam cleared his throat. "Go on. I'll be here waiting for you."

Lauren turned to look into his eyes but he'd removed his arm from her shoulder.

You don't want to what, Sam? What were you going to say?

Chapter Sixty-Eight

Chief Finch called Sam the next morning and the two spoke about the events of the day before. "I've read your report, Sam. Good job. You've been working really hard on Ruby West's case. And from reading your report, Ms. Biggs is now a person of interest in two overdose deaths." Chief Finch smiled. "I want you to take the day off. You deserve it."

"But I need to take everything to the county attorney, sir."

"Don't worry about it. I'll walk it over myself. I don't want to see your face around here today."

Sam didn't argue. "Thanks, sir."

An hour later, Sam finished the last set of bench presses, biceps quivering with the extended workout. The old overhead heater wound down, and the large shop fell silent, as if paying homage to the quiet outside, telling him to stop and appreciate Mother Nature. He walked to the window and gazed out. A windless day. The bare limbs of the cottonwood trees hung motionless. Even the juniper bushes along the north and west of the shop were still. A rare kind of day that made people who lived in Crawford tell themselves all the hurricane-force wind days were worth it to be able to call this place home.

The early spring temperatures had yet to take a bite out of the large snowdrifts between the house and the shop. He had gotten his cardio workout simply shoveling the hundred-foot path from his back door to the shop. *I really need to move my workout equipment into the house.* Sam stepped out into the sun, a little higher now in the sky as spring slowly began to devour winter. The sun made the pristine sea of white sparkle. As dazzling as it was, Sam had enough of snow and dreamed of warmer weather.

He ambled down the shoveled path, enjoying the sun on his back. As he walked into his house, he thought of the morning he'd been called out to Twila Nash's home, finding Lauren there. Sam had watched her standing in Twila's kitchen, holding Evie, and how the green flecks in her hazel eyes deepened as she kissed the baby's forehead and cooed into her ear before taking her out of the room. His mind revisited that image several times in the past month.

Was Sam ready to take things further with Lauren and make a life together with this beautiful danger magnet? Possibly have children together? The corners of Sam's mouth curved upward as the answer came to him.

Chapter Sixty-Nine

Two weeks later

Lauren attached a transcript to an email, the maneuver awkward with her right hand still out of commission. She hadn't been able to work on it herself and had to send the deposition off to a scopist—a court reporter's lifesaver—who edited it for her, then a proofreader in order to get it done. The doctor told her to keep her hand raised and not to use it, especially not on a keyboard. She hit send, the final pages now on their way to the attorneys. Lauren had farmed out all her other depositions and was all caught up with work. She flexed her fingers gently, thinking of her empty calendar.

Lauren checked the time on her computer screen. Four o'clock. Plenty of time to change and meet Sam, Kyle and Joni, and little Mason for dinner. Lauren smiled to herself, looking forward to seeing the new baby. She went into her bedroom to change her outfit, and chose a pair of jeans and the pink sweater Sam had given her on Christmas. As Lauren headed for the bathroom, she heard Maverik's excited whimpering. She went downstairs and peered out her living room window. "So that's why you're all excited." Percy was loose in her front yard.

With her good hand, Lauren gave Maverik a hand gesture, followed by a command. "Stay." He did a half sit, his body quivering. When she opened the front door, Percy raced to her. Lauren scooped him up one-handed. They were nose to nose. "What are you doing out here? I know you're not allowed out front." In answer to her question, Percy licked her face and wriggled in her arm. Lauren pulled her head back while managing to keep hold of Percy. That's when she saw a blue Honda Accord parked in Twila's driveway.

"Let's get you back home before you give your mom a heart attack. You're naughty, you know that?" Lauren said as she crossed the lawn into Twila's yard. Before she made it to the front steps, Twila opened her door and called out, "Percy."

Lauren reached the top step. "I've got him, Twila. He was in my yard."

"Thanks. He must have snuck out earlier. Come on in. Evie's here."

Lauren stepped inside. "Evie's here?"

"This is the neighbor I've been telling you about," Twila said.

Lauren set Percy down and walked further into the living room. A young couple sat on the couch. Evie sat on the man's lap, her back against his chest, his steady arm around her waist. The woman handed the man a baby bottle. She turned toward Lauren and smiled.

Lauren stared at the woman. *Ruby.* Ruby several years older but the same golden-blonde hair. Only her hair cascaded down to her waist, not short and spiky like Ruby's. She even had the same airy blue eyes.

"Hi. You must be Lauren," the young woman said.

"Yes, hi." Lauren walked over and extended her hand.

"I'm Opal. Ruby's sister." She rested her hand on the man's arm. "And this is my husband Matt."

Lauren smiled at them. "It's nice to meet you both."

Twila shuffled over to them. "My Cynthia always said Ruby and Opal were her little gems." She turned her head away, cleared her throat and continued. "We just come from the courthouse. Opal and Matt here, they adopted Evie."

Lauren's eyes widened. "That's so great. I'm so happy for you. And for Evie." Adopted by family. Opal and Matt adopting Evie would be the one good outcome of a terrible tragedy. "She gets to be with family. That makes my heart happy."

"Yes," said Opal, a sad smile rolling across her face, then quickly disappearing. She turned to Evie, whose chubby hands held the baby bottle with the help of Matt. Opal's expression brightened. "It was one heck of a process though, that's for sure. We had to fill out all kinds of paperwork. DFS had to do a home study, and since we live out of state, that took, like, forever." She rubbed Evie's tummy absently as she spoke. "But we finally got approved, didn't we, Evie?"

Evie kicked her feet in response.

Matt rested a palm on Opal's forearm and smiled down at Evie. "We'd planned on starting a family. Just doing it a little sooner than we thought."

"We were planning to drive home today but the court had an emergency hearing and the adoption got bumped to the end of the line of cases," Opal said.

Matt added, "We got lucky. The judge said he'd do the adoption today rather than make us come back Monday. Since it's kinda late, we're staying the night. We'll leave in the morning."

"Where do you live?" Lauren asked.

"North Platte, Nebraska," replied Matt.

"So not too far away," Lauren said.

"A little over 270 miles," Matt said.

"We plan on visiting grandma more often so she can get to know her great-granddaughter," Opal said.

Twila smiled, the crevices around her eyes deepening. "A little company once in a while will be nice."

"Lauren, thank you for all you've done. Grandma was telling us everything that you did. Persuading the police to keep looking into Ruby's death. Finding her diary pages. You helped get justice for my little sister."

"I really can't take the credit. The detective, Sam Overstreet, worked hard on the case."

Twila sank into her recliner and nodded. "Yeah, that's Lauren's boyfriend."

Lauren blushed. "I'm just so happy to hear that Evie is with you. With family."

The four of them chatted for a few minutes while Evie sucked the last drop of milk from her bottle.

Lauren glanced at her fitness watch. "I better get going. Would you mind if I say goodbye to her," she asked, dipping her head at Evie.

"Of course not." Opal got up and placed Evie in Lauren's arms, then made her way to the kitchen. "I need some coffee."

Twila trailed after her. "I'll show you where the cups are."

Lauren held Evie. She felt heavier in Lauren's arms, and the baby's blonde locks were thicker. Lauren brushed Evie's smooth plump cheek with her finger and whispered, "Go on and have your best life ever."

Chapter Seventy

Even before Lauren entered the Slice It Up, the familiar aroma of tomato sauce and baking pizza dough greeted her, making her remember she'd skipped lunch in order to finish the last job she had taken. Sam waved from a back booth, and Lauren weaved her way over to the group.

"We just ordered," Sam said. Lauren smiled at the iced tea waiting for her.

While they waited for their pizzas to arrive, the conversation turned to Taryn and her case. Joni turned to Sam. "Since Taryn pled guilty to killing Ruby and attempted murder on me, what's going to happen to her?"

"She'll be behind bars for the rest of her life," Sam said before taking a pull on his beer. "I think her sentencing is coming up in a couple of weeks."

"I was kind of surprised when you told us she pled guilty." Joni shuddered. "But I'm so relieved I won't have to testify. Just thinking I might have to do that made me sick to my stomach. I'm just so happy I'll never have to see her face again."

"She pled guilty to murder in the first degree of Ruby, and in exchange the county attorney took the death penalty off the table." Sam shook his head. "Taryn still contends the first overdose victim, Cammie Johnson, was not her fault. It just gave her the idea of how she could rid the world of people who she didn't think deserved to live, and make it look like an accident." Sam cocked his head at Joni. "Of course, you were different."

"Yeah, she hated my guts." Joni shuddered again. She tucked the blanket around her sleeping son in his carrier. Kyle put his arm around Joni's shoulder, pulling her into him.

Sam continued. "I gave the county attorney everything I had. He decided not to charge Taryn with Cammie Johnson's death. But without that conviction, she's still a goner." Sam picked up his Coors and downed the last drop. "Crazy bitch, that one — sorry, Kyle."

His brother snorted. "Hey, if the shoe fits, right?"

Lauren stayed quiet as the conversation centered around Taryn, who had been her friend. Seeing her out of control at Joni's house had shocked and saddened Lauren. She absently massaged the inside of her right hand. Her index, middle and ring fingers were still numb. After the doctor had removed the stitches, he told Lauren he was optimistic that the nerves would heal with time. Lauren just needed to be patient.

❊   ❊   ❊

Sam walked Lauren to her Volvo after they left Slice It Up. Before she got in, he asked, "You're still planning on coming over, right?"

She nodded. "I'll be right behind you. I'm just going to go home and check on Maverik."

"Hey, why don't you bring him along?"

Lauren raised an eyebrow. "Uh, I don't know. Do you really think that's a good idea?"

Sam reached out and tucked a lock of hair behind her ear. "I do. Bring him. It'll be fine."

There were several lights on inside Sam's house, including the room on the far end in the back. Sam's bedroom. Lauren clipped the leash onto Maverik's collar before getting out of the Volvo. "I want you on your best behavior, you got it? Sam was nice enough to invite you over, so don't blow it."

Maverik, who sat in the passenger seat the whole ride over, stuck his long muzzle out the partially open window, sniffing the air, as if ignoring her comment.

Lauren gave the lead a slight tug and he jumped out the driver's side, pulling her up the sidewalk, the slack having gone out of the leash. *This is a bad idea*, she told herself. When they reached the front door, she pressed the doorbell.

Sam opened the door and ushered them in.

Lauren gripped the strap in her fist so Maverik wouldn't drag her into the house.

"I think Maverik will be fine off-leash," Sam said. "Let him have a sniff around. I'm going to fill a bowl with some water in case he gets thirsty." Sam gestured with his chin at the death grip Lauren had on the strap, and walked toward the kitchen.

Lauren raised her voice. "I really don't think I should let him loose in your house, Sam."

Sam turned and raised his arm out. "You've seen my place. He'll be fine."

"Okay." *Don't say I didn't warn you.* "Remember what I said in the car, Maverik," Lauren said as she unhooked the clip from Maverik's collar, then hovered behind him as he trotted into the living room.

Sam returned from the kitchen, knelt by the hearth to start a fire. He grinned as he watched Lauren watching Maverik.

Maverik's nose went to work sniffing every surface in the room. When he got to the leather loveseat, he stuck his muzzle into something beside it. Lauren went to investigate. A large plush rectangular dog bed lay on the floor. Maverik stepped on it, burying his nose in its surface. He circled a few times and lay down, then let out one short bark. Lauren laughed. "Yes, I think that's for you, Maverik."

"It is." Sam stood behind her. "And I think he likes it."

"Looks like he does." Lauren turned and faced Sam. "Aww, that was nice of you."

"It was, wasn't it?" Sam grinned but his expression quickly turned serious. He took Lauren's hands in his and cleared his throat. "Listen. I've been meaning to … I want to say … What I'm trying unsuccessfully to say is that I like you." He exhaled loudly. "No, scrap that."

Oh, so you don't like me? Lauren almost blurted out but she sensed Sam struggling with something he needed to say. Now wasn't the time to be flippant.

"You know I like you. That's not what I'm trying to say." He gently placed his hands on her shoulders, holding her at arm's length. "I want us to spend more time to-gether. I want us to be together. I'm tired of your place, my place, you getting up and leaving, not spending the night here with me." Sam gathered her in a tight hug and spoke over her head. "I want him ... and you ... to feel at home here." He cleared his throat. "What do you say?"

Lauren tilted her head and met his gaze. Afraid to speak for fear of crying, she simply nodded. She relaxed into Sam's embrace, feeling the rise and fall of his chest. Lauren stole a glance at Maverik, already asleep in his new bed, snoring softly, paws twitching.

Acknowledgements

I want to thank John Schultz, Anna Lane, Dave Lerner and Mary Billiter, a/k/a the Nite Writers. You have been with me since my very first word was written. Your input and ideas have been invaluable to me. Thank you for your friendship during these past ten years.

I'd like to thank Jim Harper and Dean Jackson for answering all my questions regarding police procedure, even the dumb ones. Any factual inaccuracies are mine and mine alone.

Athena Loftus, thank you for sharing your knowledge of what goes into being a social service caseworker, and the truly hard work and dedication it takes to do the job well. Again, any inaccuracies on what a caseworker does are on me.

To my beta readers, Harry "Butch" Gordon, John Schultz, and Dan Levine, thank you for your suggestions and thoughts.

And thank you to the readers who chose this book to read.

About the Author

Merissa Racine is a court stenographer who grew up on the east coast, then moved to Wyoming, which she now calls home. When not working or thinking about her next writing project, she can be found reading a mystery, trying new recipes, and spending time with her grandchildren. She enjoys the company of her four-legged friends; dogs Maya and Roz, and her cat Zelda.

NOTES FROM THE AUTHOR

To any readers who are interested in learning more about the world of court reporting and captioning, contact the National Court Reporters Association at: www.ncra.org. It's a wonderful career.

Word of mouth helps authors succeed. If you have enjoyed this book, please consider leaving a review online wherever you are able. Even a line or two is helpful.

You can visit my website www.merissaracine.com
Find me on Facebook: @authormerissaracine
Or Instagram: merissaracine